Manistee Encounters

By Michael Ames

Copyright © 2015 Catherine's Books LLC

TABLE OF CONTENTS

1	BEAR'S WOODSTOCK	10
2	DARKNESS ON THE FACE OF THE EARTH	15
3	RECOVERY AND BACK TO WORK	22
4	ENTERTAINING JUSTICE	30
5	GUY VISITS IVY	36
6	CONFIRMATION	41
7	A LITTLE FUN, INTERRUPTED	43
8	WALT MEETS IVY	46
9	IVY CHECKING OUT	59
10	SICK OF THE DARKNESS	60
11	IS THAT KARL?	71
12	NEARING "SO DAMN GOOD" AGAIN	73
13	THE DARKNESS CRACKS	81
14	AN OLD TRIP HOME REMEMBERED	87
15	SEEING HOSS	104
16	WHO IS THIS?!	111
17	FEELING STRONG AND BEAUTIFUL	127
18	FURTHER RECOVERY ON THE JORDAN	130

19	THE BIRTH OF THE MESICK INN	134
20	THE GUTSY SHERRIFF WHEELER	148
21	THE EARLY VISIT OF MR. S AND NICK	155
22	VISITING HOSS	158
23	HOME WITH HOSS	167
24	A MEMORY INTRUDED	169
25	BULLSHIT ORDERS	175
26	THE CHARMED LIFE OF YOUNG IVY	181
27	IVY'S HOPEFUL NIGHTMARE	198
28	CAN'T BE HIM	204
29	AGENT WILLIAMS FROM DENVER TO MESICK	206
30	AGENT WILLIAMS REVIEWS HIS FILE	213
31	AN UNKNOWN CLOSE ENCOUNTER	225
32	MAGGIE AND HER LATE HUSBAND JOHN	234
33	KIRT AND BETH	257
34	AGENT WILLIAMS	314
35	CAL DROPS HIS PRIDE	318
36	ANOTHER STRIKE AT THE WALMART	323
37	THE BIRTH OFF THE VIGILANTE	326
38	TRAILING NICK	331

39	NICK'S GETAWAY PLAN	333
40	FINDING NICK	340
41	THE MEETING	346
42	AGENT WILLIAMS AND THE SHERIFF	349
43	IVY RUNS FOR IT	351
44	BAD BOY MAKES GOOD	354
45	MAGGIE TELLS HER DAD GOODBYE	360
46	MAGGIE TRIES TO HELP CY	366
47	DON'T DRINK AND DRIVE	368
48	KIRT AND MAGGIE	376
49	GUY DRIVES HOME	387
50	KIRT'S LETTER OF COMMITMENT	389
51	ANOTHER FUN EVENING	392

ACKNOWLEDGEMENTS

A first novel is often semi-autobiographical. This one is not, although it uses composites of my youth and intimate knowledge of the venues in the story. It would be wrong not to acknowledge those strong influences, especially those people who may see their name attached to a character or place. I assure you, it's all fiction.

I would like to thank my wife Cathy and son Evan for their helpful criticism and edits. I would also like to thank my first readers John Birney, Janet Ladley, Pauline Ciesielski and Marion Ames. Insight was gleaned from each. Thank you to Michigan Historical Center at Hartwig Pines and History of The Ottawa and Chippewa of Michigan part of the Native American Nations (online service). Background information was aided by the NY/NJ Freight Forwarders and brokers association.

I would also like to thank four early influencers who had a great impact on my love of the written word. My mother, Marion Ames,

who never stops reading. Two high school teachers, Mr. Fuller and Mrs. Friedenburg, both of whom gave solid instruction and encouragement. Dr. Parola at University of Michigan who helped hone my writing into something someone might actually want to read and taught me the near sacredness of the scholastic process. There are too many great writers to give tribute to here but I will mention Charles Dickens, Hemmingway, Kurt Vonnegut, Jim Harrison, Elmore Leonard and John Irving as having made the deepest impressions
on me.

Special thanks to my son Evan who used his considerable persuasive and technical skills to convince me to take the individual route to publication.
His understanding of the marketing, linking and sales process in the virtual space was and is invaluable.

In no special order I would like to thank Pastor Erwin Kostizen, his wife Carolyn and family, Paul Maier Th.D./PhD at Western Michigan University for his insight into historical fiction writing,

Stephanie Hawka PhD. and our great orthodox Lutheran theologians who stay loyal to the text while using humor and poignancy to clarify their work. Throughout my learning the classical dogmaticians have made it joyful to grow using writing skills that excel in a non-fiction format.

I feel compelled to thank the late Norman McLain whose publications near the end of his life left me wanting more. McLain had a wonderful way of communicating intense human emotion without ever sinking to sentimentality or nostalgic flights. Both <u>A River Runs Through It</u> and <u>Young Men and Fire</u> told deeply personal stories while also plunging the reader into the place and era of the story. I learned much from his approach.

In fiction little is new so revealing what remains unsaid in life is paramount. If I have learned anything it is that the written word remains, the most expansive medium to tell a story and the best way to open anyone's imagination. Thank you all who have inspired me to make the attempt.

To Cathy and Evan

BEAR'S WOODSTOCK

The Feathered Hook Lodge on the Manistee River in Mesick, MI. 1997, early May.

Bear sat motionless on the bank of the Manistee waiting patiently for the signal from Cy. If all went well Bear knew he would be called upon to "retrieve" at least two tasty browns or brookies before the late morning hatch came to an end. For the last seven years Bear faithfully sat on the banks from April through November. He was so attuned to the rhythms of the ritual that he would begin to watch the surface of the water for signs indicating the onset of the hatch. If he detected no rising or sipping, no caddis or mayfly emerging, depositing or spinning, Bear would lazily stand up and make his way back to the lodge. Cy had gotten to the point that if he saw Bear walk away he would either quit fishing or resort to nymphs and streamers. Bear was the best barometer for dry flies that Cy had ever known. If Cy decided he wanted to keep a trout he would simply say, "OK, Bear. Fish," and Bear would jump into the water, stealthily secure the trout in his jaws and take it over to Cy. It amazed Cy that the skin of the trout was rarely punctured. After witnessing any retrieval by Bear Cy would always think and sometimes say out loud, "There truly is our God." Cy's language was peppered with praises to God with an emphasis on His *I AM* nature. As a former conservative Jew now Orthodox Lutheran Christian, Cy took his faith very seriously and with deep passion. He saw nothing blasphemous in declaring the certainty of God reflected by the beauty of Bear's impeccable work. Bear was a phenomenon, a Blonde Labrador retriever that could as easily fetch a salmonoid as any piscatorial bear—hence the name. Cy did not teach this trick to Bear, merely directed his innate desire to do so. When Bear was just a puppy he would try to catch the minnows and small fry that would collect in the shallow bend of the river just next to the lodge. Cy had never seen anything like it. As Bear grew so did his fish retrieval skills. Initially Bear would lunge at every fish he saw but through careful training Cy was able to direct Bear to wait for the command before he snared the fish. After a time, Cy was able to teach Bear when he could and could not eat the fish and eventually to actually retrieve on the command of, "Okay, Bear. Fish."

For the last five years Bear had developed into quite an angling aid and to the locals and the guest's at Cy and Sylvia's Feathered Hook Lodge, Bear was legendary. Like most legends many of the stories told about Bear were absolutely true many however were developed from fanciful yarns spun over one to many "pops" at the Mesick Inn. One such embellishment was the idea that Bear and not a famous fly fisher from Montana, held the Michigan Master Angler award for the largest King Salmon ever caught in fresh water. According to the story Bear spotted the lunker during the fall run while wandering along the banks of the Manistee several miles down stream from the lodge. Upon spotting the monster Bear stealthily entered the water downstream and carefully waded and paddled for over 5 miles before attacking the giant King from behind. Bear attached himself to the King's backbone, bite down and broke the beast's back. He then dragged the King to shore and proceeded to drag him all the way back to the lodge. Along the way Bear encountered a real black bear that had designs on his prize. Bear, not to be outdone, hauled the fish up a hill to a drainage tunnel under the road and placed himself in front of the entrance determined to fight off the Black Bear. As the bear cautiously lumbered toward the entrance, Bear lay there playing dead. The bear rocked the lab several times before deciding that he was truly dead. Just as the black started to step over Bear, Bear latched onto the black's testicles and jumped backwards down the small hill leading to the tunnel. The black bear cried out in agony and ran screaming back towards the river. Bear then decided to take the shoulder of the road where he was spotted by Carl a local cherry truck driver who recognized him as he dragged the monster King along the road back to Mesick. The driver was amazed at both the size of the fish and Bear's determination to take it home. The driver also noticed a considerable amount of fresh blood on Bear's face but assumed that the blood came from the fish. Carl let down his back gate and encouraged Bear to hop on, which he did. When the driver delivered Bear back to the lodge everyone was amazed. They were also completely puzzled as to why a set of black bear testicles was lodged inside the giant Kings jaws.

"There's got to be one hell of a story behind that," Carl said as he continued on his way to Clair.

Even though Bear had indeed caught or retrieved some impressive fish, this story, (although not true), was denied by no one in town, including Cy. After a while the lie was so accepted that many people pathologically remembered witnessing the event and dozens claimed to have been there the day Carl delivered Bear, the king and the testicles. Minimal research would have placed most of them nowhere near Mesick at that time. Privately Cy referred to the story as Bear's Woodstock and estimated that over a 100 people had witnessed the non-existing event. Cy never denied the story though. He reasoned that it was a harmless tale, springing from some truth and often good for business.

DARKNESS ON THE FACE OF THE EARTH

On this early spring day, with the snow still in spots on the north banks and the river full from thawed run off, Cy felt none of the wear of his sixty-five years. As he jaunted up the hillside back to the lodge, he looked toward cabin number seven. He decided to double check on "The Hermit" if for no other reason than to nose around. Kirt, "The Hermit," checked in four weeks ago and as far as Cy knew hadn't left his cabin more than a couple times. He certainly wasn't a fly fisher, Cy surmised, or he would have been on the river given that the opening day occurred three days ago. When "The Hermit" checked in, he refused to provide identification, but did pay for four months rent, up front. Even though this was a violation of a local ordinance, Cy determined that the law was unconstitutional and took the money. Just in case, Cy and Sylvia kept a faithful record of their mysterious guest's appearance and mode of transportation. A few days later, Cy and Sylvia become concerned that they may be harboring a fugitive and contacted the local State Police post to check on the license plate of the vehicle the Hermit was driving. Once a check had been made, verification of "The Hermit's" appearance matched with the plates, Cy and Sly determined that all was well and "Mr. Hermit" had a right to be alone. Knowing what he knew about Kirt, "The Hermit," Cy felt incredible empathy and tried to give him as much space a possible.

"Has he come out today, Sweetie?" Cy queried.

"I haven't seen so much as a ruffle of the curtains," Sylvia replied.

"I am truly concerned about him. In his state of mind, who knows what he'd do to himself and I do not relish the thought of cleaning up after a suicide," Cy said selfishly and with genuine concern for Kirt.

"They say that men tend to do it in a violent way – I'd hate to think of the tragedy and the mess of a gunshot to the head," Sylvia said with tears welling up in her eyes. "Maybe we should call his doctor again, yes? I think we better call him right now," Sylvia insisted while thinking out loud.

Cy breathed a deep sigh. He was inclined to let the poor soul work it out on his own, but the conversations he'd had recently with Pastor

Cramer had convinced him that he was wrong in his assessment of how to deal with Kirt, "The Hermit." Pastor Cramer had convinced Cy that the worst thing a man with depression could do was to isolate himself from the very support he needs. The Pastor/Psychotherapist had recently taken to repeating a quote of Martin Luther who had once said, while in the throws of a deep depression: "…Please, all of you, please go on talking – It is good for me to be around people. I will just sit here and listen."

Pastor Cramer was very concerned about the welfare of Kirt and knew of where he spoke. Cramer himself had suffered bouts of clinical depression, aka "the Black Dog." A term he borrowed from Winston Churchill, who stated, "Everything seems gray or grayer. Every voice muffled drones. Making contact with others seems impossible and the damn affliction presses down day and night, and sleep either becomes something from which you never want to escape or the one thing you are unable to do. The only thing that kept me from blowing my brains out was the awareness of God's command against suicide and a gossamer strand of faith."

"I shutter to think of what it must be like for a man of no faith and no hope to endure the pangs of depression. Before the miraculous medications of the last several years, men of great constitution developed coping mechanisms to deal with "the Black Dog" until he would go away," Cy said. "Some of their tactics were helpful and healthful, and some were not. Churchill seems to have overdone alcohol and cigars while spending countless hours painting. Luther admittedly abused the local brew, and Lincoln would retreat to his bedroom for days, even weeks. Jefferson was known to do the same…."

"I didn't see him bring in a long gun, sweetie. Just an old aluminum fly rod case," Sylvia justified. One thing Cy did notice was that sometime during the night, Kirt had removed the license plate from the rear of his plate. This also did not go unnoticed by two other guests in town now watching from the window of the Mesick Inn across the street from the Feathered Hook Lodge.

Inside the confines of cabin number seven, Kirt sat peering out a crack in the curtain of the back window overlooking the Manistee. This most recent event, this "situational" response, although understandable, did not explain the same response he had had to more minimal stress or loss or no stress or no loss at all. "The illness seems to have a life of its own," echoed his psychiatrist's words in his head. On the stove sat carefully prepared homemade spaghetti sauce and dried out cooked ziti. It was one of the side effects of his affliction that he often had difficulty concentrating on even the smallest of tasks; consequently, the focused effort needed to prepare the meal was wasted as he had forgotten its preparation and now sat in an unfocused gaze. The clinical unipolar depression suffered by Kirt at least a half dozen times in his life was triggered by stress, loss, or nothing at all. *This* time around he knew exactly what the trigger was, but truly wondered how he would recover given that his wife had always been there before and this time she could not be there to support or reassure him. The news of her and their two daughter's fatal accident near Telegraph and Twelve Mile Road left him bereft and so disconsolate that he truly wanted to cause his own death. He had contemplated it several times in the last four months since their accident. Looking at the Manistee now beginning to sprout forth in full spring array did little to lift his sprits. The many times spent on this river in solitude and at peak peace and contentment now seemed illusory. He loved the solitude and the haunting beauty of the wandering river. *Maybe I had merely imagined those days – Maybe I invented them?* Maybe life after all was best enjoyed while ignorant of the realities of loss, pain and death. His Christ, whom he yet and fleetingly knew would somehow pull him through, seemed angry, two faced and indifferent. Maybe isolation, prayer and exercise could bring him around to some degree? The Welbutrin seemed not to be working now. Even as he had experienced the ineffectiveness of other anti-depressants that had worked for years and for some reason lost their effectiveness. Maybe his faith in their effectiveness is what was working and loss of trust in them caused them not to work? All he knew was that the Manistee, that in the past had been such a source of comfort, now was viewed as an inky run through a half dead landscape. The river ran gray; it seemed to him. The bank merely shades of white and gray like some ill-conceived noir film. In reality, the banks fairly teemed with yellow-green sprouts of crocus, violets, trillium, wild leeks, lilies and grasses reflected in the slightly copper tea colored water as it rushed over fallen logs on a bed of rocks in shades of red-brown, black and dark green. Hatches of small blue winged olives created reactions on the surface as lunker browns sipped them from the surface film and the immature dinks splashed as they haphazardly broke through the surface. Herons, eagles, and hawks waited—each in their own camouflaged way, for the opportunity to snare the most careless of the trout. None of this was apparent to him now. What made it more painful was he knew he should be seeing the beauty, the tranquil splendor. It was a damned awful feeling. He used to be able to lean on Beth during times like this, it was easy for her to understand; they had become so intertwined. She was so wonderful, so grounded, so affirming when he needed her to be. When he was whole, when he was not depressed, he was the epitome of balance. No highs, just a calm, crisp and strong spirit. His confidence seemed to know no limits when he was whole. His children respected him because they knew "the Black Dog" was not the real daddy they so loved – they respected his tenacity his strength to gut the dark times out and his commitment to them. He bore the illness well, which often reminded him of Hemingway's phrase: "You put up with it because you know how damn good life can be."

RECOVERY AND BACK TO WORK

Even as he stared into the tea colored Manistee, Officer Guy Veitengruber could still remember the anguish on his partner's face while on stake out outside of the newest addition to the Birmingham, MI downtown community. The street level view of the Pax town homes gave one the impression that they may be on some quiet side street on the upper west side of Manhattan, New York. Guy Veitengruber and his partner of four years, Cal Thornton, were waiting for the appearance of a highly connected drug lord, Joel Cantor, to exit the building. Their goal was to make sure a series of standby local and Detroit police were prepared to trail him to his destination. They had been informed that a meeting between Cantor and a Yemen contact, who supplied southeast Michigan with a very potent heroin, (likely from the Afghani region), was to take place at one of the many upscale hotels in the area. *The* hotel was in at least one of the six various sections of the suburbs— Where the *real* action takes place in the greater Detroit area.

Guy had just picked up a couple of Asian chicken salads, iced teas and a quart of strawberries from the "Merchant of Vino." Both he and Cal were fairly conscious of their health and wellbeing. Being able to have the best produce and free-range chicken not only kept the calories and cholesterol low, it also just tasted plain good. Both men were forty-three years old and had entered The Bureau when they were thirty-eight. While working together on a bust of an angel dust production facility in Ann Arbor, MI, their boss found that their individual instincts and skills sets were highly compatible and decided to pair them up for any future such investigations. Guy was extremely expressive, Cal analytical. This may be a compatible arrangement regarding the outcome of a bust, but could at times be a highly combustible relationship. Often Guy would get downright pissed as Cal could sit for hours on end without saying a word. Guy found it frustrating that the two of them could discuss any myriad of issues and that Cal's response would often be monosyllabic. Guy, however, had enormous respect and emotional attachment to this highly talented, loyal and supportive partner. Cal's loyalty to Guy was legendary. Not only had Cal saved Guy's life at least twice, but he also became closer to his children and wife than most of Guy's own family. He always provided the right gift and words of advice. In Cal's own emotionally closed way, he expressed a love for Guy that he could only compare, as many cops do, to that of his wife's. Guy's respect was mutual. The relationship of these two men reflected a bond only law enforcement could understand. The role of "protector" filled by these men exposed them to more dangerous situations than those engaged in a declared war. Their enemy was often unknown. The life-threatening situations came in shifting forms. One could only trust their partner, as only he understood the nuances of any given situation. They required this intimate knowledge of each other to survive.

As they sat quietly eating their salad, they heard Joel Cantor over their surveillance signaling to his driver to bring the car around. Both Cal and Guy carefully closed the lids on their salads and the tops on their iced teas. From their location, two blocks down the street, they were able to see if Cantor pulled out. Additionally, a camera placed in the garage revealed who was actually entering the vehicle, thereby avoiding a tail on a decoy. The electronics for this purpose had been planted earlier this morning, as it wasn't unusual that these bastards would discover the electronics fairly quickly. It was essential that the devices be planted as closely to scandal meeting time frame as possible. On the screen inside their vehicle they could plainly see Joel Cantor slip into the back seat of the bullet proof Lexus. As Cantor exited the building, Cal and Guy watched to see which direction he would turn. It came as somewhat of a surprise that they turned north toward Main Street. Once on Main, they continued to Woodward Street, made a "Michigan left" and headed north once more. In a calculated attempt to guess their destination, Cal began calling all posted police and FBI to keep them informed as a redundancy to their own on board-tracking device. Uncharacteristically Cal blurted out in frustration, "Where is that son of a bitch going?" Guy acknowledged, "I don't get it either, Cal. I thought we had the odds fairly well calculated. Most of the time, Cantor stays tight to the Metro area."

They followed the Lexus north on highway I-75 past The Great Lakes Crossing Outlets, Grand Blanc and Flint. "Where the hell is he going?" Cal said again. Finally, Cantor veered off the highway and took Exit 131 Clio/Montrose, heading west toward Montrose, MI. "Okay, Cal. Call the State Police and notify all locals ASAP. I don't want us to handle this alone," said Guy. The Lexus then turned north onto Seymour Road, which follows the 78.3-mile-long Flint River. It was autumn, and the indigenous Michigan trees were beautifully arrayed in various colors. Cal thought it ironic that on such a beautiful day, on such a beautiful autumnal display, that in the midst of all this beauty traveled one of the lowest, most repulsive humans on the planet. The Montrose area reminded Guy of some of the New England areas he had visited with his wife. The Lexus turned left into the Montrose Orchards. *Of course,* thought Guy. *Large crowd, people moving around like hypnotized cows. The bastard is going to do the exchange right here. But where would the drugs be, in the trunk? And why would Cantor do this himself?* The Lexus parked on the western side of the gravel-covered parking lot. Immediately, the doors opened and Cantor stepped out. From the other side of the vehicle stepped a young man attired in a pair of blue jeans and a hooded navy blue sweatshirt. The two exchanged words and Cantor proceeded to go back into the car, and the Lexus pulled away. Cal radioed the State police and directed them to follow the Lexus until it stopped again. Both Cal and Guy stepped out of their vehicle and carefully tailed the young man. The hooded sweatshirt traveled inside and around the Orchard's crowded Bakery/Concessions building. This quiet observation went on for several minutes. The young man picked up a gallon of cider, some cinnamon donuts and a raspberry pie and patiently waited in the checkout line. Cal went outside and Guy stayed inside the building. When the hooded sweatshirt departed the building, he moved toward a Channel 12 television van and climbed in.

Meanwhile, the Lexus had pulled over at a rest stop several miles just south off of highway I-75 North. Inside the Lexus Joel Cantor viewed two screens: One focused on the Channel 12 television van, and the other inside of a small building where three of Cantor's men sat across from two others at a table. Cantor's men were holding a bowling bag full of cash and had their own monitor screen of the Channel 12 television van. As soon as the hooded sweatshirt in the van gave the "Okay," Cantor called his men to turn over the bag of money. By this time, Cal and Guy were standing by either side of the van. Cal signaled his intention to enter the van. Guy nodded and entered from the other side. As both Officers opened the doors, the young man in the hooded sweatshirt turned toward the van's partition, thinking that only Guy had entered. The young man pulled a Glock and fired off a round at Guy, who dodged and also returned fire at each of the young man's legs. Guy's intention was to bring the man down and keep him alive in order to question him regarding the whole fiasco. The action paid off and the hooded sweatshirt fell to his knees, screaming in agony. Guy then directed the FBI backup who arrived to call an ambulance. In the heat of the action, Guy failed to notice that not only did the young man fall to the ground, but also did Cal. His partner was in a controlled state of shock while gripping his bloody groin in pure misery. One of the shots fired by Cal may have ricochet or passed through an exit wound of the intended victim's knee, entering Cal's groin—piercing and exploding one testicle, and settling in Cal's inner left thigh. As soon as the young man in the hooded sweatshirt was stabilized in handcuffs, Guy called out to Cal. When no response was forthcoming he rushed around the front of the van only to see Cal curled up on the ground in a frozen fetal position. Cal cried out to Guy, "Why in the hell would you shoot? It was a possible crossfire!" A rush of circulating blood immediately left Guy's brain inducing a serious panic attack. He hyperventilated, and passed out, going against all of his law enforcement training. The very thought of harming his partner sent him into an intense awareness of guilt and fear. How did he not consider his partner's position on the other side of the van? When the backup team arrived, they came upon a peculiar scene: Guy passed out, Cal writhing on the ground, the hooded sweatshirt in handcuffs screaming in agony and a boat load of Afghani heroin in the back.

It was a bittersweet time as the bust went down even better than planned. The young man spilled his guts, leading to a conviction that placed Joel Cantor in prison for the rest of his life. Cal and Guy were honored with the "Creative Investigators Medallion" on a podium in front of a thousand agents, including their supervisors. Inevitably, Cal remained so depressed and so angry that nothing Guy said or did would suffice. As they left the podium, Cal screamed at Guy for all to hear, "You flaming asshole!"

Guy sat, months later, looking into the tea colored Manistee River. He stood up and walked back to the Mesick Inn. As he walked back to his cabin he thought, *"What the hell good is this doing me? I might as well go back home.*" Then he saw a *ghost* across the street.

ENTERTAINING JUSTICE

Ivy decided he was going to dine in the Mesick Inn's dining room. Picking up his menu, he noticed a man outside dressed in nondescript spring-weight clothing and a ski mask pulled tightly against a pair of wrap-around sunglasses. This eccentric man approached an old Ford truck that was parked in a handicapped-parking zone closest to the entry of the Mesick Inn. Ivy watched as the man removed the valve stem caps and carefully unscrewed each one, allowing air to escape from the tires. The man did this to all four tires on the vehicle, including the spare inside the box. Then the man moved across the street and did the same thing to three vehicles parked near the grocery store. As if on cue, a highly overweight man left the Mesick Inn and climbed into the Ford truck. The man started his vehicle, revved the engine and commenced to jack rabbit onto Boardman Street. Ivy choked with laughter as the seals on the tires were broken and the truck driver stunned and flummoxed sat motionless for several seconds. Finally, he jumped out, went to the front of the vehicle and opened the hood. The man could see no reason for the abrupt stop to occur, so he reentered the vehicle and gently tried to pull forward with obvious results. He jumped back out took ten steps away from the truck, letting out a, "Son of a bitch!" so loud that all the diners in the Mesick Inn's dinning room turned their heads to see what was happening. Ivy, by this time, was laughing so hard that he began to feel lightheaded and tears ran down his cheeks. The man with the truck then reentered the Inn bitching and complaining so loudly that Ivy nearly wet his pants. Of course the whole incident was a mystery to the rest of the guests. Almost instantaneously, the man confronted Ivy and shouted, "Just what is so damn funny asshole? You do that?" Instead of responding, Ivy just passed out and his head hit the table. The hostess dialed 911. Walt Johns, the owner of the Mesick Inn, hovered over the table to investigate the status of Ivy's level of consciousness. Breathing and pulses existed, yet shallow, irregular and quick. The symptoms indicated a possible heart attack or vasovagal syncope—Symptoms Walt had seen several times back in Hamtramck, MI during his former career.

Walt had worked his way up the Engineering ladder. When he was only fifty-two years old, he retired as President of TriMotors

Engineering. TriMotors took their name as a reflection of the former domination of "The Big 3" automotive manufacturers in Michigan. As a young graduate from General Motors Institute (GMI), Walt had witnessed several such medical signs and symptoms on the factory floor. Those affected at that time were generally male, clinically obese and sedentary, with multiple co-morbidities and around fifty years old. Back then these workers would work half a day and have someone else clock them out. When Walt would witness these men endure similar syncope episodes, he had little pity for their plight and hoped that the incident would permanently take them out of the work force. They were almost impossible to fire, given the irrational power "The Big 3" had, due to the union. Ivy, however, did not fit the typically ill-appearing characteristics. He was tall and lean, and though his face said he was late forties his body portrayed possibly thirties. *Why would a guy of his stature pass out?* Within ten minutes, the Emergency Medical Technicians (EMTs) arrived, captured several readings and administered oxygen while strapping Ivy onto a stretcher. As Ivy settled onto the stretcher, a black PK380 handgun slid quietly onto the ancient wooden floor of the Mesick Inn dining room. Walt quickly picked up the gun and discretely placed it into his back pocket. He left the dining room and hid it in a safe under the loose floorboards in his office. After ,the ambulance rushed to the Munson Medical Center in Traverse City and all of the guests and employees calmed down, Walt approached his hostess demanding, "Come back to my office. Now."

Entering the office, Walt locked the door behind them and turned to Maggie. Maggie was forty-four years old, widowed and everyone's friend in Mesick. She enjoyed her genetic gift of appearing at least fifteen years younger than she was. The envious women in town would often say she stayed that way because her daughters kept her young of mind. Deep down, they all knew that that was not the reason. Maggie's mother bared similar traits, looking like she was sixty at the age of seventy-five and retained her slender figure after having three children. She worked long hours by her husband's side on the family farm in Traverse City, MI, producing a fine living and a comfortable nest egg for their three growing girls. Maggie stood there puzzled in Walt's office. He lifted a piece of floorboard; pointing at a shiny object, "Look here. See what he dropped out of that man's pocket?" Walt inquired. He picked up the black handgun.

"This is a PK380, a damn fine weapon. Hand crafted by those genius Germans. The thing must have cost over $5,000… Maybe he is with the CIA, the FBI? I don't know."

"Why did you pick it up?" Maggie nervously asked.

"I don't know. I just couldn't help it. I've wanted one of these for a long time."

"Why don't you just buy one? You can definitely afford it."

"Don't know. I just couldn't let go of the bucks," Walt said with his eyes glued on the handgun.

"Ya' got more money than God, Wally!" She was the only one to call him that.

"I'm gonna do it," Walt blurted.

"Do what?"

"Buy one of these… Come on, let's go to the hospital."

"What for?" Maggie asked, hesitant to go.

"To see where he bought this WW2 tool. Maybe he got a deal."

"You go, Wally. I'll stay here." She had no interest in Wally's stupid venture. *Jerk,* she said to herself.

GUY VISITS IVY

Guy Veitengruber sat outside the hospital room trying to decide what to say to Karl. He decided on the assertive approach: "Karl, is that you?" Ivy sat up in his bed. He couldn't believe his ears. He had not heard his real name used in years. It startled him and Guy could see that it did. In an attempt to keep up the act, Ivy said, "No, afraid not buddy."

"Well I'll be damned. You look so much like him. Of course it's been over twenty years, but he was one hell of an athlete. Sorry to bother you, but you look so familiar. I just had to ask."

"No problem," said Ivy. "Everyone seems to have someone they look like."

Guy walked out of the room. He didn't buy it, none of it. That guy in there was Karl and he was going to prove it. Ivy sat stunned. *Guy Veitengruber? I can't believe it. Holy shit. I have to get out of here, complete my contract and get back to New York.* He called to his nurse and asked her to page his Doctor ASAP. Just as he was about to get out of bed, Walt the Mesick Innkeeper walked in.

Guy's mind was clicking like a strobe light. He reasoned through any possibility or reason why Karl was lying in that hospital room. He decided on a parallel approach that required a high-resolution photo and matching DNA. He would cross-reference it with Law Enforcement Information Network (LEIN) and the FBI database to find any matches.

Walking by the nurses' station, Guy said, "I hope the Physician taking care of Karl is good."

"Oh, he is," said the nurse. "Dr. Brandise is a great cardiologist."

"Is he the specialist from Ann Arbor, MI?" Asked Guy.

"Oh no," she said. "Dr. Brandise is now a cardiologist based in Traverse City. He was originally from St. Vincent's Hospital in Indianapolis, so no Ann Arbor connection, I'm afraid."

"Well, thanks. He sounds like a good man... Glad to hear Karl's in good hands."

He continued down the corridor, mind racing as he walked. *I need to get those medical records. I can't use my FBI status on this,* he thought. *Maybe I can pass as a Doctor? I'll need DNA. I'll need to take a couple photos while he is asleep. DNA, DNA... Damn. How do I get that? Could a reporter get that? Would his mother or father have any of his old items around? Maybe old shoes, a brush or comb, his old golf club grips, or a lock of his hair?*

Guy opened his cell phone and called a reporter from The Detroit News. "Bob? It's Guy. I have a favor to ask... I need you to conduct a story on parents whose child was the first and only one to go to college. At least you can tell them that."

"What am I looking for, Guy? DNA, huh?" Bob asked.

"Tell them you are doing a story called, 'The First members of A Family Attending College.' Maybe you can get some hair or something?"

"Am I on the FBI's payroll here?" Bob asked.

"No, but I'll buy you a nice dinner," Guy offered.

"Okay, Guy. I'll give it a whirl. Where am I going and who am I seeing?"

Guy closed his phone, stood outside the hospital's secured phlebotomy lab until the door conveniently opened. He was dressed in a white lab coat to blend in. Guy approached a phlebotomist behind the counter, "I need to see the blood samples for a patient named Ivy. I need to verify his last name."

"I've got it right here. What's the problem?"

"I'm not sure. Doctor Brandise ordered me to retrieve one of his lab samples."

The phlebotomist gave him one of the four blood vials with Ivy's name and medical record number on it.

"Thanks," Guy said with a smile.

Guy walked out of the hospital with the white lab coat on. He rushed over to the FedEx office, carefully packaged Ivy's vial of blood and sent it overnight to the FBI Biologist headquarters in Detroit. Guy opened his phone and dialed the extension number to Jim, the Biologist in Detroit. "Jim? Hey, it's Guy."

"Hey, Guy! How's the vacation?" Jim asked.

"Interesting—Hey, so, I am sending you a vial of blood via FedEx. I need a rapid DNA test performed. I hope to send you another type of DNA sample soon to see if they match. See if you can find any database matches on this blood, okay?" Guy explained as he frantically left FedEx.

"What's up, Guy?"

"It's a long story, but I need this quick."

"Okay, okay. Try to have some fun, please?" Jim urged Guy.

In a way, Guy was doing just that. He jumped into his car and drove to North Port, MI. He ate a wonderful breakfast at The Warm Kitchen. He ordered Eggs Benedict, a side of very ripe cantaloupe and a grilled cinnamon roll. He bought a dozen cinnamon rolls to go. He walked over to a nearby post office and mailed the rolls overnight to his wife with a note saying he would be home in a few days. He drove back to the Mesick Inn.

CONFIRMATION

Guy's phone rang.

"Guy? It's Bob. I have what you need about Karl," said The Detroit News Reporter.

"Hey, great. What did you get?" Asked Guy.

"Well, his mother had kept a lock of his hair from his first haircut and I snatched a few strands when she left the room to get me a drink. She's still haunted by it all."

"I can't imagine," Guy concurred.

"The mother discussed Karl's acceptance to Harvard and his success up until his disappearance. The ugly evidence of his life broke her heart. I could still see the pain in her face. I told her I wouldn't mention her son's name in the article."

"And the Dad?" Guy asked.

"Pretty closed off. He has a love/hate memory of his son. It's evident he misses him, but he is pissed at the way Karl threw it all away."

"Bob, I owe you. Please FedEx your documents to the address I left on your voicemail."

"Guy, I'm happy to help, but this visit was draining. Clue me in next time. I'm gonna go home early to be with my family."

"Thank you, Bob. And sorry, next time I will," Guy said before hanging up.

A LITTLE FUN, INTERRUPTED

The next morning Guy asked Cy where he could get some fly fishing lessons.

"I always wanted to try it," Guy said.

"Try the fly shop in the city of Beulah," said Cy. "I'm told they are very good, tell me how it works out for ya'."

"Thanks," said Guy.

Guy drove over to Beulah via M31. The hours of the shop were listed as 8:00am to 12:00pm and 3:00pm to 8:00pm. Since it was already 2:00 pm, he decided to drive into Frankfort and grab some lunch. Heading west he saw the arch over the road welcoming visitors to Frankfort, MI. It had a large model of a freighter smoke stacks, lights and all at the top of the arch. At the top of the hill he pulled over just to take in the view. He blew off lunch and went back to the fly shop.

"Most fish are caught within 30 feet so long casts aren't really necessary. You can develop a double haul in due time. For now, just work on the cast between 11 and 1, smooth karate chop, feel the line load," said the fly shop owner.

"How am I doing, generally," asked Guy.

"Pretty good. Now let's talk about reading the water and fishing a stream. It's a lot different than this still water."

"Sounds good…"

Guy's cell began to ring.

"Sorry, just have to catch this."

"Hey, Jim. How's it going? What did you find out?"

"They're a match. I don't even want to know what you're up to. Hey you just got a freebie at breakneck speed. The databases kicked up a match for a young guy named Karl Schroeder. That was twenty years ago though and they say he is dead," Jim said.

"Well, guess what? He is very much alive. Don't worry about the under the table request. I called into the office right after I called you and they know what's going on, 'even sending an Agent from

Chicago who knows this case as well as anyone. I'll tell you all about it when I get home. Thanks again," Cy said, hanging up.

"Sorry, Jim. Gotta go. Thanks for the lessons. I will be back. Ship me any gear I will need to this address, use this AmEx."

"'Could run around six hundred or so all told, that okay?'"

"Yeah, whatever is entry level but not cheap. I gotta get back to my room and my lap top ASAP. Thanks a lot Jim." Cy shook his hand heartily. His investigator juices were in full boil.

WALT MEETS IVY

The Emergency Department at Munson Medical Center in Traverse City (TC) was fundamentally as sound as any good hospital in the nation. TC was not a hick town—it was the hub of the playground of the Midwest. Tourists came from all over the world to tour the NW corner of the state. The storied haunts like the fish town of Leland, the pollen free areas of Harbor Springs, the early resorts of Bay Harbor and Petoskey. Historically speaking, this was a moneyed area and therefore a sound hospital was a given. Over the years not only did the wealthy of New York and Chicago come to visit, but also a healthy number of upper and middle income earners as well. The area provided an ambiance for every rustic taste from low cost motels to multi million dollar second homes on the Harbor Springs peninsula. Walt checked at the front desk to see where Ivy was. "Can you tell me what's wrong with him?"

"No," said the nurse," only the immediate family can gain that information."

"I am family," said Walt. "He's my nephew visiting here and his mom and dad expect me to see him," Walt continued the lie.

"He is in room 347. You ask him what is wrong. Visiting hours are over at 8:00 pm on that floor." Walt stopped by the gift shop and picked up a couple magazines and a local paper, then stepped into the elevator on his way to 347.

"Hey," said Ivy. "I can't thank you enough for getting me here."

"Don't mention it. What do they say is wrong?"

"The doctor says it is low blood pressure."

"Low pressure? I thought that was good."

"Yeah, but if it is too low that ain't good, buddy. I have had high blood pressure and high cholesterol for a long time according to the doc and my body just rebelled. I told him I run every day, and he said so have many athletes who have died from undiagnosed HBP. He also said I have only three heart chambers working at full capacity... probably that way all my life and the exercise helped to offset this without my knowledge. I haven't been to the doctor very often in the last 22 years so I guess they now have the technology to see the heart. He said I am lucky I haven't died."

"So what now?" Said Walt.

"Well, I need to reduce most stress in my life. Right. I can do that," Ivy said sarcastically. "I will have to get a handle on this somehow, or die."

"What does he suggest besides reducing stress, drugs, and surgery?" Walt asked.

"A combination of both reducing cholesterol and blood pressure."

"I thought you said it was too low?"

"Well, it is. But it's complicated." He said, trying to get away from the subject.

"If you don't mind my asking. Where did you get the PK?" Cy asked as he handed him the gun.

"I bought it in Germany a few years ago. I like the way it feels in the hand and it conceals easily." Ivy said.

"Where in Germany, if you don't mind my asking?"

"Call this guy," handing Cy a card, "I get asked all the time."

"Thanks. What did it cost?"

"I paid six thousand. Pre WWII and like new."

"Wow, well I'm going to treat myself and get one. Are you in law enforcement?" Cy asked.

"No. Just consulting ,international logistics , but I get into some antsy areas some times and need the protection. I have used it twice and it saved my life. Long stories."

"Well, I won't trouble you any longer. Thanks, Ivy. By the way, is that your real name?"

"Real as any," Ivy smiled.

"Do you have any family, Ivy? Would you like me to get a hold of them?"

"No, just a sister in California," he lied.

Walt walked away wondering who the hell this *guy* was, this "Ivy". *Consultant my ass*, he muttered to himself.

Ivy's role was quite solitary now and to him, his family was dead. He had learned the process of blocking memories and emotion that did not fit into his pragmatic and secretive work. When Ivy was eighteen years old he was the hero of Clio high. He was a highly skilled basketball player and golfer. He was equally gifted in academics. His Germanic good looks made him ruggedly handsome, appreciated by men and women. He had a scar on his chin from an accident while baling hay and a larger one on his forehead that ran diagonally from his upper left forehead down to just above his right eyebrow. As one of his favorite female teachers said, "Even his scars look good!" He won the medalist award for the Big Nine and became the state champion medalist at the State high school tournament held at Oakland Hills, MI. His scores at Oakland were 69 and 67, a Michigan record in 1982. The Michigan PGA had offered to sponsor his attempt to get a tour card and make it through PGA school. Meanwhile, MSU offered him a full scholarship to play basketball. At 6'2" he was not the tallest player but moved around the court like the reincarnation of Pete Marevich. But the dearest offer to Karl, (his real name is Karl Schroeder. The moniker "Ivy" came much later), was the one he received from Harvard, a full scholarship to play golf for the team. Karl had his sights set on becoming a professor part time and working full time in archeology. Archeology fascinated him ever since he first read about the Dead Sea Scrolls and the history of ancient Egypt. His father was also passionate about the discipline and read all he could about the finds, history and the dove tailing of many Middle Eastern and Persian finds with the Biblical records. Karl's dad was not particularly religious but considered the bible as useful as regards reference to historical information. The Old Testament was of particular interest. Karl and his dad would review specific chapters trying to understand the locations of particular cites, rivers or other geographic landmarks. Unbeknownst to Karl's dad Karl had become fascinated by the many finds that *confirmed* both the Old and New testaments. The ancient city of UR was of particular interest, as it was the home land of Abraham and most likely all the early biblical populations. In preparation and as bait for Harvard attendance Karl was invited to a summer long dig in UR before his senior year. The bait worked and Karl accepted the offer at Harvard. No one in the greater Tri City area had ever been accepted to Harvard. Karl *was* the hometown hero, not just a cliché. Although Karl could have any girl he wanted, he merely dated fearing that attachments would get in the way of his dreams of digging in the dirt. Karl's dad and mother admired his grit and tenacity but often lamented his single mindedness, which could exclude him from others socially. He was not antisocial, 'just found no need for great doses human contact. Karl had a healthy sense of wry humor and once on a raucous night after winning the Michigan Medalist he stood on a table and did twenty minutes of standup humor mimicking everyone from the principal, his coaches, Rodney Dangerfield and Iggy Pop. His coach was laid flat ,gasping for breath, as Karl killed him with his mimicry. Because of this display, he was asked and begged by his English teacher to play the role of Nathan Detroit in his senior year play. He was of course excellent. To tell the truth his apparent effortless success annoyed the hell out of many, but his down to earth attitude usually diffused their jealousy. The fact was it took hard work to be as successful as he was. When at Harvard he would study archeology under the school of Anthropology connected to the famous Peabody Museum. In addition, he would be able to study abroad at University of Cambridge in England under a partnership program. He was ecstatic and could not wait to play the august courses of the United Kingdom. And he knew how to get extra cash to take with him.

Ivy's greatest weakness was his addictive tendencies. Archeology, golf, pot, alcohol, whatever. If he liked it, he really, really liked it. Pot was one of his favorite addictions and, if not for his high energy, it would have interfered with his studies and his golf. He became a connoisseur of marijuana—Kona, Mexican, California, Big Bud, Northern Lights. He knew his Indicas from his Sativas. He could identify each by taste and smell and the punch of its THC. No one ever ripped him off with inferior quality. A local dealer recruited him to sell the stuff to his high school friends. He was especially effective because he was such a high achiever even though he smoked his own product. Soon his selling ability became a new addiction and he stopped smoking himself, in any substantial way and focused just on selling. He applied a system of distribution that allowed him to clone his efforts through the Big Nine schools. He selected his own sales staff and multiplied his production 100 fold. His supplier in Ann Arbor rewarded him handsomely.

Ivy paged a nurse to his room. He then removed his IVs and stood up. He was a little woozy but soon found his balance and stood solidly vertical once again. The nurse walked in his room and looked a little puzzled. "What are you doing, Ivy?"

"I am checking out. Please have my bill prepared and I will pay before I leave."

"Ivy, you can't just leave like this. Have you talked to Doctor Denson?"

"No, not yet, but I *can* leave, and that's what I'm doing," he said with a smile. "Sherry, you and the other nurses have been terrific, but I need to manage this on an outpatient basis. I have too many obligations."

"Okay," said Sherry, shaking her head knowing it was not really okay.

Ivy opened his wallet and left four, one hundred dollar bills and a little note that read:

Thank you so much Sherry, Belinda, Barb and Carrie.

One for each of you. Spend this on yourselves, only!

With my admiration,

Ivy

Ivy grabbed his clothing from the small closet, hung them on the shower rod, turned on the shower and closed the door. Waiting for the steam to do its work, he put on his underwear and socks. Sherry stuck her head in his room and said, "The bill should be ready soon. I called Doctor Denson. Oh, and by the way, nice outfit!" She smiled, as did he, and she left. As she was leaving, Ivy said loudly, "Thanks, Sherry."

"Your welcome," she replied.

Ivy opened the bathroom door, pulled out his shirt and pants, and waited for the steam to dispel. He looked into the mirror and saw how tired he looked. He had a somewhat stylish two-day growth of beard. He washed his face, brushed his teeth, and slipped on a Merino wool mock sweater, black. Then he put on his light gray slacks. Fastening his belt, he slipped into his black loafers and started walking toward the front desk facing Front Street. He stopped, remembering to go back and get his wallet and keys. When he entered his room, an attractive young woman was adjusting the IV fluids. Ivy noticed her because she was so damn stunning. She said hello and walked out. As she walked away, Ivy noticed a butterfly tattoo on her right calf. Any attraction he felt abruptly went away. He hated all tattoos on women. 'Made them look tacky at best. *Why do they do that?* He said to himself.

"Ivy? Where are you going?" Ivy was surprised to see Doctor Denson there so soon.

"I'm leaving Doc. I appreciate all you have done, but I need you to tell me how to handle this as an outpatient."

"Ivy, look, you have an unusual condition. We don't see this very often and I need more time to put you through some additional tests so I can prescribe a course of treatment and an outpatient plan."

"Okay, so I will schedule the tests and get you the results then…"

"Ivy, promise me you will do that. This is not something to trifle with. It requires regular observation, at least for a few months…"

Ivy took one of Doctor Denson's cards and shook his hand sincerely. "Thank you Doc. I really appreciate your skill and dedication. I just have to get back to my work. By the way, can you can send the info you now have to a cardiologist I will name for you? 'Be in New York."

"Sure, just send me the request and we will get it over. Good luck, Ivy. I will look for your request for patient records. SOON."

Ivy could not grasp the cost of his five-day stay. The total exceeded $10,000. At any other time he would have tried to renegotiate, but instead he just pulled out his AmEx and gave it to the cashier. The cashier was a little taken aback, as she had never seen anyone pay his or her bill in full with a credit card. She was further amazed when the large amount came back approved. He signed the receipt and walked outside to a 68-degree day bright with sunshine and an almost cloudless sky. Grand Traverse Bay was arrayed in colors of deep blue, light green and turquoise. It reminded Ivy of the water in Acapulco, Mexico but without the annoying salt. He wondered how he could feel so good yet be ill.

Now, he thought. *What is Guy Veitengruber up to?*

IVY CHECKING OUT

Jane picked up the phone and called Walt.

"He's back here and he wants to check out."

"Keep him there I'll be right over," Walt said.

Ivy had parked near the front door of the Mesick Inn. He kept a quiet relaxed demeanor. He said hello to Jane, and told her that he and Vincent would be leaving in a few minutes. Ivy stopped and looked across the road at the Feathered Hook. "Vincent, is that guy over there our guy?"

"I don't know Ivy. He hasn't been in his room for a few days so I haven't been able to find out."

SICK OF THE DARKNESS

Kirt turned and looked at the stove, noticed the food that he had forgotten to eat and began to sob. He sobbed because it had come to this ,strong loss of focus and an inability to do the smallest things; he felt he might need hospitalization, which scared the hell out of him. He could hear his wife saying, "Get out and run, Kirt. The exercise always helps." He sat there crying for several more minutes and then went over to the sink, washed his face, wet his hair and slicked it back. He then put on a white headband, some heavy cotton sweats, and his favorite running shoes and stepped outside into a cool clear morning. Before running he went into his car and grabbed his sunglasses as the sun seemed excessively bright, and he did not want to make eye contact with anyone today. He did not warm up, he never did. He started walking slow, then faster and then broke into a fairly strong jog. He was heading west along the old railroad line that had been converted into a biking and running trail. He liked the feel of the synthetic brown mulch. It cushioned his feet and knees. It was made of shredded tires. The company that made the mulch was the brainchild of a local who had found a way to make a living and stay in the area he loved. Most full time North Michigan residents lived very meagerly or devised inventive ways to make a living from tourism (Michigan's second largest industry) or found a way to milk the state for assistance. The truth is that more "welfare" goes to rural residents than to those in the inner city. Many storeowners worked the assistance system and would close for the winter and collect unemployment until it was time to open their shops again. Everyone who came here wanted to live here, and why not?

The land rolled heavily from a moraine that spilt the Northern part of the State somewhat down the middle. The creeks, streams and rivers flowed off the moraine to the west into Lake Michigan, and those to the east into Lake Huron. The Manistee River came down to the west side, and from its initial headwaters the river ran cold, clear and without restrictions. There were no low head or standard damns to restrict movement of the wild strains of trout and char. In an effort to restrict upward migration of the highly successful lake runs of salmon and steelhead, a stout weir was placed a few miles from the mouth. This allowed for their reproduction, and stopped lake runs from mingling with the brookies, browns, and rainbows above the weir. This river was classic trout fly-fishing water and the main reason why Kirt had so often come to the area. He had never come here with his wife and girls, as they had no interest in the sport. He came at least twice a year, even if only for a couple days. He might come alone or with friends, either way it was his river.

This was the first time he had stayed in this particular establishment, as he did not want to bump into anyone he may know. He did not want to talk about it with anyone. He wanted to work it out, just him and God. At least he wanted to try to do it this way. Besides, what damn difference did it make anyway? He had nothing left to struggle for. How many times had he sung the verses from Luther's hymn, "Goods, fame child and wife? Let these all be gone…" He had, on occasion, asked himself if this was the kind of trust he had in Christ. He was now finding out that Christ was the only one left in his world.

Kirt looked up to see that he had passed the three-mile marker and knew he should turn around and sprint/jog back two miles and walk off the last. If he didn't, his muscles would knot up like a climbing rope. He was not yet used to running past six-miles, and to increase too quickly would not be good. He finished up and took a long hot shower followed by a long, hot soaking bath, while listening to the radio. He thought about his home in Clarkston. *How can I ever go back there?* He visualized the nightstand on Beth's side of the bed. On the stand were the books, mirror and hairbrush she used just before lights out. He envisioned Bonnie and Julie's room with its large space, the full-size beds on each side, a desk at the foot of each bed, the games and books on the floor, and baptismal certificates on the wall for each. His daughter Bonnie loved acting and music, and at age fifteen was considered on her way to a career in the Arts. The Interlochen Center for the Arts in Northwest Michigan had given her a scholarship and invited her for the last two summers. She was an excellent guitarist and had even been asked to do back up work for the acts that came to the Pine Knob Music Theater. She was backup for Don Henley, AC/DC, Lyle Lovett and Bob Seger last summer. His daughter Bonnie was talented, confident and as Henley had said, "A very beautiful, talented and sweet young woman." Kirt began to sob again and he did not stop for a long time. Then he thought of

Bonnie again and the fact that she was so much like his beloved Beth. He had wanted to see her married, successful as a person and a Christian. He would never see her in this life again. He exploded into sobs again. After crying he felt absolutely exhausted. He stepped out of the tub, dried off and went to his bed. He could not get to sleep. The endorphins from the run were at war with the draining grief. He felt deceived physically and emotionally. He sat up in bed and screamed, "Is this what you want, you bastard? I thought you were my friend! I know you are, but I am so fucking angry! I can't focus, I can't sleep I can't even get a lift from running! I know I should not cuss like this but you already know what I am thinking so I am gonna let you have it! I know you can take it and I have to say it out loud… Give me a break. Let me sleep!" He then lied back down and began to sob again saying, "Father I am sorry. Anger and my grief are warring with my trust in you. I cannot do this alone; I need your help. I need to sleep." Exhausted and drained of all emotion, he then felt nothing, nothing at all. He was numb and comfortably so. He turned on his sound machine, set it to "Ocean Waves," which reminded him of the sound of Lake Michigan waves. He drifted slowly and quietly to sleep. He slept for over twelve hours and when he awoke, he still felt tired. He called the local pizzeria and ordered a medium pizza loaded with meat. He also ordered a large Greek salad. He turned on the TV and began to watch David Letterman. The pizza arrived and he began to eat. Surprisingly, he ate almost all of it. He even laughed in a natural way at several of the jokes offered up by Letterman and his guest, a comedian named Pablo Francisco. He got up and went to the refrigerator, grabbed a pint of Guernsey Farms Dairy butter pecan ice cream. He savored its salty, sweet and rich flavor. Then he remembered a night when he and Beth shared a sampling of several butter pecan ice creams. They both determined that Guernsey was absolutely the best. He remembered her laughter as they sampled and joked about their indulgent behavior. He cried again and asked God to help him get past the pain. He then lied down and again fell asleep. When he awoke it was early morning. He grabbed his fly rod and gear and walked into the Manistee River. He did not move. He stood and felt the pressure of the river current against his shins. He watched as Cy's dog, Bear, sat on the bank watching him. He stepped out of the water, sat down on the bank. Bear strode over and Kirt reached out to rub Bear's neck. Bear sat next to him and he began to massage Bear's chest and neck. Bear looked up at him and licked his hand. Kirt wrapped his arms around the dog and began to sob. *This sobbing is getting disgusting and futile,* he thought. Bear did not move, but simply let him hug him. From the lodge, Cy could see the scene. Cy stepped outside and walked down to the river.

"…He's a sweet dog," Kirt said.

"Yes, he is," said Cy.

"I recently lost my wife and two daughters in a car accident," Kirt said.

Cy said nothing. His eyes welled with tears and he offered his hand to pull him up.

"I can only imagine," said Cy.

Kirt said nothing. He slumped and tried to regain his composure so as not to embarrass himself.

"How long has it been?" Asked Cy.

"About fifteen months," said Kirt.

"What have you done to reorganize your life?"

Kirt was a little pissed, "What do you mean? Just getting through life is all I can do right now."

"Sorry. I meant have you been able to work to maintain any kind of schedule?" Asked Cy.

'No, dammit! Didn't ya' HEAR ME!"

Cy stepped back and said, "I did not mean to upset you. It must be unbearable. Let me ask you, do you have a Pastor or someone you could talk to?"

"Yes, I do, but it doesn't seem to be helping. Exercise isn't helping, medication isn't helping, I can't sleep and then all I can do is sleep. I can't let them go. All I ever wanted was to be a good husband and daddy—it's all I ever wanted in this life. Meant more to me than anything. I love fly-fishing and golf, and now I can't enjoy either one. You would think with all the excess time I would. I always wanted more time and now I have it, but it, it… it is so numbing."

"Can I ask what religion you are?" Asked Cy.

"I am Christian Orthodox, dyed in the wool Lutheran Christian."

"That seems like a pretty adamant confession."

"Yeah, I still trust and yet I don't. My prayer is always, 'I believe; help my unbelief'."

Cy's voice cracked, "I know that prayer. I used to say it a lot, and you know what I found out, even after my faith and confidence in Him grew?"

"What?"

"I still say it. Only now the unbelief feels far less than before. We are simultaneously sinner and saint, or we are just sinner. Those that can say the prayer are in his care; the others don't care. Their grief never ends when they leave this life. Was your wife as strong in her confession as you?"

"Yes, and the girls too. They would sit on my lap and tell me what they had learned in school about the Old Testament stories or the basics of the Ten Commandments. They believed like children, and

I often prayed for that kind of faith. I don't seem to have come too fa-fa-farrr…" Kirt's voice trailed off into tears.

"'Damn hard to see the changes when you are in the middle of a trial. I do know you cannot do this alone and Christ does not expect you to. If you ever want to talk you know where I am." Cy walked away.

"Thanks, Cy."

Kirt sat there for several more minutes and then sank back on his back and fell asleep. Cy kept watching and stepped out to get Kirt off the cold ground and into his bed. "Kirt, you need to get up let me take you to your room." Kirt sat up and walked back with Cy. Cy put Kirt to bed and took a look around the room. It was a mess. He felt depressed just looking at it. He moved over to the west wall and opened the door adjoining the next cabin. Kirt looked at Cy saying, "I feel like such a weak bastard – a burden."

"God sent an angel to Elisha one time, Kirt, when Elisa deserved to be whipped. The angel woke him and fed him and helped him back to strength. Just think of me as that angel. It is my privilege to serve one of my brothers in the faith. Maybe you will do the same for me or someone else one day." Kirt started to cry again, felt embarrassed, and said thank you Cy. Cy picked up the phone and called his wife over to help him clean up the mess. Then he too began to cry, "Help me help him Lord. You are so caring and concerned about our final destination. Help him move through this life until we see you together. And, oh yeah, thank you for giving me Sylvia, who taught me how helpful it can be to cry once in a while –you are something Lord."

IS THAT KARL?

Across the street inside the Mesick Inn, Guy saw what he thought was a laughing Karl Schroeder, an old high school friend. Guy and Karl were fairly tight back then; both having been on the golf team, both of Teutonic ancestry and both quite successful. In fact, Guy was about as close to Karl as anyone could get. When Karl went off to Harvard and Guy to the police academy they never heard from each other again. But the visage was unmistakable. *Same clear eyes, same rugged good looks and,* Guy thought, *same scars?*

There had grown a mystery around Karl after his sophomore year at Harvard. He went missing and was never heard from again. It had been extremely painful for Karl's family, especially his dad; no closure was ever found. Being the oldest son of three boys Karl was sought out by his brothers and the community. They hired two independent investigators who never turned up a clue. It was determined that Karl had involved himself in an east coast drug ring and had sold upwards of half a million dollars of recreational drugs on campus. Students began to come forward, admitting their purchases, as they feared more for Karl's life than being admitted buyers. The news of his trafficking puzzled his family and yet the reality of the corroborating evidence was unmistakable—Karl had become a campus dealer, scum in the eyes of most. There must have been a reason, thought Karl's dad. It just doesn't make sense. Karl had a full scholarship; he had spending money… Why would he do it? They assumed the east coast syndicate had murdered Karl, probably because he was leading law enforcement to them in some fashion. Towns folk hung their heads low and murmured, "Why, why?"

It was possible, thought Guy. *It could be him.* Just then, Guy noticed a driver of a pick up truck bolt out of his vehicle, only to find his tires had all gone flat. Moments later an ambulance pulled up—Loading unconscious "Karl" into the ambulance on a gurney. Guy's natural curiosity got the best of him. Guy ran across the street and asked the waitress whom the man was. She replied, "I have no idea." He inquired as to where the ambulance was going. She told him Munson Medical Center in Traverse City.

NEARING *SO DAMN GOOD,* AGAIN

Kirt awoke from his sleep feeling unexpectedly refreshed. First time in weeks. He noticed that it was daylight so he turned on the TV to see what time it was. Some soap opera was on so he knew it was not early morning. Soon a newscaster broke in to announce the upcoming noon news. That meant he had slept for at least 19 hours. He noticed that his room had been cleaned. Everything was back in order, the dishes washed; the sink and kitchen counter spotless. He felt more at ease in these clean, orderly surroundings. He decided that he would take advantage of the new strength and went for a long jog in order to kick in the endorphins. He slipped on a pair of heavy cotton gym sweat shorts, a heavy sweatshirt, a headband, (with an extra one in his pocket), and his best pair of Serengeti's. He stepped outside his door and headed west on Front Street. When he reached a seasonal road headed north he veered off down that road. After about three miles, he came across a small feeder creek, which likely fed the Manistee. Knowing that these small feeders often housed some gorgeous brookies he decided to stop and take a look. Peering into a few holes of five to six feet that only appeared two feet deep because of the gin-clear water and the excellent polarization of his lenses. He saw a brookie of about ten inches tucked up against the bank in the bottom of the hole. He made a mental note and decided to come back later to dapple in the creek for these fish that always seemed cloisonné by God. He decided to follow the creek back east to see where it feed into the Manistee River. The banks of the creek were classic meadowland.

He thought as he walked, that this would be a great place to try some terrestrial imitations in July and August. About half a mile east he came upon two gentlemen roll casting and dappling the water. In an attempt not to disturb them with vibrations from the undercut hollow bank, he moved further away as he continued east. At once one of the men asked him, "Have you fished this water much?"

"Never," said Kirt. "Just scouting it right now."

"Well, I will tell you one thing. These brookies are gorgeous." He held up a stringer of four, fifteen-inch brookies.

"Wow," said Kirt. "Those are beautiful; I would keep them too!"

"I normally release, but I have caught so many of these I decided to keep a few big ones to broil. You know, sage butter and lemon." He said this smiling, as both he and Kirt knew just how delectable the mild, flaky brookie could taste.

Kirt asked, "Mind if I come over?"

"Sure," he said, and invited his partner to wade across the creek to join them. When the man moved across the creek, Kirt recognized him immediately. It was Pete Solon and his partner, the legendary Lefty Kreh. Solon was a Pro Golfer, and Lefty a Fly-Fishing Expert. Kirt hated seeing people clamor whenever a celebrity was spotted. He hated the way folks fawned over someone just because they were in the public eye so he underplayed his enthusiasm.

"Pete Solon and Lefty Kreh. Can't hide, can you?" Kirt said, laughing. "What in the heck are you guys doing out here?"

"Well," said Pete Solon. "Lefty has been giving me tips all week up here and he wanted to show me how to dapple and fish the small water. Most of my fishing has been on the wide rivers out west. I have caught over seven brookies here in the last hour, ten to fifteen-inches and each absolutely beautiful. They're in full glory here."

"I guess I am scouting the right water after all," said Kirt. "Mr. Solon, I have always admired your skills, but even more how you have handled the cancer scare. Mr. Kreh, you must have financed your latest trip with the books I have bought from you over the years. I really enjoy your fly-fishing knowledge and passion in expressing it. I always thought you were the real thing and now I have witnessed it for myself." Both men smiled broadly and said thank you. "Where are you headed next guys?"

"I thought I would take Pete to the Jordan River and to the small stream Hemingway used to fish as a kid," said Lefty Kreh.

"Can you believe I get the full guided tour from the fly master here?" Grinned Pete.

"I can surely appreciate that!" Said Kirt.

"Would you like to join us?" Asked Pete.

"No, that would not be right. This is your time to be alone and I would not want to interfere."

"Another fly man interferin', not possible," said Lefty.

"Guys, any other time I..."

"What do you mean any other time? What is so darn important that it supersedes fishing?" Laughed Pete.

"Well, I am here kind of getting over the death of my wife and daughters."

"What happened?" Asked Pete. Kirt resisted, but decided to tell them the whole sad story. Pete spoke up after a period of awkward silence. "Being alone right now is not a good idea, Kirt. Believe me, I know. I know that up here," pointing to his head. "And here," pointing to his heart.

"Does it feel good talking with us right now? Asked Paul.

"Yes. It does," said Kirt. "As a matter of fact, it is the best I have felt in a long while."

"What's stopping you from having a good time, Kirt?" Asked Pete.

"Good question, Pete. I don't know."

"At the risk of sounding like a shrink, I bet you do know." Almost as quickly as he spoke, he said, "I'm sorry. I'm outta line. I am sure you are getting enough advice."

Kirt sat there motionless for several beats. "…Yeah, a lot of advice, most of it good, just hard to implement. To tell you the truth, for the last hour or so, I haven't even thought about them." He welled up.

Pete, trying to help, suggested, "I think your wife and girls would like you to enjoy yourself; do the things you like to do."

"You're right. That is what they would want."

"Are you feeling guilty about the free time you enjoy now? Like maybe you finally got your wish but don't like how you got there?" Asked Pete.

Kirt felt himself on the verge of a sob, but was tired of hearing himself do so. He forced the sob down. "That's it. That's really it.

I'm enjoying myself in a solitary way and I find myself completely forgetting about them and I don't want to."

"Kirt. Did you think about your girls every minute of the day when they were alive?"

"No, of course not."

"Well, you can't do it now that they're dead either. You're gonna think about them often and the pain will lessen, but you still have to function in the *here* and *now*. Heck, they're not in this bubble of time and space anymore. They are in eternity with Christ. When you think about them, think about 'em that way too."

A creeping calmness began to settle in. "Thanks Pete," Kirt said. "Thanks for listening. You've given me another way to think about this."

"It won't go away all at once, Kirt, but it will subside and joy will come again. Our God is a living God, and so your girls are still alive. I will be praying for you." Kirt shook his hand and as he did, Pete reached out and gave him a one armed hug. "So, Kirt. Why don't you take advantage of the expert here and let's hook up some brookies for dinner?"

"Damn right," said Lefty. "I know a stretch coming up here where we can…"

Kirt interrupted, "…Dapple?"

"Well hell, Pete! I think this guy knows what he's doin'. Ya' up ahead around those poplars is a stretch where there are three or four long deep runs, one for each of us. We can dapple those for a while and see if we can pull up a few more," said Lefty.

Kirt smiled and said, "Hey, Lefty. Let me see that rod of yours. What is that, a 3 weight?"

They continued to fish until nightfall, shared a meal of brookies, with American fries and asparagus, and washed it all down with a few beers. Kirt was beginning to feel other emotions again and it felt okay. He remembered one of Hemingway's comments on depression, "You deal with it because you know how damn good life can be."

THE DARKNESS CRACKS

The sound was so familiar—giving him a calm, crisp and strong feeling. It gurgled, riffled and flowed westward off the moraine down to Lake Michigan. He realized that he felt peaceful and calm. The awareness of it drew out a sense of relief and fear, relieved that he had finally felt whole again, yet fear it would not last. Kirt rose to his feet and looked out the window at the beauty that was *his river*. The water that seemed so dark and inky was now gin-clear, and he could see the colors of the bottom rocks. It was all so familiar. His sense of well-being was not a "high." It was as though his dry sinew had been rehydrated from his legs up leaving him feeling normal, grounded. It felt so wonderful to feel normal again. He sat back down on his bed and began to pray as tears rolled down his face. Tears filled with joy, carrying away some of the toxins of grief. "Thank you, Abba, thank you," he prayed. "I am still afraid of what comes next. Hang in there with me." He smiled to himself, realizing that God already knew these petitions, but God demanded prayer for his sake. He picked up his phone and called Doctor Hawks, his psychiatrist. "Hello, Mary, this is Kirt."

"Kirt," said Mary spiritedly. "Where are you? How are you?"

"I am in Mesick and I am feeling fearfully well."

"Fearfully?" Asked Mary.

"Long story…Is Doctor Hawks in?"

"No, but he wants you to call him at home. He has been very worried."

"Okay, I will give him a call."

He punched in the cell number. "Doctor Hawks? It's Kirt."

"Kirt, how are you?"

"Well, I am not sure." He relayed the experience he had this morning.

"Well, Kirt, I do believe you are turning a corner."

"My thoughts are still a little jumbled and I am afraid that it won't last."

"It won't," said Doctor Hawks. "But the oppressive periods of sadness will shorten."

"I feel solid again. My body is more relaxed, yet more secure."

"The body often follows the mind," said Doctor Hawks. "You know the kind of anxiety you feel before you go into a depression? Something in reverse. Let me tell you, Kirt, I am damn mad at you right now. You took off not letting anyone who cares about you know where you went. Pastor Knaus is very worried too."

"I thought I could work this out up here, where I have so many great memories of being by myself."

"So, did being by yourself help?"

"No. It wasn't until I started talking about the girls with a couple guys I met on the river and the owner here that things sort of broke loose."

"You mean Cy? Asked Doctor Hawks.

"Yes, how did you know?"

"He's the one who told us where you were. He saw you remove your plate and took the number down."

"I took that plate off in the dark and Cy was not at the desk when I registered."

"Right. He was across the street walking back from the Mesick Inn. He saw you remove the plate, and one of the small lights on the string gave off enough light for him to see the number."

"I thought I was so careful."

"You were, but when he saw you removing the plate your plan fell apart. God has you surrounded."

"What? I know. Pastor Knaus, Cy, and his wife, all trust in Christ."

"That's right, and we all care about you. Sometimes when our trust in Him is challenged, we find Him again in the love of His people." There was a long pause—at least it seemed long.

Hot tears of release and joy were running down Kirt's face. "I really did hate Him. I questioned everything again. Why evil? Where did it come from? Why suffering? At the same time, there was a small flicker telling me to keep it in perspective. I guess I'm looking at all this from a larger perspective, thank God."

"You bet, you bet. You know I can identify. Look, do your old Pastor a favor and give him a call. He is very concerned about you and damn it, Kirt, failing to call him has been cruel on your part."

"Yes, I will. Thanks, Doc."

"Take your time. Stay there awhile longer and relax, fish, allow yourself to enjoy again. Oh, yes, and call me after 5:00 pm on my cell number."

"I will," said Kirt.

"Good. Pastor calls me often just to check and see if we have had contact. He's a great guy for a Lutheran, not a bad Christian."

Kirt had grown accustom to the Lutheran cracks and knew the doctrinal differences between them. Doctor Hawks being a Baptist was respected and Christian love was at the core of their relationship. "Yes he is Doc, and so are you. Keep me in your prayers." Kirt put on his waders and wading shoes, threw on his vest, grabbed his rod and walked down to the river. As he was walking he noticed someone dressed in a hooded sweatshirt and sunglasses kneeling beside a Mercedes-Benz backed right up next to the Mesick Inn office door. Shortly, Kirt heard air escaping from the tires. Seeing that the person driving the Mercedes had parked in a "no parking zone," Kirt just laughed and kept walking to the river.

"I'll be darned," said Cy. "You've been hit by the valve stem vigilante." The man with the new gear, who probably had no idea how to use it, Cy thought. Did not find it at all humorous.

"Why would he steal our valve stems?" Said the taller of the two who owned the Mercedez-Benz.

"Oh, he didn't steal them. They are right next to your tires there on the ground." Kirt was trying not to laugh but then broke out in an eruptive guffaw. "You see gentlemen, when you park in the wrong spot in Mesick, the vigilante strikes. Here, you better call a wrecker to bring you some air. Probably will cost you fifty bucks," he said as he laughed his way up the steps to the office phone. Then he just couldn't resist, "That'll teach ya'."

AN OLD TRIP HOME REMEMBERED

The rain pelted his windshield with such force that he had no choice but to pull over until the front passed. The sky had that eerie green look. West across the flat valley there seemed to be no end to the front. The temperature had hovered around 90 degrees all day and the humidity must have been at least that high. This weather had persisted for the last several days and everyone in Michigan knew that when it broke, it would be dramatic. Kirt pulled over to wait it out. He was headed back to Clarkston, MI after a weeklong trip to the northwest. The trip was a biannual one. He always looked forward to visiting his VIP accounts of the north. The trips were combinations of intense business follow-up and great evenings spent on the Manistee, Boardman or Betsie Rivers. The July heat had prompted a hopper hatch the likes of which he had seldom seen. He caught a mess of browns and brooks in a three-hour session on the Manistee. His favorite fishing partner was also one of his largest Northern accounts. Bill Jacobsen, ("Hoss," he was called), was a burly man, sturdy, over 6'4" and tipping the scale near 300 pounds. He was massive, intense and incredibly gentle. His frame held his weight with ease and though he could afford to lose some fat, he was as nimble as any man could be. Kirt was always amused to watch Hoss crawl on his knees to peer into a hole, slowly sit up and deftly roll cast a 4 weight rod to some of the most selective trout in the world. Hoss tied all his own flies and when Kirt visited in the winter they would spend hours over their vises tying until their eyes hurt. Hoss's fingers looked like bratwurst and yet he delicately tied even a size 20 Adams with no apparent awkwardness. Hoss shipped over 100 ton of sewer grates and covers with Kirt each year. Kirt admired his entrepreneurship and the freedom of living in Jordan year round.

Hoss came by his freedom the hard way. He took an aging foundry and renewed its production and market in just six short and difficult years. "Without the river, I would have given up a 100 times," Bill had often said. But he did not give up, he built a wonderfully profitable business that employed over three hundred people, all of whom preferred to live and work here rather than the Detroit metro sprawl. Kirt longed for the day when he and Beth could live there too. His heart always sank a bit when he had to return to Clarkston.

The trip south always depressed him. The land became flatter as you traveled. Flat land depressed him. It seemed characterless and empty and the Saginaw Valley storm was making this even worse. Looking west, Kirt became concerned. After sitting in his car for twenty minutes no letup occurred. His lightening filled radio cracked with updates. Several tornadoes had been seen and the storm line ran all the way to Chicago. The national weather service said the storm was stalled and might hover over the area all night. Kirt picked up his cell phone to call Beth to tell her that he would have to spend the night in Saginaw. This was the final kick to the head, Friday night in Saginaw of all places. He began to edge his way back onto I-75 and decided to make the best of the circumstances. He decided to stay in Frankenmuth; at least he could eat a great meal and wash it down with some local brew. He called all the local hotels and was just able to get a room at the Bavarian Inn. It seemed the storm had caused many of his fellow travelers to also get off the road for the night. Frankenmuth was about fifteen miles away and it was difficult to go much faster than 35 miles per hour. Kirt turned off the radio and put in a Dave Brubeck CD. The sounds of the jazz quartet made the rain bearable. There was another reason the flatness irritated him. When it rained, there was no place for the runoff to go. It just sat there until the ground held all it could, and then spread out covering the flood plain like too much syrup on the last pancake. When he was a kid, growing up in this area, he vowed he'd leave as soon as he could. Before he was twenty-five, he did. This was the land of the United Automobile Workers (UAW) and Teamsters. His whole family had made their living off the automotive industry. They had lifetime jobs, *real jobs*, they would say, as he tried to explain why even talented sales people would move with or ahead of the market, going from one company to another. He had tried to explain the process of representing a company and being paid to move their wares. They did not understand him; he was a foreigner in his hometown. He was no longer one of them.

It was as though Michigan consisted of three distinct areas: the hills and lakes of southeast Michigan, the spectacular geography of the north, and the mundane central region with its miles of factories and farm fields. Kirt spent the last several years working as a Sales and Support Representative for Great Lakes Logistics, and made a good living doing so. His work took him out of town quite often, more often than he wanted. It was a source of conflict for him. In order to pay the bills, he needed to visit centers in Vincennes, Indianapolis, Peoria, and Davenport in Iowa. While he was gone, the full load of parenthood was squarely on Beth's shoulders. She never complained, but he resented his situation because no one could be kept fully satisfied by it. His girls missed him; he missed them and Beth. The greatest satisfaction he derived from the travel, aside from the road and the income, was the kind of people he would meet along the way. Unknown to most of them he included their stories in a book he was writing called, "On the Plane Again." It was a thinly disguised autobiographical story about the life of a family man, on the road, as a window on the world of the "road warrior."

In Vincennes, he met a truly quirky couple. The owner of the center, Billie Ray Cuthbert, turned out not to be the owner after all. He was simply a front man for the real owner, his wife Trudy Barrows-Harkston-Cuthbert, the seventy-two year old wife of the former and dead Senator Harkston of the Harkston family agricultural empire. Senator Harkston was in her words, "A good for nothing, lying, lazy, son of a bitch who made his living through obfuscation and twisted Southern banter."

Harkston had died twenty years ago when his wife Trudy was only fifty-two, who looked to be thirty-five and with the constitution of a ninteen-year-old runner. Trudy managed the "farm,"—four thousand acres of prime land on top of a massive bluff overlooking the Wabash River. She was a spectacular businesswoman equipped as she was with her rock hard body, natural jet-black hair and piercing green eyes. Her mom was Cherokee and her father Italian. She could hold the attention of even the most difficult banker or field hand. She was a royal pain in the ass but she got results. Five years after the "bonehead" died, Trudy started buying a herd of cattle which "bonehead" objected to when he was alive and she promptly hit pay dirt. Her beef was raised to be USDA Prime and was sold through places like Lobels and the Allen Bros in New York. Trudy was fond of saying that she only needed a man for two reasons: One, to do what she could not do physically, and two, to give her the "tremors."

Billy Ray worked for her as a Ranch Manager and lived in the quarters provided for him. The Ranch head quarters were located about half the way up the three fourth-mile driveway on a ridge extended from the limestone bluff. The quarters were comprised of a long ranch house, a tool barn and a small swimming pool. Trudy hired Billy just before her husband died. Billy eventually married her and moved up to the big house at the end of the driveway. The home had been built in 1927 and had been left to her late husband because as she told it, "His parents took pity on the dull of mind," making sure he had a roof over his head. The big house, as Kirt referred to it was a massive forty thousand square foot craftsman ranch with a giant horseshoe bar situated so that you could look out over the Wabash valley through crystal clear windows that stretched from floor to ceiling across a hundred foot span. Trudy was always sure to point to the river and say, "Right there is where Lieutenant Colonel George Rogers Clark carved the British a new ass hole." Trudy had of course received rather generous amounts of the tremors from Billy long before the dullard had died. On the property adjacent to the big house were four large farm ponds that had been stocked with Crappie and Largemouth bass that grew as large as the species could.

When Kirt met Billy he had been placed as the manager of Red Logistics, a nod to the favorite local boy made good, Red Skelton. Trudy, not knowing what to do with the handsome, strapping but rather dim-witted Billy, decided to give him the role while making sure his second in command took care of things. Trudy made sure Cyril, the second man, was well compensated in cash and tremors. Now Billy was a natural athlete and spent most of his time playing golf with the customers. Being a local high school hero, the locals loved to play with him. Trudy kept a membership for this purpose at the River Glens Country Club. She was a mean golfer herself and she and Billy originally met there before she persuaded Harkston to hire him making it easier for her to have access to her tremors. Kirt walked into the situation and soon learned that he had to make Billy think that he had made the business decisions even though Kirt made sure he communicated everything to Trudy. At this time, Trudy was seventy-two and Billy fifty-two, with a potbelly and a bad left knee from his football years. Trudy arranged Billy's clothing so that he never had to think about how to coordinate. Trudy took a liking to Kirt and why not? He was fairly attractive, still young and, of course, warm and moving. Kirt at first did not recognize her overtures as sexual, but figured it out soon enough. Kirt made sure Billy was with him whenever he would visit with her. On one occasion, Billy and Kirt drove to the big house together so that they could change into their golfing attire. As Billy changed, Trudy came on to Kirt and he gently let her know that he was a happily married man. "If I hadn't been," he once said, "I swear that would have been the first seventy-two year old woman I would have given the tremors." Such was the strength of the sap coursing through Trudy's veins. Kirt liked her and respected her business head but he knew she would die lonely given her undisciplined appetites. "Don't laugh," he told his Regional Manager. "She is hot regardless of her age." After meeting her, the Regional Manager confirmed Kirt's opinion and she became a legend in the Chicago office. When Billy came out dressed in a pair of cut-offs and a Willie Nelson t-shirt, Trudy tore into him like he was a 13-year-old boy. She was merciless and right in front of Kirt. Kirt pretended not to notice but Trudy turned to him and said, "Sorry, I guess he just can't be trusted." Billy came out dressed appropriately for the country club and he and Kirt headed off. The River Glen was an old course, traditional by US standards, built in 1923 by an unknown architect.

It was a pretty piece of land and a good test of golf. Kirt shot an 82 and Billy shot a 71 while under considerable influence from the ice cold Southern Comfort he brought with them in the cooler. Billy was gifted and had a skill for consistency on the course. He loved it too and he truly liked people. After the round, they returned to the big house as Trudy had insisted Kirt stay with them when he was in town. Kirt consented and always placed a dresser in front of his door at night so Trudy would not try to visit him for some night tremors. "I love that room," Kirt told his boss. "It is absolutely beautiful overlooking the Wabash and beyond to a wide open west. Trudy keeps every kind of drink on hand. I swear, Greg, in the low light that woman looks forty-five."

Kirt kept these stories tucked away on several legal pads inside his briefcase. Beth loved to read about these characters and Kirt made sure he brought home photos of his clients so she could put the faces with the names.

"Maybe you better not stay at Trudy's," Beth said, as she she stared at a photo of Trudy, Billy and Kirt at the Harvest Ball held at River

Glen. Beth smiled, "Wow, what a looker. I should look so good at her age. Keep your distance, I'm the only recipient of your tremors,"

"Of course," said Kirt.

Laughing, Beth said, "What's a tremor?"

"I'll show you tremors," said Kirt, as he tickled her to tears.

Beth and Kirt were far from the perfect couple; they were a committed couple. They took a realistic view regarding romantic expectations and were able to put their sex life on hold for children and responsibilities without the usual guilt or blame. Many times they came together and it was as though they were twenty years old again and Kirt was seeing the woman he loved afresh. The travel eventually took its toll and Kirt was able to arrange for a smaller territory consisting only of Michigan and northwest Indiana. Occasionally, he was able to take one of his daughters on the road with him. He was not happy with his work any longer and he felt trapped. What else could he do? Maybe he needed to view work as a means to gain time with his family. Beth and he had lived well, maybe too well. They were over extended with credit, but as long as the income kept coming they could work their way out. Waiting for a change seemed no longer an option to Kirt.

"Beth, we have to talk. For the first time in my life, I feel trapped."

"Trapped by what?" Asked Beth.

"By our lifestyle. I mean, we are up to our necks in debt. Our girl's tuition is killing us and I…" He took a beat, "I hate what I am doing. I know, I know. I should have said something a long time ago. Now we are in so deep we can't get out if I quit, if I change careers."

"What do you want to do?"

"I don't know. Give writing a shot. Brewer says I could pick up a reporter position at the Free Press. It would pay about half of what I make now but I could also write on the side. I've been researching this for months. I think we can do it," said Kirt.

"Honey, I can't take seeing you like this. We can fix this."

"How?"

"Well, let's sell the house and buy a smaller one in town. It could cut our mortgage way down. We could pull the girls out of St. Paul's and put them in the Clarkston system. That's quite a chunk right there."

"Wait. The girls are really at home there. They receive God's word every day."

"Yes, but we can make sure they continue to get that here at home. Better yet, I could home school through Con Lara. I've been very interested in how to do that for some time."

"I don't know, sweetheart. Home schooling? That's seems weird to me."

"But it's not. These kids rank extremely high on the entrance exams, SAT's and ACT's. They seem to do great."

"But what about socialization? Time with kids their own age, athletic teams?"

"The Con Lara has athletic teams and they coordinate with some of the most successful travel teams. The kids get together all the time and it wouldn't be that weird. How many times in your life have you been surrounded by people only your own age? Now that's weird," she smiled.

"How do you think the girls will take it? I mean, a new house and new education?"

"First they'll be in the same area, same town. They'll actually like going to church close to home instead of the drive every day. Bonnie is ready for more focused training on her guitar, more than any school can give her. We can then afford to send her to Charlie Packers music school. Jane wouldn't care either way. We can make sure they see their best friends often. I can work Kirt. To tell you the truth, I am sick of this debt burden. And, oh yeah, we can work with a credit counseling group and reduce our interest rates and pay down the card debts."

"So you've been thinking about this too?" Kirt smiled.

"Yes, because of the debt. I knew you were starting to hate the job."

"I do. Last week I was driving up to see Hoss. I had to pull off the road in West Branch because I thought I was gonna have a heart attack. I went to the hospital and they told me I had an anxiety attack. I could feel a depression coming and this time I gave some serious thought to how much life insurance, if I were to just check out. I couldn't do it but it was so overwhelming. Normally a depressive episode comes for no reason and I work my way out of it. This time I thought, 'okay, you'll work your way out just like before,' but this time I would only work my way back to a trap. Trapped by debt and a job I hate." Kirt was sweating across his forehead, behind his ears, across his chest and back.

"Kirt, sweetheart, it's not worth it. Work out an exit plan and let's get the ball moving. You're right. We can make this work. In fact, it might even be better. We'll all be home more. We'll save a ton of money. The load will go away. Let's write a plan."

Kirt reached over and kissed her passionately on the mouth as both shed tears. Their love had pulled them through again.

"Do you want to go to the bedroom?" Beth smiled.

"Yes, but let's do the plan first."

Four months later, Beth and the girls were headed north on Telegraph just north of I-696. When they came to the intersection at Twelve Mile Rd., the light had turned green and traffic was moving through. From the left, to the west, a man named Carl Gorlic, who was drunk of out of his skull, came speeding through the intersection at well over 60 miles per hour and plowed into Beth's minivan. The van was no match for the jacked up truck that crushed them like an aluminum can. For a brief moment the thought of the accident passed through Kirt's mind and set up a level of guilt Kirt had never felt. When he heard the news he wanted to rush to the morgue to see them. Bob and Carol Swanton, their best friends, discouraged him from going. They had been told of the indistinguishable mess of the bodies and didn't want him to see them.

"Oh my God, my sweet Jesus. What will I do now? My girls, my Beth," Kirt broke down and sobbed. Then in his mind, an unexpected thought, *they're gone now. No more debt load, no more worries, you're free.*

Kirt sat up in the chair with fear written all over his face. *Where did that come from? I never wanted this. What's wrong with me?*

Carol said, "What's the matter?"

"What a dumb ass fucking question. My girls are dead, God damn it!"

Carol and Bob were shocked to hear Kirt use profanity. He rarely did.

Carol whispered to Bob, "It's just the grief, honey, the God awful grief."

SEEING HOSS

Kirt called Hoss. Hoss the hulk of a man, a core of muscle with a heavy layer of fat, fingers like bratwurst all puffy and wrinkly. His piercing green eyes sparkled like the bay waters. He laughed fully with no apologies for the boom it made; the laugh coming at once from the gut and the sinus cavities. When he hugged you, as he did everyone, you could not help but be a little startled. Prepared for a bear hug, he would give you gentle ones followed by a gentle tap on the shoulder. Hoss reminded Kirt of Whitman internally and Hemingway externally: full of life's juices and adventurous as hell. At sixty, he looked more like fifty, but even at age thirty-five Hoss looked fifty. Of course he had little hair, what was left was around the sides, a remnant of red from the few years he had hair like a horse's mane. Now most of his hair was on arms, back, chest, shoulders, legs; everywhere but his head. *The opposite of me,* thought Kirt. He could use some of Hoss' juice right now.

Hoss had managed a couple of foundries down state, actually downriver of Detroit. He made some intriguing innovations, not the least of which was to let in more natural light so the place did not feel so much like Hades. He got wind of an Iron Works in Jordan being for sale fifteen years ago. He went to the bank in Jordan, presented his business plan and credentials and he and the bank kept the furnaces going. He also kept two hundred jobs alive in a job-deprived market. In order to avoid unionization, Hoss created an employee commitment program whereby each employee could gain a percentage of the profits based on years of service including those already accumulated with the previous owner. It was very agreeable with the employees and most stayed on, at least those that you would want to stay on. Some key folks came to Jordan with Hoss to help him run the place. The foundry produced all kinds of iron casts. They were most known for their manhole covers, which were seen all over the world. Hoss loved to fish and hunt, as did his adult sons. He just wanted to be near the big lake and all of its tributaries. It was the land of Hemingway's youth after all. Kirt used to visit with Hoss every fall and spring. Kirt at that time managed a sales team that sold logistic services in and around the auto industry. One of his northern reps had signed Hoss on and the business was terrific. When Kirt first met Hoss they connected right away. Hoss would take a couple days off and he and Kirt would go fly-fishing, sometimes for brookies, and sometimes for steelhead or King salmon. It didn't matter much, as the bonding was the purpose of the outings. Hoss once said if it were not for the terrain he would retire and move back down state. "It's the water, the sweet waters. You cannot find this anywhere else in the world."

Kirt would always stay at Hoss' when he came up. Several times he came with his wife and girls in January. Everyone would ice skate, maybe ski, ice fish in a huge shanty Hoss hauled out on the lake every year, all would totally decompress rapidly. Kirt and Hoss tied flies for the upcoming season. Kirt marveled as Hoss worked under a magnifier tying even the smallest of flies; his puffy fingers as agile as a jeweler's.

He had not spoken with Hoss since the funeral. Now that he was feeling better he missed his company again. It felt great to feel joyful again.

"Hoss?"

"Yes? Is this Kirt? You son of a bitch."

"Yes it is."

"How are you doing buddy? I have missed you."

"Well, better but still a little wobbly."

"No doubt it's a long process, I know. Well, not that I ever experienced the situation you have. I often think about you guys and I miss your ladies an awful damn lot."

"It's been a son of a bitch but God is walking me through it."

"Well I'm glad you have that Kirt."

Hoss was a kind of deist without an explicit label on it. Carol and he talked about Christ but Hoss remained unmoved.

"He is all that gets me through. Hey, if it's not too much trouble, do you have a few days you can take off?"

"I was hoping you would ask. Damn right I do. Hey, last fall I promoted a young local guy to superintendent. I have him getting some technical training on line with Walsh and Lawrence Tech. I cut him in on a bigger piece and now I have more time to fart around. I have a guy now!"

"I was thinking we could go on the little Papa trail."

"You bet. When can you be in Kalkaska?"

"Probably tonight. I'm in Mesick right now."

"Are you fishing without me, you little shit?"

"Yes, but it doesn't mean anything. You're still my fish wife." They both laughed. There was silence for a moment. "Hoss, I missed you. I seem to be out of it now. Anyway, I need fish wife with me on the little Papa."

"Okay, Kirt. I'll see you at the bakery in Kalkaska tomorrow at 9:00am. Don't use a hotel. You're staying with us after the trail run!"

"See you then, Hoss…Wait! Do you have any BWO, size 20?"

"How insulting. I won't even answer that!" Said Hoss.

The little Papa trail was the name Hoss and Kirt gave to a fishing tour they sometimes took. The trail was based on short stories and histories they had read about Hemingway's childhood tomes around northwest Michigan. Hemingway and his friend jumped on a train in Oak Park Illinois and departed. Hours later they arrived in Kalkaska. The boys were around fourteen years old or so. They fished north of Kalkaska, went on to the Boardman River and also fished Horton's Creek that flowed eastward down into Lake Charlevoix. The creek was narrow and ran through trees in some areas that blocked out the sun. Hoss and Kirt would dapple flies into the pools that still held some decent brookies. As the creek neared Horton's Bay of lake Charlevoix the two would exit at the bridge on Main Street and walk a half-mile or so to the general store and the Fox Inn. The two remaining business in the tiny village. They would buy some beer and sausage and set on the porch of the Inn and talk about what it must have been like in those days on the verge of the twentieth century when native Americans still lived an original lifestyle in Michigan. They would often walk down to the old spring still bubbling ice cold, clear, clean water. The spring was mentioned in Hemingway's Nick Adams series, especially the one about one of his early romantic encounters. They might even walk all the way down the hill to the docks at the bay and work their way along the shore to where Horton's Creek flowed into the lake. Several times they had caught some hefty browns hanging around the mouth of the creek. It was a trail only young men or big boys would enjoy. They were both.

"Hey, Hoss lets work that meadow stretch on the Jordan. Maybe a couple beaver ponds?"

"We'll hit 'em all. Use my house as home base. Let's hit the wine trail while we're at it, up Old Mission."

"First time I have felt this excited about anything in a long time."

"You always come back, my friend, and this will be no exception. I'll see down to the river. See you at the bakery."

Kirt hung up the phone and walked down to the river. He took Bear with him.

WHO IS THIS?

Before leaving, Kirt decided to get a full meal. His eating habits had been so meager, so infrequent that he now found himself famished. He decided to go across the street to get some steak, salad, potatoes and pie alamode, maybe a couple beers too. As he crossed the street, he noticed a man cursing at his vehicle, as both front tires were flat. In the alley between the Inn and the hardware was a man in a hoodie with his hood pulled up wearing sunglasses, watching the cursing man and trying to stop his convulsive laughter from erupting. What was that? He wondered. Stepping inside the Inn he was greeted by Maggie. She had on a pair of knee length green shorts with green and white seersucker short sleeved shirt; the top three buttons undone. Her hair had been pulled back into a ponytail. She had on bare minimum makeup and her hazel, copper, specked eyes seemed to pop right out at you. Kirt could see she was no youngster; she had a few wrinkles that were quite faint and soft especially around the eyes.

She smiled and said, "How many in your group?"

"Huh?" He felt a little stupid. "There is only myself. Could I get a table by the front window?"

"Sure, sweetie. Please follow me." She was the kind of person who could get away with calling a person sweetie, honey, darlin', whatever. Her authentic warmth earned her the right.

"What is the best steak here?" Asked Kirt.

"Well…" She paused to give the question real consideration. "I love the rib eye, cowboy rib eye, but it's a lot of meat. Second best I prefer the filet and the 24 flank."

"What's a 24 flank?"

"Well, all our beef here is prime and when you take a piece of prime flank and marinate it in our black pepper sauce for twenty-four hours, grilled medium you get a steak for half the price of the filet and equally as good. I love it and so do my girls."

"You have girls?" The phrase was so common to his ear as it was the very one he used to refer to his wife and daughters.

"Yes, three. Two newly out on their own and my last one going to University of Michigan."

He wanted to express his surprise over the fact that she had daughters of that age without sounding corny or like it was a come on. He decided to say it anyway, what the hell. "I have to say, I am surprised that you have daughters that age. You must have had them when you were fourteen." It was not the first time she had heard that but coming from this guy she took it as a genuine compliment. "Must be the Northern air," said Kirt.

"I had the first at twenty-one, and two right behind her."

"Must come from some hearty stock, attractive stock, too I'd say." He blushed at the fact he had said the last part. He hadn't blushed in years. It just came out because for the first time in a long time he actually noticed an attractive women and one with character at that. Maggie saw him blush, saw his discomfort, leaned closer to him and said, "thank you very much, I know you meant that."

"I did," he said still blushing. He hated that he had blushed.

"What about your family?"

A deep piercing pain stabbed him and caused his throat to grow thick. He realized he still had his wedding ring on. "Well…" He slowed his speech. "My wife and two daughters were killed in an auto accident down state about eighteen months ago."

Maggie instinctively sat down across from him in the booth. She reached over and lightly touched his hand and said, "oh, honey I am so sorry." Her empathy caused him to well up and over onto his cheeks.

"That's why I have been up here the last few months. 'Just trying to come to grips with it. The good news is I turned a corner in the last few weeks. I'm ready to go home and get on with my life."

"Oh my Lord that has to be a blow. How old were they?"

He took the time to give her all the particulars. Jane saw Maggie's intensity so she seated people for a while. "To tell you the truth I am comforted by the fact that they all trusted in Christ otherwise I see no real reason to be comforted at all."

"We grieve, but not as those who have no hope," Maggie said out of memory.

"Yes, that's exactly it. Are you a Christian?"

"Yes, yes I am," said Maggie. She seemed a complete package just like his wife had been. They sat and talked for over an hour while he ate the 24 flank. It was as good as she said it would be.

As he got up to leave, he heard himself saying, "Maggie would you mind if I called you, maybe go out to dinner or something?" He blushed again.

She leaned over to him, "I would love that, Kirt," kissing him on the cheek.

"Are you coming back up here soon?"

With a smile he said quietly, "I am now."

Maggie smiled and she felt appreciated, for far more than just her appearance.

"Do you fish, Maggie?"

"I grew up on the Manistee, Kirt. What do you think?"

"Okay, let me put it this way, do you like to fish?"

"You come back up and I'll show you a few spots on the river you have never seen. Bring a 5 weight and some hex nymphs."

Grabbing his heart, Kirt said, not blushing at all, "A woman after my own heart."

They exchanged phone numbers and set a date in June before the Hex hatch when the nymphs would be at their peak. He did not want to leave now. She did not want him to leave. As he left, he thought to himself, *how wonderful that I met her when I was already feeling better.* There would be no mistaking that she was not the reason for his recovery. Maggie was a wonderful, beautiful icing on his cake.

Now she had to break the news she had been putting off for months—she needed to tell Walt she was going to break it off. He was a good man but she needed something more, she needed someone to be with, have fun with and Walt's idea of sedentary fun was not hers. She was not at all sure where things might go with

Kirt, but she thanked God for providing her with a boost of fortitude to break it off with Walt. She had no illusions about the challenges of competing with a dead wife and daughters, but she would not compete. She would complement if at all possible; she let her fantasy unfold. Kirt seemed so authentic, a real guy, a real family man. She was sure his wife had received plenty of pleasure from him. Usually when Margaret saw a man of that caliber he was already taken. Not this time. She walked up to the front and Jane said, "Wow, Maggie your radiating." Maggie thanked her for covering for her and asked her to finish her shift for her. Maggie ran home and opened her "far and fine" case. She had been given the old bamboo by her grandpa years before he died because he loved to watch her cast and Grandma would not let him fish while wading anymore. Oh how she loved her grandparents. "'Gonna catch a few gramps," she said to herself. She replaced the old fly line with a new one and rigged it for nymphing. She still loaded it with silk line because she loved the action and because she was so used to it even though she did have a few graphite rods that used the newer lines. She sat down at her tying vise and began tying Clark's squirrel hair nymphs to imitate the hex. She was forty-four, from a very small town that she had seldom left, and God had allowed her to meet a well-traveled man of substance who appreciated her; she felt twenty-five. She said a Te Deum and kept tying into the night.

When Kirt got back into his vehicle, he could still smell her, still felt her full lips on his cheek, saw her attentive coppery eyes and that warm authentic smile. He hadn't felt this way for years not since, not since he met his wife. He began to cry again, damn-it. Was this unfaithful behavior? If he just felt a sexual draw it would be different but this was far more holistic. He felt so incredibly guilty. Just a couple of weeks ago he could not get his wife out of his every thought and just now he had almost forgotten her altogether. He did not know how to think or feel about it. He picked up the phone and called Pastor Craemer.

"Hello?" Pastor Craemer said, recognizing the number on the ID. "Kirt, is that you?"

"Yes…I, uh, I need to talk with you."

"Go ahead, Kirt," Pastor Craemer said with that fully attentive voice.

"I just met a woman and I made a date to come back here in June to go fly fishing with her."

Smiling happily to himself, Pastor listened as he had of course been through this with other men and women. "So a woman who fly fishes? Right up your alley!"

"Yeah, but I feel so incredibly guilty and so unfaithful. I love Beth still. What do I do now?"

"Your confused feelings are very normal, Kirt. You took seriously your vows and always had a genuine love for your wife and girls and that will never go away. They are with Christ and outside of space and time; we are still on our way. Because we're pilgrims here, God provides us with love and companionship no matter what our circumstances. Look, we don't know what will come of a date with this woman but isolating yourself from other women and other people will never let you focus on positive aspects of the gift God gave you in your girls. Keep your date. Does she know about your situation, your depressions?"

"Yes. I told her everything and she just listened. It didn't seem to scare her away."

"Scare her away? Hell, Kirt. You're what a lot of women look for but can't usually have: a family man with genuine loving dedication. What did she tell you about herself?"

"Well…" Kirt went on to tell Pastor everything he had learned about her ending with the fact that she was Christian.

"Whoa, Kirt. She may not be your next wife, but the Lord really set you up. Is she attractive?"

Kirt reflexively blushed like a child. "Yes, she is; auburn hair, attractive freckles on her nose and arms and on her chest, hazel coppery eyes, full lips, just the faintest smooth wrinkles in all the right places; a smile that is so intensely warm with that, you know, that internal fire that seems to radiate every part of her."

"Well I see you *really* noticed," and at that they both laughed.

"Take the lass fishing boy, and tell your wife and girls about it. You know full well they really don't hear you but do it anyway. It will help you be honest with this transition. I miss your girls extremely, but believe me, if they knew you had found a lady like this they would be the first to say go for it."

"You're probably right. I just never imagined feeling like this about someone other than Beth. Honestly, I have had sexual thoughts about others before, but this is stronger and much more…"

"It can be another gift from God. Till death do you part and you are apart for now. The level of understanding and perspective we'll have in heaven will more than handle all of this. When you link up with this woman when all of us get to heaven we will praise God for it, including the girls. If the shoe were on the other foot, that is what you would want for Beth, right?"

"You're right. "Love ya', Pastor," Kirt said.

"You know I love you, Kirt. God's blessings."

After hanging up, Kirt prayed for a long time. As he drove he talked with God, he told him everything he was feeling and thinking and he asked God to give him the strength to deal with all this and stay close to him. Request for strength had always been his habit but for the last two years it had been his breath it seemed to him. Pastor Craemer said a prayer as well for what God would deem best for Kirt and Maggie and the strength to deal with it all.

Jane told Walt that Maggie was not feeling real great so she was filling in for her. "She wasn't sick, was she? Walt asked.

"No, not really sick but just pretty tired. She works awfully hard you know."

"That's for sure. She looks so damn good sometimes it's hard to tell when she is exhausted. I better go check on her."

"No!" Jane blurted out a little too loudly. "She, I mean, she's probably sleeping; better let her sleep."

"No, I better go check."

Jane had seen both Kirt and Maggie leave and she was afraid this new guy might be over at Maggie's right now, not that Maggie was the kind that would be having a fling, being so religious and all. But heck, you never know, and she didn't want Walter to barge in. It looked like he was going over anyway. As Walt left, Jane phoned Maggie and told her he was coming. Maggie said, "Yeah, so what?"

"Well, the way you looked at that guy and the fact that he is coming back to fly fish with you I thought maybe he might be over there right now."

"Jane. Do you think I would just bed down some stranger?"

"No, no, Maggie. He just seemed like a nice guy and you being such a nice woman I thought…Well, Maggie, you deserve a little sex, dammit!"

"Thank you, I think, Jane, but I don't play that and you know it. Anyway, Kirt is not over here he has gone back home to Clarkston."

"Okay, Maggie. Love ya'."

"Love you too, Jane, and thanks for filling in for me."

"What are you doing anyway, Maggie?"

"I'm tying flies," and Maggie hung up.

Maggie heard the incessant knocking and it irritated her. She wished they would just go away. She got up from her tying bench and walked from the rear of the house through the living room and to the front door. She opened the door and there stood Walt. "Maggie, you ok?"

"Yes, Walt, I am. I just needed some time to myself."

"What's the matter Maggie? You never need time to yourself."

"Yes I do, Walt, and if you had an empathic bone in your body you might know that. I am not a machine; sometimes I need to just have some time to myself. Can you understand that, you damn blockhead?"

"Whoa," Walt said. "Where the hell did that come from? I just wondered if you were Okay."

Feeling a little guilty she said, "Walt. I shouldn't have snapped at you. You're a good man but I need more. I need someone who likes me and wants me around just because they want me around. I'm just not comfortable with our relationship and I should have told you months ago but I didn't have the guts. I love you, Walt, but not in the way a woman should really love a man. We have been playing this strange dating game for several years and it is never going to go anywhere, is it?"

"What's wrong with the way it is Maggie? I love you. We have a good arrangement We like each other."

"Walt you are a good man, but you are not a passionate man, at least not when it comes to people. You are passionate about your business and politics and that's great it's always needed just not by me. I want a man to love me passionately, and I do not mean like a damn lovesick teenager, I mean the kind of passion that is always there even when you piss each other off, even when things are not going well, even when you might not have all the money in the world. The kind of passion that goes way beyond romance and sex…You know what I mean, Walt?"

"I think I do. Are you saying I am not like that?"

"Walt, I am saying just that, and I know I don't want to be that for you. We are different people, and I guess because I have isolated myself with work and raising my girls, I just kind of settled for you—Not in a bad way, but we are two lonely people who need different kinds of people. It's best discovered now rather than if we let ourselves drift along or get married."

"Okay, Maggie. I can see you have been thinking about this for a long time. I know you well enough to know nobody's gonna talk that beautiful thick Irish head out of it."

"Oh Walt," she said with a smile. "I will always love you in the way deep friends love each other, and I want nothing but the best for you, but I have to move out on my own."

"Maggie, I hate to agree, but I do and I love you too, kid."

They embraced and Walt left. Maggie felt much lighter.

FEELING STRONG AND BEAUTIFUL

A major southwest blast of air from Mexico blew into the upper Midwest and Michigan. Northern Michigan blossomed into a rare combination of a 75-degree, low humidity early summer day. No clouds could be seen and the sun shined brightly into the cedars and pines. Maggie decided to breathe a little. She put on her favorite summer dress of lily green with lemon grass accents. She looked into the mirror and was grateful for what she saw. At forty-four, she was taut, still firm, and her breasts had fallen only slightly to the south. Maggie wore this for herself, and if truth be told, to impress other women. She harbored little arrogance given her youthful condition, she felt thankful to have inherited such genes. Her auburn hair pulled into a full ponytail retained a healthy glow with the aid of a few "naturally" placed highlights. Her freckles, hazel clean penny specked eyes and full mouth still looked young, and so she flaunted a little, knowing full well that all the hard work she had done raising three girls alone and working in unskilled positions would catch up with her and would begin to reflect in the coarsening of her complexion; the fine lines around her eyes and neck becoming legitimate wrinkles. She was glad she never picked up the habit of smoking saving her skin from its accelerated aging effects. She felt wonderful and very much a woman. She grabbed a small purse and headed for the Inn. As she walked along the old wood and brick sidewalk the warm breeze and penetrating sunlight felt so good. The freedom from coats, boots, wool hats and gloves gave her a sense of lightness and strength. No longer having to carry the heavy gear of winter was one of the most pleasant transitions of living in the North. Of course she noticed, although she pretended not to, the cross section of men who halted to take a look at her. Her calves were strong and gently muscled. Her back and arms were lithe yet strong. Her neck was long and the ponytail was mustang-like. The summer dress fluttered and waved like the gentle riffles of the section of the Manistee at Hodenpyl Dam Pond. She came by her body honestly having never lifted a weight in her life. She ran a few miles a week but mostly the hard physical labor had carved the form for her. A man in his forties smiled at her a little longer than appropriate and when she passed he turned to catch a view from that side. Willie Henderson was hooking up another tow and when he looked up he said, "looking even prettier than usual Maggie." He said it with a combination of lust and respect. "Thank you, Willie. This weather makes me feel pretty too." Carol Hanckles, the owner of The Honey Hole, (a gift shop aimed at fly fishers), looked at Maggie and waved, thinking humorously, *she makes me sick.* The valve stem vigilante at work beside a truck parked illegally in the alley felt his temperature rise, and it wasn't because of the hoodie or the southwestern wind. Her father-in-law of her deceased husband stopped and said, "I'm gonna call the cops, Maggie. It's illegal to look that good; you look terrific, sweetheart."

"Thanks Dad." They both remembered her dead husband in a passing thought. Seeing Maggie in this attire was unusual, as normally she was fairly practical, not that practical attire could hide her allure, but today she thought, *what the hell.*

FURTHER RECOVERY ON THE JORDAN

He got down on his hands and knees and slowly crept toward the earthen outcropping that protruded over the Jordan on the south bank. He tried to mimic the patience of the Great Blue Heron—sit and search for trout activity. There was no hatch but he knew that most of the fish's diet consisted of food eaten below the surface. At first he saw what appeared to be a brown, down and across the water below the opposite bank. Upon further examination he realized it was a shadow angled from an undercut. He started to notice some whirling action just below the surface. He scanned intensely until he saw what he thought was a flash of white. He lay there until the flash was seen again. It was a sizeable brook trout. He had grown quite fat and larger than most brookies in the Jordan. The brookie would venture out and attack his prey and quietly dart back into the undercut. The dark cold water under the bank provided him with cover from birds of prey and other enemies. Slowly the big boy moved out partially into the light but not too far from his cover. Kirt became enthralled with the fish. He could see his eyes, clear and observant. He marveled at the wormy blue/green/gray color on his back and the spots on his sides. The fins were tipped on the underside in crisp bright white. This was the white flash he had seen. Under the brookie were rocks of various sizes in whites, browns, greens and reds. It appeared as though the brookie had morphed from the bottom of the river, his camouflage was so complete. If Kirt had not taken the time to search he would not have seen him at all. A pattern began to emerge as the fat boy would move out and then back. Upstream about 20 yards was a slight riffle as the water fell over a small ridge. By the time the water reached the big boy it had slowed down and a seam went right past the undercut. Kirt could not see what the brookie was feeding on but whatever it was it was coming by regularly. He guessed it was a hatch that was about to happen or maybe nymphs cut loose from the rocks and he simply grabbed the nymphs before they rose to the surface. He rolled over and tied an attractor nymph to the end of his tippet. He moved carefully downstream and still on his knees casted up and over to the north side of the bank just beneath the riffle. The nymph was pulled down and sank into the seam. He could still see the fat boy as the tippet continued past the undercut. He did not respond. He cast again; again nothing. No wonder the old boy was so old; he was a careful selector, rare for brookies. They usually attacked just about anything that floated by. He stopped and tied on a larger hex nymph. He cast up and across again and watched the tippet follow the seam until, SLAM! The old fat boy was on. Kirt played him a bit as he did not want to tire him out. On his feet he stepped into the stream and brought the brookie in. He reached down and passed the rod from one hand to another. He removed the hook from the lip of the brookie. He thought twice about releasing him. He decided not to and placed the fat boy in his creel. He could see himself frying him in butter, sage and dried cherries. They could eat him tonight at Hoss's. He was gorgeous and measured about 18", large for these streams. Remembering a recent article he had read recommending keeping the larger fish and that keeping a few was better than releasing them all; 'gave the smaller fish a chance to grow. Kirt had never kept more than a meal or two. In his mind brookies (not technically trout but char) were the gold standard of all, trout family cuisine. Their meat was slightly pink pale yellow, flaky and mild. He had come to love them best in sage and butter, although over a grill wasn't bad either. They would have to stop and buy some fresh small potatoes and broccoli. He would buy the vegetables and his dear friend Hoss could blend his cheddar sauce to cover them. He was determined to eat nothing the rest of the day and keep his palate clear for the meal he was dreaming of. He was so thankful to have his senses return along with some energy as he lifted from the melancholia. He remembered the description of melancholia from a fellow afflicted, Robert Travers M.D. during a group session at Beaumont Hospital in downstate Michigan. He liked the word better than the word depression. It seemed to more fully capture the experience of it. It was not simply a depression, a dip or hole but an experience of being enveloped in sadness, hopelessness and isolation, shrouded in it. As he continued to remember he felt oddly upbeat. He gained hope knowing that there was someone else who knew what it was like. They were in the brotherhood of the melancholia and they could learn from each other. There was a way to escape after all.

THE BIRTH OF THE MESICK INN

"You think those guys are homos?" Walt asked Maggie.

"I don't know. How the hell would I know?"

"They're kind of unusual, don't you think?"

"Damn, Walt. You're getting like an old woman," said Maggie.

"Strange. The tall one is so fastidious and the short one is kind of a slob."

Maggie looked at Walt with a mixture of irritation and puzzlement. "Holy crap, Walt, get a grip."

"What?" said Walt, as he watched the two from NYC walk away. Gertrude was a lovely woman. As a recent immigrant she had set up a solid business in Michigan on the Manistee. It was a business she was quite familiar with from her former life in Philadelphia. She spoke English fairly well, stood around six feet tall, blonde, medium boned, with womanly curves and firm bosoms that stood up above her bodice. She was in her thirties and was pleasantly pretty with a wide smile, green eyes and deep dimples on both sides of her face.

She had learned to go where the boom times were and the lumbering boom times of Northern Michigan in 1841 were just what she wanted. She had convinced thirteen women to come with her to Mesick, MI from Philadelphia to set up her whorehouse. It was said they were the most beautiful whores in the west. The women went with Gertrude because they had come to trust her to defend them against the abusive ones and she was fair with the ladies financially. The Mesick Inn had twenty ample sized rooms for entertaining, five large rooms for housing the ladies and five full sized baths with pumped in water, each with its own waste water pipe and a long shafted commode with a flush system fed by a central water tower which was fed from catching water from a waterfall on the creek, or if the waterfall was too slow, from a deep pool at the bottom of the waterfall using a pump located behind the stone wall that was the wall behind the large central fireplace. The waterfall source was ingenious as the force of the water into the catch pipe was pushed through decreasing sized pipes and when the valve was opened inside the building, the water would come out with substantial pressure. The pump was indoor and stayed unfrozen during the winter from the warmth coming off the back of the fireplace stonewall. On high platforms beside and above the roofline, were three, large water holding tanks open to the elements to catch rain and snow and also receive pumped in water when needed. The tanks were tarred on the outside to catch sunlight in the spring and summer to warm the water, otherwise in the winter water had to be heated over the fireplaces. At the base of each tank was a screen that needed to be cleaned from time to time. In addition, George Carmine had built a structure with double log walls. The interior of the walls facing each other was heavily tarred to help keep out moisture, seal out air and repel insects. There was a 2-foot space between the walls. The double walls made the whole building cooler in the summer and warmer in the winter. He provided each room with a fireplace and a large double paned rough glass window with screen inserts for the summer. Around the top of each wall were small windows covered only with a fitted board, which could be removed as needed. He had the same small windows in the smoking room downstairs to draw out the cigar smoke as it rose to the fifteen-foot ceiling. The rest of the structure contained a large dining room, a well-stocked, expansive bar with billiard and card tables and a porch out back that stretched along the back wall giving a view of a large creek that fed into the Manistee. All lighting was from oil lamps and mirrored sconces. A large second building outback housed the kitchen, which was connected to the main building by a long covered porch. The kitchen also was fed by a separate water catch providing running water also backed up with water tanks. George also put an indoor toilet in the kitchen building for the cooks and waitresses. The whole setup looked rather utilitarian on the outside but the interior was very tasteful and more refined, refined by logger's standards. True, the wallpaper colors were in keeping with a whore house, but not excessively gaudy. It was a nice piece of rustic elegance in the middle of nowhere and nearly every lumberman wanted to visit there for one reason or another. Sometimes it was just the baths and the food. Other men partook of the ladies but whatever the reason it was a wonderful break from the hard life in the pines. It was not cheap, in fact it was quite pricy for a frontier outpost but it was worth the extra coin and many made it a monthly or even weekly ritual. The supervisors and owners of the companies went there often. But if you had the money Gertrude and George treated you like a king and gave everyone considerable respect, even those who needed hygienic attention and could not write or read or speak effectively. The ladies scrubbed them all down before the fleshly proceedings even when it was more than a little repugnant to do so. Gertrude demanded that the men take the first whack at it by bathing themselves and then the ladies would follow up to make sure all the seen and hidden places were clean and pink. "Hell, I love it there. I never been so clean. Now I can't stand myself when I get a little ripe, they spoil me so. And lovin' never felt better than when your cleaner than when you came into the world and the ladies are always polite and clean and smell so good," a regular customer said. There was never any trouble at the INN either because George and Gertrude never let the men get excessively rambunctious. The only time there was trouble was when one of the ladies was physically manhandled by one of the lumbermen until Gertrude put a double barrel 0.28 gauge to his head and ended it. "He just wouldn't stop," she told George. "Serves him right," said George. They brought his body down the open stairs so everyone could see it and George said loudly just one time, "This is what happens to anyone who beats on any of us. Put the son of a bitch on the fire out back." The retelling of the story kept things quite peaceful. The owner of the logging company sent the abused woman an apology letter and a substantial amount of money as a peace offering. "Vas ah dahm classy ting ta do," said Gertrude in her High German accent, as the lady showed her the letter and the money. Gertrude always took time to eat dinner with that owner when he came in after that. He never partook of the ladies, just the food and drink.

Gertrude was self-taught, but well educated and carried with her a collection of books called Classic World Literature. Her mother and father gave the collection to her when she made her confirmation along with a King James Version of the bible with many illustrations. Her parents had connected themselves to the Lutheran group The Magisterium of Pennsylvania and Adjacent States. They were both murdered on a small street while in downtown Philly. They left little else for their only daughter as they were newly emigrated and had just recently establish a small dry goods store in Gettysburg. Many in the church rallied around to help young Gertrude but she had always harbored greater desires to see the rest of the continent. She turned her first trick in Philly in a fulsome facility owned by Jane Stein. "It was not at all a bad experience," she said. "And the gentleman was not only sweet and kind, but quick."

So she progressed and when Jane was murdered by one of the clients Gertrude took over the place and changed everything at a hasty rate. By the time she was twenty she owned and operated the classiest whorehouse in town. After some ten years, she met an innkeeper named George Carmine and he shared with her his plans to build a beautiful inn in Mesick on the knowledge that the lumber boom was just coming into its own and the loggers would have plenty of money to spend. George's dream and Gertrude's desire to see the country was a perfect combination and the two set out for Michigan. George put up the money for the inn and Gertrude provided the enticements. Gertrude kept the income from the ladies, who received free room and board, and George kept all the other profits. Gertrude did not peddle her own soothing wares and George and she shared each other's amorous affections from time to time. Gertrude was able to entice her most beautiful ladies and a few tolerable looking ones to come with her by offering them an additional cut on their earnings and maybe the chance to homestead a piece of land of their own. Truth was many of the ladies thought their chances of marrying up might be greater with less competition around; the whore's retirement hope. Sometimes men did fall in love and marry their whore, sometimes. George also took in a young Ottawa woman he called Sunshine because he did not really understand how to pronounce her native name and because she was very pretty with a seemingly constant smiling face. Sunshine's family had died from small pox and she was living a meager life when George and crew moved into the area. She was an expert gardener and was soon able to grow many of the vegetables used in the cuisine at the Inn. She also netted fish for the same purpose. Gertrude and the ladies adopted her and helped her make the transition to a white man's world. Sunshine never became a prostitute as both her former native and current Christian religion forbade it. Sunshine and her family had become Christian long before the small pox epidemic. Most of the remaining of her tribe went to Kansas as part of a treaty agreement. Sunshine stayed back alone because of her love for Michigan and she also knew she could find work among the lumbering whites. She actually admired much of the white man's world even though she felt a little guilty about it from time to time. She adapted well. Gertrude was teaching her both English and German and Sunshine was teaching Gertrude the Algonquin language, which was the language of the Ottawa with some exceptions. The two could often be heard speaking to each other in the different tongues as they practiced their pronunciation. The guests and George loved to hear their exchanges. George came to love Sunshine like a daughter and "gave her away" to a compassionate Indian Agent at their wedding. They moved to Montana. George cried off and on for the next week. He made a trip to visit her one summer and she and her husband reciprocated a few years later. Their correspondence became legendary and now resides at the University of Michigan 's archival facility. George was right about the boom as more men were made millionaires from Michigan's lumber boom than those from the later Gold Rush. George and Gertrude eventually married and Gertrude quit the whore business as the lumbering decreased and tourist began to come to catch the native Grayling and brook trout. They became quite rich, not as rich as the Lumber Barons but very well off. Fisherman came in trainloads. Men cast multiple leaders and often caught three grayling at a time that were stacked like cordwood in the river. Grayling with their tall dorsal fins and delicate flavor were prized and uniquely they smelled of thyme when caught. The combination of the loss of habitat from gravel gouging logs, sand brought into the river by the logging covering up the gravel used for egg laying and the over fishing (sometimes as many as 700 a day by a group of four men) caused the Grayling to disappear and they have never returned. Companies loved staying at the Mesick Inn because of its history. People had pictures taken standing next to George and Gertrude and they still hang on the walls, Walt later had them restored and carefully framed for preservation. The Inn was left to Sunshine who gave it to her two daughters and they ran it for many years and then the Inn was sold to other owners until purchased by Walt. George had one of the beams hollowed out on the north side of the Inn. He took a piece of pipe and put it in the center hole. Inside the pipe he hadplaced a copy of the local newspaper, a list of all his employees, photos of patrons and the ladies. An assortment of information he wanted to be left as a kind of time capsule. He plugged up the hole with concrete and propped the beam back into place and secured with the original long nails. When Walt bought the Inn he discovered the treasure and framed and mounted them to preserve them as much as possible. The carefully written narrative that George had written was on display under glass beneath the other items. It took up a lot of space. Patrons loved it. The place felt like a trip back in time; the photos were a real hit. In some of the photos you could see a small oak tree that seemed to be the giant currently in the front yard. Maggie fashioned this editorialized history and Walt let her hang it next to the pictures, which read:

The saloon at the Mesick Inn was maintained as much in its original form as possible. It connected from the more log cabin like dining room through a set of hickory swinging doors still mounted on the original heavy spring loaded hinges. The building had been erected in the mid-1800s to serve travelers between southern and northern Michigan. At the time of the logging heyday when the fishing tourism was replaced by town like camps full of workers serving what then seemed an endless supply of pine and hardwoods for the fast growing new Republic. The Inn at that time converted its saloon to reflect a kind of high end "parlor," a euphemism for brothel. In the beginning, mostly the owners of the lumber companies utilized the services there but over time more and more of the rank and file splurged to spend a night with the comely ladies of the Mesick Inn. Walt bought the place partly because of the historic nature of the building and its intact saloon/parlor. The room's ceiling was covered in an elaborate almost Victorian tin, painted pearl white. The walls were paneled red oak with floor to ceiling mirrors here and there. The bar stretched across a wall of sixty feet and was made of white oak and carved in the shape of an oversized Au Sable River boat inlaid with panels of red oak in the shape of the lower peninsula of Michigan and alternately trout and Grayling. The glassware racks still hung suspended from the 20-foot ceilings. On the west side of the room was a stairway that led up to the rooms designed to be comfortable but with high turnover in mind.

Walt had restored the paint, blood red velveteen wallpaper, white glass chandeliers and sconces and porcelain bar sink. It gave an accurate feel of walking into a rather upscale whorehouse of the 1800s. Some say, "It gives them the creeps, all those lost souls trying to class up their depravity." Pictures of some of the ladies of that period hung on the walls along with some of the clients and the owner, Gertrude, a Madame who had helped build the original building when she moved here from Philadelphia. Although Gertrude had kept her girls as "clean" as possible the place was still a source of venereal diseases in this part of Michigan and many women back home were given the gift that keeps on giving in the form of gonorrhea or syphilis when their men returned to the more civilized environs of southern Michigan. "The most beautiful ladies of the woods" was the original slogan Gertrude had used to describe her women and from the pictures on the wall it did appear that many of them were actually attractive unlike many of the sad looking ladies seen in other pictures in other histories Walt and I have researched.

Walt wanted a written blurb he could put on his menus to describe the place, and Maggie was able to talk him into allowing her to add the following sentences to her history that was hung by the entry door of the saloon: *Most of the prostitutes came from Philly with Gertrude and did not live to be more than thirty-five, most of them. They died often from sexually transmitted disease or other infectious disease caught from such intimate contact. Their deaths were often long and painful due to lack of medical treatments for such infections.*

It was impossible to have a drink in the saloon without thinking about the people who long ago inhabited the very room. It was a kind of living history of the area warts and all. No self-respecting Michigander or traveler would fail to tip a couple at the Mesick Inn's Saloon. Maggie and her husband had gone there on occasion before Walt bought the place, but found it too depressing to frequent.

Maggie, looking over the old bar, thought about the history of the Inn and her own life. "Life is bittersweet music. You know, Walt? I sometimes find myself smiling and crying at the same time. It's peculiar, hyper real."

"It sure is, Maggie," said Walt.

THE GUTSY SHERIFF WHEELER

Sheriff Wheeler reached over with his long, lean banana fingers and picked up the printout. His slit-like eyes opened as wide as they could. "Carla!" He yelled. "Come in here!" Carla entered his office. The Sheriff's office was appropriately decorated for a semi-retired down state cop. There were plaques and photos everywhere. The walls were covered with photos of fish caught on the fly, golf courses and grandchildren. His numerous citations from his work in the Detroit and Farmington Hills police departments were also on the wall, but took up very little space. "That's what I do for a living. This is just a hobby," he was fond of saying. Sherriff Bob Wheeler decorated for valor three times in Detroit only to be unceremoniously booted for "beating" a black crack addict on Cass Ave. He had been a victim of diversity and police brutality mentality gone amok. Even before the case went to trial, the city paid the family $6 million for the loss of their son, brother, husband and father; a typical move for the city in those days. His arrest had been captured on video from an angle that made it appear as though the blows from his flashlight were more severe than they were. Bob thought the addict might have had a zip gun or knife in his right palm as the addict refused to open it. In an effort to get the hand open, Bob placed several blows to his knuckles and the left side of his head. When the *perp* suddenly lost all muscle control, defecated and wet himself, Bob knew something was wrong. He called the precinct and asked for help. An ambulance was sent and the body was taken to the coroner. Bob never liked to see anyone die and in addition, this was such a dreadful waste of life. He punched out early and rushed home to tell his wife.

The next morning, Bob and Cindy were greeted with a call from their Pastor. "Bob, are you all right?"

"Yes, why did you call?"

"You don't know?"

"No, I don't. What?" The press is convicting you of murder, film and all. Turn on the TV, see what I mean."

"Okay, Pastor." He hung up. A building flood of heat and needle-like prickles on the skin began to cover his body. His forehead became tighter than a zip tie. His breath stopped at his chest bone instead of flowing up and down from the diaphragm. "Cindy, turn on the TV now." The set came on right at the tail end of a discussion about the death with the Chief of Police, the Mayor and a neighborhood spokesman. "It's very troubling," said the Mayor. "We will conduct a thorough investigation and then we will know what really happened."

"What the hell do you mean? Can't you see the video does not lie?" said the spokesman.

"What video?" Bob blurted. Now the heat across his body was pure anger. He started to channel surf, determined to see the video. Then, there it was. A short wide angle shot. Bob was repeatedly hitting the man about the arm and head. Then the *perp* collapsed.

"That's it!" said Bob. "Hell, that is so text book…the guy died, but not because of the blows!"

Cindy let him vent then stood up and encircled him with her arms. She and he started to cry.

"Damn," he said.

Cindy picked up the phone and called Joel Seaver. He was the best damn defense attorney a cop could have. Not only did he empathize with clients, he once was a cop. Twenty years ago, he left to become an attorney and did a great deal of pro bono for cops. Cops have little income and welcomed his expert advice.

"Did you see it Joel?"

"Yes."

"You know he is not responsible for that man's death."

"Yes, I do. I've seen trauma from that kind of force, but what else could he do. No, the *perp* deserved the hits. Tell Bob I am already on it. I called the coroner and also requested an autopsy from an external expert. He was a crack head. He had a heart attack, for God's sake. I know, the *perp* being black and Bob being white and the Mayor and Chief of Police political *maggots* makes the situation highly volatile."

"Well, what?"

"What? The Mayor is on the tube already."

"I know the outrage you feel over this senseless murder. I have suspended Bob and he will be prosecuted to the fullest extent of the law. I will not stand for this kind of brutality on my force!"

Bob and Cindy sat dumbfounded. Joel would not believe it. On the phone Joel was whistling to get Cindy's attention. Cindy heard and put the phone back to her ear.

"Cindy, this guy is an evil S.O.B. Tell Bob to talk to no one. Send me a dollar for the fee."

"Thank you, Joel," tears ran down her face. She hung up and turned to Bob, "Joel says stay home and talk to no one."

The circus unfolded before their eyes as they watched the TV as the updates came in. The Fraternal Order of Police cried foul on the escalation of Police force and explained that the action was likely justified and the death due to some underlying health issues. The family and friends of the *perp* cried on cue for the cameras. A makeshift shrine was erected for the *perp* at the site of his death.

When the *perp* died he was gaunt; teeth missing, eroded nasal tissue and smelled repulsive. The picture hung up at the shrine was of him when he was married fifteen years ago before cocaine and crack had done their work. He looked like the typical young groom, bright-eyed and well groomed. The public outcry was racially mixed, but only reported as along racial lines; whites against, blacks for the *perp*. Many in the white community did not side with Bob and many blacks did, but editorial manipulation painted a different picture. The *perp's* Uncles and cousins said he deserved the beating. Some upscale white liberals decried the police brutality. Bob was undone. He sat still for long periods of time, or he lay down on the couch. Cindy handled the phone calls; the press, friends, union, Mayor's office, Chief of Police all called. She referred each to Joel. Around 6:00 pm. that evening, Joel came to visit. When Cindy opened the door she began to sob and Joel hugged her and sat her on the sofa.

"You know what the number one negative side effect of crack usage is?"

"No," said Bob.

"Heart failure!" "The coroner says the *perp* died from cranial blows and hemorrhaging. My guy says there was evidence of hemorrhage but not enough to kill him. He says he died of heart failure due to damage from crack."

"So what you're sayin' is that I did not kill him and it can be confirmed?"

"Yes, sit tight. I intend to have a conversation with the Mayor, the Chief, and of course, the press."

"Thanks, Joel."

"My pleasure," he said.

Joel's efforts paid off and Wheeler went to work for the Farmington Hills police and wrapped up his tenure as Chief. It was a miserable situation that worked out well for Wheeler and Joel, but not for the taxpayers of the city who lost six million to the sad family of the dead crack head. The mayor and chief retired with full pensions and benefits.

THE EARLY VISIT OF MR. S AND NICK

East of Grayling and north of M-72 can be found a nice low-key, fly-fishing lodge. Gill's Lodge had been there so long that most people couldn't remember when it wasn't. It was very typical. Several cabins with comfortable back porches, each sitting just yards from the Au Sable, that ran downstream from the main office. There was a diner that provided excellent hearty cooking and a fly shop containing an assortment of flies tied by locals who knew the seams and riffles of the "Holy Waters" as this stretch was called. The proprietor was friendly and even if you had all the gear you needed one always stopped in to get advice and buy some flies and a book or two. Gilly, a fourth generation Gill and current owner described his guests as strangers who often become lifelong friends and many did.

"I remember when I discovered that Mr. Spalding was a world renowned heart surgeon. He had been coming for years, sometimes alone or with his boys and friends. He wore practical, economical gear. He used the same Paul Young bamboo rod for as long as I knew him. One day a guest began to vomit in our restaurant and passed out on the floor. He then woke up suddenly and complained of pains in his arm. I asked my wife to call an ambulance and asked if anyone in the diner was a doctor. Doc Spalding was coming in the door to eat breakfast and by God he went to work on the guy right there on the floor. He gave me his keys and asked me to go get a hinged leather box out of his trunk. When I saw the box I first thought it was a layered fly box. You know one of those fancy ones? Fly boxes attached so they slid out. I brought him the box and he opened it. He took out a needle and a syringe and pulled some kind of medicine from a glass vial. He asked me to have the ambulance service connected and he told the drivers what was going on and what they might need. He then asked the man who his GP or specialist was and I got him on the call too. The two doctors talked and Doc Spalding jumped into the ambulance and went with the man to the hospital. It was inspiring to see him work. The man survived and Doc made sure he was setup with the right cardiologist in Traverse City. When I went over to pick Doc up after the event, I just looked at him and said, 'you son of a bitch. You're a Doctor!' He laughed and explained that he tried not to make a big deal of it because people treated him differently if they knew. He's a peach of a man. When he walked up to the Lodge a crowd of guests and locals were there to applaud him for his successful treatment of the poor man on the floor. I found out later that Spalding never billed the man and Doc paid off his costs relative to his local treatment, because the man's insurance did not cover all costs. The man with the heart attack still comes in her and he still mists up when talking about old Doc. Anyway, the point is nobody is anyone special at Gills. Everyone is a fly fisher looking for trout and fly fisher camaraderie. It was an unwritten rule that no one talked business at Gills. Once a computer salesman who sold those big IBM mainframes tried to ingratiate himself with some guests, 'hopes to sell them or get referrals. He got nothing but the cold shoulder until he finally caught on and apologized. It still took him a couple seasons before people could trust him."

Gill's lodge provided guided fishing as well, both float and wading. On one particularly fine afternoon, two Hyde riverboats floated up to the dock. In one boat was a Mr. Stringini with his guide, and in the other a man named Nick the Greek and his guide. Nick loved the area.

VISITING HOSS

As Kirt drove east on M-72 toward Kalkaska, he stopped to fill up. He loved these northern fill stops as the gas stations usually doubled as a kind of general store. He decided to feed the two old black bears that were in a massive cage behind the store. The owner had rigged up several trees inside the cage and a large stainless steel water trough. He to the station and bought a lug of frozen blueberries and washed them outside under the hose until they were slightly thawed. This was one of their favorites and he wanted to give them something better than the feed you could buy from the vending machine. He and his girls had often fed the bears this way. The owner recognized Kirt as the "blueberry guy" and said, "Where are the girls?"

Kirt told his story as the shopkeeper stood there mute and frozen.

"So many lives pass through here and so many stories. I am so sorry to hear about this. Those ladies were so special, even a stranger could tell."

"Thank you," said Kirt. "I'm dealing with it much better now, and just know they would never forgive me if I didn't get some berries for the bears."

"I bet the bears remember you too. You are the only one to feed them the berries. They cost so much more than the feed."

"I'd like to think they do," said Kirt.

Kirt grabbed two paper plates and put a load of berries on each. He placed them under the fence into the bears. The bears ate the berries hurried and licked their chops, while groaning asking for more. Kirt obliged. He gave them several plates until they lay down and made a kind of satisfied rumble.

Kirt sat on the bench facing M-72. He watched the cars going by in the early morning light. He imaged the lives inside some of the passing cars. They all needed the same fundamental things, they all felt pain and joy. Because of his loss he was developing a greater empathy and connection to people. It was a good thing and the vastness of all the lives God must attend to overwhelmed him and he shook off the thought as one might when contemplating eternity.

Pulling into the bakery in Kalkaska, with his windows down, Kirt could smell the unusual but satisfying odor of donuts and a massive outdoor char grill. The Bakery functioned as a cultural gathering place and provided simple, hearty food for breakfast, lunch and dinner. Their specialties for breakfast were Eggs Benedict and wheat berry pancakes. They were known for macaroni and cheese and meatloaf at lunch. At dinner, their savory marinated rib eyes with seasonal side dishes or their dried cherry and sage butter trout were all that they served. They had only two desserts: Peach Melba ice cream pie and dense brownies with or without ice cream. The owners had installed a highly effective and quiet exhaust system so that anyone could smoke anywhere they wanted and the smoke would rise into the filters and not bother anyone. Kirt loved the smell of the place. It smelled like honest food, warmth and integrity. The walls were old 1940s knotty pine and covered with newspaper articles about the place form all over the world. The furthest an article came was from New Zealand written by a travel writer who spoke so highly of the place that if they were anywhere near New Zealand, you would never get a seat. Hoss was seated at the donut/liquor bar. He had a giant bear claw, a cup of regular coffee and a cheroot cigar in front of him.

"How can you do that?" Asked Kirt.

"It's a real palate pleaser. You oughta try it," said Hoss.

Hoss loved his cigars. He smoked a wide range from the overpriced premiums to the lowest of quality. At home he had converted a closet into a humidor. In that humidor was a substantial supply of cheroots from Kentucky, the kind the Italians often smoke. He smoked too many each day but kept his breath and teeth very agreeable. With cheroot in his mouth he looked like a villain in a spaghetti western. He had eaten bear claws almost exclusively since Kirt had known him.

"Why don't you try the nutties, Hoss? Walk on the wild side."

Hoss grinned, "I like my bear claws, buddy."

The Waitress smiled and refilled his coffee.

"Thank you, Charlotte," he said as if he had known here all her life. He had a demeanor that invited conversation. He was transparent and people just sensed his friendliness was genuine, which it was.

"She's up here for the summer to work. A friend recommended her. She's only twenty and already working on a Masters in pharmacology. She said she needed a mental break and decided to work here for a few months before returning to Indianapolis to finish her masters and intern at Eli Lilly. She is single and has not dated for a couple of years; even as attractive she is, because she wanted nothing to interfere with her studies. She said she would date a little while here. I told her I would send a few guys her way. She said…"

"Whoa, Hoss. Did you find out about her hygiene habits, her favorite music or her family history?" Said Kirt.

"Yeah," smiled Hoss. "Her family is Maltese and she is the first in her family to get a college degree. You know me, buddy, people just tell me stuff and ya' know, it's always damned interesting." Hoss stood up and gave Kirt that huge gentle bear hug. He hung on a little longer than usual. When he let go, his tears were about to roll over onto his cheeks. He quickly wiped his eyes to prevent a public display.

"So, Hoss. How is the foundry business? Any challenges lately?"

"Just the usual government shit; getting the sand supply we need that kind of routine pain in the ass."

Kirt smiled and ordered some Eggs Benedict and a grilled pecan roll. They finished their food and headed over to the forks on the Boardman River. They stepped into the cold water around 11:00 am just as a nice blue winged olive hatch was coming off. They caught a few dinks, but then tied on the deeper probing streamers, hoping to pick up a larger brown or two. They tried every streamer they had from weighted wooly buggers to Mickey Finns. Hoss hooked up with a twenty inch brown and they kept it for dinner. Hoss reached down inside his right wader leg and said, "Take a pull?"

"What do we have here? Asked Kirt.

"I just happen to have a Reserve Dry Riesling from Chateau Chantel; semi dry and cold as the Boardman."

They sat and drank the wine with the sausage and cheese Kirt had brought. Kirt lay on his back and stared at poplars swaying in the mild breeze. A large group of yellow finches then hopped down to a patch of thistle growing under the trees. Kirt turned on his side and watched as they gorged themselves on the Niger seed. Overhead a blue jay squawked like a drunken sailor. Kirt sat back up and looked at Hoss. "He made all of this. Not a sparrow falls that He is not aware of. He knows every hair on our heads."

"That's easy on my head," laughed Hoss.

These "religious observations" and vocalizations had a mixed effect on Hoss. He admired Kirt's sincerity and confidence in a present loving God but it also made him a little uneasy. Sometimes he felt Kirt was a bit of a "Bible Thumper," even though Kirt had never tried to push it on him. Kirt's trust and confidence also kind of annoyed him. *How can he be so damn cocky? I mean, who does he think he is?* Hoss thought.

"Sorry if I made you feel uncomfortable, Hoss. I get such great comfort knowing my girls are with Him right now that this life is so tiny a slice of eternity. I just don't know how to hide that sometimes."

"You seem to do that very well when you are depressed," Hoss tried to dampen him a little.

"True enough. But when I am whole and the chemicals are balanced, which is most of the time, I get a sense of calmness with strength and a kind of crisp energy. In the Mesick cabin a few days ago, you would not have recognized me. I was despairing so deeply and yet the words 'fear not for I am with you always' kept coming to mind. It was the most drastic feeling of duality I have ever had. 'Can't trust the feelings as they 'go up and down but Christ is always the same whether I feel it or not. It's nice when the feeling are there but not necessary."

Hoss looked at him and smiled back. Kirt was one of the last honest men he knew. He was who he was, no fake piety.

"How do you know what you believe in isn't a bunch of wishful thinking?"

"Tell you what, let's fish for a couple more hours and pick this conversation up at your place. For now, I will just say because I know who I am trusting and that He is who He said He was, and there is more than reasonable evidence to prove it. My faith is not blind. It is based on reasonable evidence."

"Deal. Keep the next two browns we catch and I'll pan fry 'em tonight."

"Can we slip over to your house tonight and hit the Jordan tomorrow instead of staying in Traverse?"

"How else can I pan fry if not at home?" Said Hoss.

"I want to tie some of your modified Mickey Finns. I brought my tying stuff."

"Okay, a new fly for you."

And they said in unison, "First try for the box, the second to fish with and the third one to put on your hat!"

HOME WITH HOSS

"Is that you Hoss?" Asked Shirley, Hoss' wife.

"Yep, brought our man home with me."

Shirley walked over to Kirt and embraced him, "So glad you are here, Kirt. I have been worried. Don't shut off like that again okay? You stubborn German Irish, stoic drunk."

Kirt smiled and kissed her on the cheek. He smelled the raspberry pie in the oven. He saw a large bowl of broccoli slaw drenched in garlic dressing. At the end of counter was a big stack of long thin potatoes strips ready for the deep fryer. On the table were two bottles of cherry port and some Padron cigars.

"Damn this place smells great as always, Shirley. I can see you made our favorites."

"You bet! All we have to do is put those browns in a pan and we'll be ready."

"I miss them so, Kirt," said Shirley. She started to cry. They all did.

"Do you mind if I clean up a bit? Catch a quick nap too, first?" said Kirt.

"Sure, take the Hermit Hole. I've already set up your bed."

The hermit Hole was Hoss' retreat. It had everything: wide screen TV, fly tying desk, computer desk, two walls full of books, a bed, stuffed chairs with hassocks and an air cleaner for his cigar smoke. The view from the windows looked out over the hills and Lake Charlevoix. A few pictures of fishing and golfing trips hung on the open wall spaces. An aerial view of the Foundry was framed and mounted on the inside of the door. Sitting on the bookshelves was a picture of Hoss, Shirley, Beth and the girls sitting around an open campfire on the banks of the Jordan. Kirt remembered that night, and was taken by the wonderful group capture and the light in the middle of a black night. Kirt unpacked his gear and took a long hot shower. He felt great.

A MEMORY INTRUDED

A memory intruded. It came with such clarity that it startled him. It was this meadow... Kirt heard the clear, clean, and gentle horn of Chet Baker coming from the reel-to-reel and Klipsch Horn speakers he had splurged on that previous winter. The song "My Funny Valentine" was flowing as they lay on the wool blanket under the stand of poplars. He heard the leaves flutter as only poplars do. He felt the warm, slightly tanned skin of her sun-induced freckled face. She was taut, firm, naturally, as only young women can be. Kirt pressed his mouth on hers and the kiss was at once passionate and elusive. He cupped her breast under her loose sweatshirt. They threw over another large blanket and made love until they were drained. She smelled of clean hair and fresh skin, perspiration, and sex. He knew no experience in this life could compete with this. Later they calculated that their first daughter was likely consummated right there under that blanket. He remembered that on that same day after they were exhausted, he welled up with a hollow feeling of when he would lose her. That day would come, he thought, but he could not envision it nor did he want to. She smiled with radiant warmth and satisfaction and he knew she might have experienced that same hollow ache. Intense love is so gratifying and the pain you feel with its loss is often more intense than the love itself. They lay on their backs, watching the late spring sky and listening to the gold finches as they fed on the thistle and the ever-present flow of the Jordan. He told himself that this was a series of moments that he needed to remember. So he had.

"What's up? Asked Hoss.

"Just a great memory of Beth. I can see it so clearly. It's wonderful, but it hurts like hell."

Hoss sat silently, as he could not imagine what his friend was going through."…So you two were here before?"

"Yeah. Oh Lord, were we ever. We had a great day right over there under that stand of poplars. It was about five years after our wedding and probably where Bonnie was conceived. We were listening to Chet Baker, drinking stream cold beer. You can envision the rest."

Hoss choked up as he remembered his own moments like that. He knew the romance, love and intimacy of those times. "I think I can identify with that. Toast to our beautiful ladies?" Hoss held out his bottle and they clinked them with gusto.

"I'll see you again, Beth. And you too, girls. We are blessed," Kirt said quietly.

Hoss listened to the delivery of his words. They were not enough to express his gratitude but Hoss could feel his conviction. "Yup, to the ladies," said Hoss, and they clinked again.

"Thank you, daddy," Kirt said very quietly.

"Daddy?" Queried Hoss. "Yeah. Scripture speaks of how the Holy Spirit groans for us in words we cannot express for ourselves so that our Abba, which means daddy can hear us intimately."

"That's a pretty intimate name for God."

"We have an intimate God."

"I like that. Daddy, not just Father, but Daddy. It's beautiful. Where is that in the Bible?"

Kirt told him where.

"I'll look it up. I like that."

Kirt said, "I think I am starting to get it. I mean, giving God thanks in all things."

Hoss interrupted, "Now it's getting too deep," and he shook off the uncomfortable feeling he was getting. "So Kirt what are your plans now?"

"Not sure yet. I haven't even thought about it. I suppose it's time I did."

"Why don't you pursue some of those passions of yours? Find a way to make a reasonable living."

"I might now that money is not so important.

"Think about doing any acting?"

"I may have lost my chops, and I need to lose some weight."

"Listening to you I can see your passion for teaching too maybe even preaching."

"Preaching? Heck no, that's not me. Teaching, maybe."

"You know your Bible. You're a good teacher," said Hoss.

"I would have to attend the Seminary for several years and I'm too old for that. I prefer to leave that to our professionals and I can support them as a layman. No money in it either."

"I think I would like to write fiction and do some theological teaching with the support from one of our Profs at the Sems. I guess I just can't think about it right now."

"I love this valley; I love this river," said Hoss

"Me too, it's so damn beautiful. I love these meadow sections; Beaver ponds, braided flows narrow and wide sections. I love those brookies, love to look at 'em, love to eat 'em too."

"You're gonna have to go back to Mesick and check out, you know. Why not do it and stay with us?" Said Hoss.

"Thanks, Hoss. If you don't mind, I'd like to spend a few days here then go back and check out. I have to get back home to see the folks who I have worried to death."

"Good people there, Kirt, the best."

"Yes they really are. Why don't you guys come down and help me with all the stuff in the house?"

"You haven't done that yet, Kirt?"

"No, but I can now. I want to leave some special photos out and pack the rest. Maybe sell some items they would have never missed."

"We'll come down. I'll take a week off now so I can leave it in the hands of my *guy*."

"Thanks, Hoss. We can get some dinner at McKinnon's, maybe play a round at Oakland Hills if I can still get on. You can meet Pastor C and some others," said Kirt.

"It's a plan, buddy. Now let's catch some more trout and how about handing me another beer."

BULLSHIT ORDERS

"Shit," Ivy said. "I hate these bullshit orders. It's not enough to have to chase this guy across the country, but he wants to exact his additional pound of flesh like some hard ass, ego driven idiot."

Vinny started laughing, "He is a hard ass ego driven idiot, but he's our idiot."

"Vinny, he's gonna go too far and get himself caught."

"You mean git *YOU* caught."

"No, I don't get caught because I direct the attention far away from me. They know it when they hire me."

"How so?" Asked Vinny.

Thinking he had said too much Ivy said, "I have contingencies to assure some folks know exactly who hired me and why. Stringini already knows this. Why do you think I'm still alive?"

"That's some pretty dangerous shit, Ivy, but smart. I guess that's why you're the best."

"Yeah, the best. The best has had enough..."

"You gonna quit? You can't get away with that."

"Oh yeah? And who got away with taking out Senator Cosette?"

"That was you?"

"Yes," said Ivy. "Look, my point is, I have enough dirt to protect myself and I'm getting close to bailing. You know Vinny, I loved a woman once, but I had to walk away, for her sake. I can't do that ever again. I can't live like this. I'm alone I mean fully *alone*!"

"You gotta figure I might talk about this, so why tell me?" Said Vinny.

"You remember how I got into this?"

"Yeah, I do."

"I kept working because I was good at it and I made the job clean, and as painless as I could. But they don't always make it possible to be clean and pain free. I'll get caught by some smart detective or the FBI. There's a limit to how much death a man can get away with. I don't care how good you are, you're gonna leave a clue somewhere. I've had that agent from New York now out of Chicago, Williams, he's been on me like stink on shit for years. He's obsessed. I've done everything I can to shake him. It only takes one Williams or one Vietengruber…I'm always gonna be alone. Who would want me once they know what I have done? I accept that I can never have a normal life, but at least I can get away without having to worry about being followed."

"How can you not be found?"

"Oh, I can be found, but if I die, a shit load of documents on Stringini and the Euros will be sent to the Feds, Williams first. It'll be sent to them from over twenty different locations. Stringini knows that. It's a mutually destructive situation. Neither one of us wants to pull any triggers."

"You talkin' about papers, pictures, recordings, like that?"

"Yes."

"Nice knowin ya', Ivy," Vinny said with a smirk, not half joking. "Again, why tell me this?"

"Who else am I going to tell? People just have to talk to people sometimes."

Ivy looked tired. He was springing a lot of leaks. Even his pants were losing their crease. He was eating like a lumberjack instead of his usual healthy self. Vinny thought he looked distracted, stuck on distracted as though he had to force himself to focus. Seeing Vietengruber gave him some fresh, strong memories of his youth and his parents. He was a little stunned. It scared Vinny because Ivy was the expert and if Vinny was left to do this alone he might screw it up. Ivy was going to bolt. He hoped he would do it after they took out the Greek.

"Ivy, you're not gonna leave before this job is done, are you?"

"No, Vinny, not that soon."

"Glad to hear that."

"I bet you are," smiled Ivy.

Ivy ordered another side of pea meal bacon and a triple espresso to go.

"They got good espresso here, eh Ivy?"

"They do."

"Better than New York."

"I think you're right."

"Must be that ancient machine Walt uses over there."

It was a big, sexy thing with all the steam, knobs and copper tubing.

"Must be," said Vinny.

"It's beautiful," Ivy said.

They left the Mesick Inn filled with pancakes, pea meal bacon, crispy American fries and espresso powerful enough to stall your heart. Maybe it was the talk, maybe it was the food, but Vinny thought Ivy was perking up a bit. As they left, Vinny spotted the valve stem vigilante across the road, pulling the stems from an old micro bus Volkswagen.

"There he is again," said Vinny.

"I have to admit, he's an inventive S.O.B."

"Be careful, Vinny, you're becoming a jack pine savage," said Ivy.

Vinny laughed hard and his jowls shook as he did. Ivy smiled.

THE CHARMED LIFE OF YOUNG IVY

Karl Schroeder, aka Ivy, woke up early to peddle his bike over to Seger's Grocery five miles away. It was a typical Michigan late summer day: hot, humid, little movement of air. You could hear everything with clarity: the birds, the deep growl of the bullfrogs, and the crunch of the tires against the gravel. A half a mile away, Ivy could hear the sad sounds of Fred Culver. Fred worked at a bakery on the third shift. As long as Ivy could remember, he heard Fred almost every morning, all seasons. Fred would open the side door to his home onto a wide set of cement steps with a small landing. The screen door would slam with authority and he could hear it particularly well today. Then Fred would begin several minutes of violent coughing, hacking, and wrenching. The joke was that one day Fred was gonna cough up a big chunk of lung with some diaphragm attached. Once this lung purging was complete, Fred would fire up a filter less Camel and pull in the smoke like it was a life giving elixir. On winter or fall mornings, you could often see the glow of the tip of his cigarette. Next, Fred would use a bottle opener to pop the cap off a quart of beer, Pabst Blue Ribbon. Then he would pour the beer down his gullet at an amazing rate; seemingly, while still breathing. Then, he could sit down, finish the cigarette and beer and enter his detached garage. In the garage was his latest vehicular project. He was an excellent mechanic and was always working on several projects at once. Outfitting and rebuilding race cars were his specialty, and many drivers brought their cars to him. He also worked on the constantly demanding snow mobile that never seemed to work for very long. He worked on lawn mowers, tractors, and anything on wheels, or that had a motor or engine. He picked up extra income doing this. All day long he continued to sip on a glass of Seven Crown or Black Velvet until he became so tired he just went to bed; often without a shower. Fred's wife, Betty, pretty much raised their three girls by herself. She was a Registered Nurse and worked about 36 hours at Flint Osteopathic Hospital. Their daughters were seventeen, sixteen and thirteen. Everyone in the neighborhood loved them. Carla was seventeen, and in her final year of high school. Caren was sixteen, and was an all-state sprinter for Clio High School. Cindy was thirteen, cute and a stereotypical baby of the family.

During this particular summer, Karl Schroeder, aka Ivy, was fourteen and intensely interested in all things sexual; not unlike fourteen year olds everywhere. He was not at all successful in his timid attempts to explore a girl's body. He felt desperate to at least see actual breasts. He had no idea how to make this happen but this summer he tried another approach, the direct approach. Although the street he lived on was in town, it stretched out into the fields and forest on the west edge of town. It was in fact a very rural setting living on the fringes of the town limits. Often, in the warm summer nights, the neighborhood kids would get together to play hide and seek. Played at night, the game took on new dimensions. Everyone played if his or her parents would allow. The kids ranged in age from twelve to sixteen. The real object of the game was to scare the shit out of the seeker even if it meant you were caught. They would hide under parked cars, up in a tree, in a ditch, behind a large Oak or Elm and ambush the seeker. Karl had climbed into the big oak at the end of his driveway and when Caren came by, he dropped down in front of her so she let out a scream the whole neighborhood could hear. Occasionally, a couple would pair up and slip off into the woods or in some secluded outbuilding to neck. It was during one of these evening games that Karl tried his direct approach. Connie and Caren were the most physically developed girls in the neighborhood. Karl guessed that Connie would have nothing to do with him because of his age. When you are a fourteen-year-old boy, a seventeen-year-old girl might as well be thirty. She just wouldn't lower herself. At fourteen, Karl was already six-foot-tall and had a muscular frame from athletics and outdoor work. He was also very bright and fairly mature for his age. Ivy also had a confidence about him instilled by his parents and family. He had a great sense of humor and he was, in fact, quite funny and had a flare for using humor in the right settings. He could tell that Caren found him appealing but his age was a barrier. Karl's real talent was in golf. He power walked 18-36 holes almost every day in the spring, summer, and fall usually before and after work or school.

Now as the seeker counted down, Ivy said to Caren, "Come with me." His tone was so authoritative that she actually followed him. Just behind her home stood Fred's garage. One of the rules of the game was that all buildings were off limits; you couldn't hide around or in any building. Ivy opened the side door and pulled Caren in behind him.

"Karl, this is against the rules," said Caren.

"I know, I know. Look, I wanted to ask you something."

The slightly sweaty dew from running around in the dark clung to both of them. Karl had no idea what perfume she had on, but it blended with the sweat or the heat of her body and drew him in closer. She was both musky and clean smelling. Her skin was smooth and taut.

"Caren, can I kiss you?" Asked Karl.

Caren was truly a good young woman and was put off balance by the question. "Karl, stop it now."

"No, Caren. I'm not joking. May I kiss you?"

"Have you ever kissed a boy before?"

"Yes, once."

"Did you like it?"

"I guess it was okay, he was not very good at it yet.

"How's a guy supposed to get good if he has no one to practice with?" Karl said. "Why don't you teach me?"

"It just doesn't seem right Karl, you're fourteen and I'm sixteen."

"So what? I see married people several years apart yet it works. Not that I am talking about marriage."

"Of course not," said Caren.

"I thought that since you are such a good friend and you are so pretty you wouldn't mind so much, unless you think I'm ugly?"

"No, Karl, you're all right."

At that point Karl pulled her close and he kissed her with an open mouth a little too hard.

"You little shit," said Caren.

"Was that good?" He said with an earnestness that melted her heart.

"Not bad. You need to not press so hard though, and don't force your tongue into my mouth so hard."

"Can I try again?"

"Yes, be firm but gentle."

Karl leaned over and put his hands on either side of her face. He looked at her beautiful brown eyes and said, "You are easy to kiss Caren. You're so pretty." Then he kissed the way she wanted him to kiss and they held for a few seconds. "Was that alright?"

Caren gently pulled him close and began kissing him again. He could taste the hot dogs, mustard and onions they had all eaten earlier. He loved it. She moaned very slightly and then gently pulled away. "You're a fast study Karl. That was wonderful. But you can't tell *anyone* that we did this, okay? I mean it!"

"Okay," he said softly, and put his arm around her shoulder. They sat down on a bench seat of a car Fred had worked on that day. "Thank you, Caren. I will never forget this." She blushed with both embarrassment and a sense of guilt because she was getting as much out of it as he was.

"Karl, please don't tell anyone."

"I won't, I don't want to hurt you. Nobody would understand anyway."

She smiled and leaned into him, "Karl, I really enjoyed your kisses. You are so caring and romantic."

"Caren, can I touch your breast?"

"Come on, Karl. Don't push it."

"I just thought that we could learn more. I don't mean intercourse, but maybe touch each other." Caren wanted to, but felt it was wrong. She then told herself she could control the exploration.

"Ok, Karl. Do you know how to remove a bra?"

"What do you think?"

"Ok, raise my shirt. In the back are a couple of small hooks. Just undo the hooks." Karl did what he was told and Caren snaked out of her bra.

"What size are you, Caren?"

"I'm a 34 B, not very big, not small."

Ivy put his hand on her breast. It was firm but smooth and gave easily when squeezed. Her nipples were erect and shaped like the tip of his middle finger. She moaned slightly from his touch. He kissed her while holding her breast. She fumbled for his zipper and Karl pulled back.

"What are you doing?"

"I've never seen one before. I thought you wouldn't mind," she said it with such earnest innocence that he said, "Let me. I'll get it out." Caren looked at his erection with amazement, almost clinical in her interest.

"It's so strong looking." She touched it carefully with her right hand. "It's so soft. I didn't expect it to be so soft on the outside." She continued to touch him until he released right in her hand and all over her arm.

"Karl! What…"

"I'm sorry!" He said in a begging manner. "I couldn't help it!"

"I thought you were supposed to last longer than that."

"You are, but I haven't had any practice." He grabbed a new shop rag from the tool table and wiped her off.

She watched as he embarrassingly cleaned her. "There's nothing to be embarrassed about Karl. I'm sure with your will power you will be able to control it longer." She reached down and held the flaccid penis with wonder given its new state. Then the flaccid member began to grow in her hand again. She just couldn't get over the process. "It's amazing how it grows and shrinks."

"No more so than your nipples!"

"And you have a wonderful touch, Karl."

"You have beautiful breasts, too. More beautiful than any picture I've seen."

"Thank you, Karl." All the while his penis became erect again and was now throbbing in her hand. Karl tried to reach into her pants.

"No, Karl, no."

"Well, I let you touch mine."

"Well, this is different."

"Why?"

"It just is."

"It's not. But if you say no, no it is."

"Thank you, Karl."

They held each other for a while and said nothing. They kissed and Ivy kissed her breasts. Caren seemed to like his kisses on her breasts.

"Okay, you can hold me down there, but don't try to put your finger in." Karl just kissed her and reached down to unbutton her shorts. The shorts were made of pure cotton and opened easily. Karl put his hand beneath her panties and felt the heat radiating from her. He explored her labia with his fingers.

"Stop, that's enough," said Caren.

"Why?"

"I'm afraid I'll do the same thing you did."

"Women don't ejaculate."

"But it feels like, like I'm losing control."

"That's how it's supposed to feel." He continued to rub her until she had an intense orgasm, kissing him hard and squeezing his penis. He let go as well and both shivered across their bodies.

"Oh, Karl! That was so strange and so, I don't know how to describe it…"

"Me either."

She kissed him over and over again and then she leaned over and kissed his slightly limp penis. "You can't tell anyone, remember?"

"No one," he said, and began rubbing her clitoris with vigor. This time she laid back and received it, losing herself in the orgasm, once again grasping his penis as he kissed her breasts. Then she lay in his arms until they began to hurt. "I'm gonna have to ask you to shift your weight," he said in a whisper.

"We better get dressed and get out of here," she said.

"Remember, please Karl, you can't tell anyone and you can never do this again."

"Why not?" said Karl.

"Because I'm afraid we'll go all the way and I am saving that for my husband."

"Oh, right. Okay, but we don't have to go that far, we can just...."

"It's not you I'm afraid of, Karl, it's me. It's just better if we just see this as a favor between good friends."

"You're more than a friend," Karl said.

"So are you, Karl, and this will always be special to me, but we can't go on."

They did not go on, but the lessons he learned stayed with him and tempered all of his relationships with women. He could not have sex without first truly liking the woman even if that meant waiting a long time until he knew them.

~

"Come on Schroeder, that's bullshit," said the kid from Eastern University.

"Hey man, can't be helped, it cost what it costs. Have I ever sold you bad product? Isn't it always the best?" Ivy sold the blonde Lebanese hash to a kid from Eastern University, down the road from University of Michigan. "Use a sharp knife to cut it. It's oozin' resin, man,"

The student took the whole brick and intended to divide and sell it at Eastern. "That's why they call this 'Jew U'," said the student as he peeled off the agreed upon amount. Ivy was the farthest thing from being Jewish.

It had been a very profitable weekend and Ivy took off to meet Jane Merchant down at Bimbo's on the Hill to grab some pizza before going to Hill Auditorium to see Jethro Tull. Jane was a tall, leggy blonde and always braless. Her breasts usually firmly jiggling inside a halter-top tied at the neck and the small of her back. If you were lucky, you could glimpse one of her breasts as she leaned over to pick something up. The gap in the side of the halter would occasionally reward the person a fine view. Ivy was sure she knew and enjoyed the attention. She was one of those girls who liked to toy with men using her sexuality as bait and power. Guys made fools of themselves over her, but not Ivy. In fact, Ivy found her kind of a bitch, a user. She was a woman of low self-esteem and she just wanted attention. So when he told her he was twenty and a junior at University of Michigan, she bought it easily. He recruited her to sell pot for him and she was good at it. Ivy visited University of

Michigan from Clio about twice a week his senior year. He continued to pass as older than he was. He was smart enough to know that the real money was in Ann Arbor. The Flint schools were okay, but nothing compared to the money he could make at the University. All told, he had ten people selling in Ann Arbor and four in Flint. His supplier was from Texas and he met with him every month to get his supply. They met in Flint. Ivy met Carlos Menara while visiting the Long Horn campus last year. Carlos was urbane, handsome and extremely well spoken in Mexican, English and French. He was forty years old, a graduate from Texas A&M and had never worked an honest day in his life.

At seventeen, Ivy was about to leave high school with a 3.9 GPA, a full scholarship to Harvard through the golf team, Biblical Archaeology sponsored digs and one of the biggest dealers of marijuana and hash in Michigan. Using the car he earned from his summer and part time work, he was able to pull off his dealer work secretly and quietly. He figured he could sell a little at Harvard just to give him extra spending money. He was different than the usual hippie dealer. He had control of his business and did not use the products. He even had short hair. He was getting ready to live his dream and intended to slowly put this kid shit behind him.

IVY'S HOPEFUL NIGHTMARE

He sat up almost involuntarily—the vision still vivid; the dream so tangible, so visceral. The vision that wakened Ivy left him weak, panting. He could feel and hear the pounding of the carotids in his neck. In an effort to manage the emotion, to pull him back to an awakened state, Ivy stumbled to the front door and walked out into the crisp spring air. Vinny in the adjoining room could not ignore the disruption, so he too got out of bed. He reached under his pillow and pulled out his .38 revolver. When he saw the door swinging in the wind and Ivy standing there in his briefs, all of his "gangster red flags" went up.

Maybe someone had trailed them, maybe the FBI? Vinny thought. *Had to be some kind of law, why else would Ivy have his hands clasped behind his head? If it were a wise guy they both would be dead by now, probably under bloody sheets...* His mind ticked with possibilities.

In an effort to maintain some kind of tactical advantage, Vinny moved quietly outside through the side door of the cabin. His efforts were in vain, however, as it was impossible to be cryptic what with the aged pine flooring that comprised the porch that linked the side door to the front. Realizing that it was too late to view the situation, secretly he gripped his revolver tightly, and for a short robust, built man he deftly jumped and rolled all the while keeping his eyes focused on the corner that would soon reveal the front porch. With the same skill with which he jumped and rolled, he just as abruptly stopped and stood straight up with both hands on the gun pointing directly at Ivy. The dream had plunged Ivy into a memory he would have rather forgotten and now *this* added surprise nearly caused his heart to stop. Looking straight at Vinny with as much of a calm exterior as he could muster Ivy said, "What in the FUCK are you doing?" The use of the "F" word startled Vinny, for he had never heard a foul word from Ivy in all the time he had known him. "I'm sorry, Ivy! I thought you were bein' arrested."

"Arrested? What the hell gave you that idea?"

"Well da door swings open, you're standing on da porch in your whitie tighties and your hands behind your friggin' neck! What would you think?"

"I'm sorry, Vinny," said Ivy as he exhaled and tried to pull his breath back in with an over tight diaphragm. Vinny saw the emotions unraveling in Ivy's face.

"What's da matter with you, Ivy? You Okay?" Asked Vinny.

"Yes, I just needed some fresh air. I should have been more respectful of you sleeping."

It was clear to Vinny that he was not going to get a straight answer from him so he simply said, "Got enough fresh air now, Ivy?"

"Ya, I believe I do. Let's go back to bed."

Now the weird behavior was emblazoned on Vinny's brain, and he knew that both of them knew he was concerned. From here on out, it would be extremely important for Vinny to be even more observant should his partner crack again, maybe at some more important moment.

Quietly both went back to bed without saying another thing about it. They each lay there for a couple hours not able to go back to sleep, at least not deeply. For Ivy the vision replayed repeatedly in his head. He was trying to figure out what was so freighting, why his reaction? Finally, it seemed to make more sense to him. He started to do something he had not done in years, not since his first hit or maybe when he left her, he cried. He cried like a small child mourning the loss of a parent, like a husband learning of his wife's unfaithfulness, he sobbed. He tried to do it into his pillow so Vinny would not hear. For the most part he was successful, but Vinny did hear some of the sobbing and decided that in the morning he would have to call New York to report the behavior. What was this vision that terrified Ivy?

Ivy dreamed of a young man fly-fishing on the Jordan River. The dreamed unfolded with what could only be described as an aerial shot in an epic movie. The camera starts flying from the center of Lake Michigan slowly headed east toward the Great Sleeping Bear dunes. The image moves closer to the ground now, maybe less than 500 feet above the ground following the contours of the landscape. In the sweeping Northeast view ahead could be seen the hills and valleys of Leelanau, Grand Traverse and Antrim Counties. The dream scanned across Glen Lake, across the hills and farms of Omena Bay and the west and east arms of Grand Traverse Bay. His dream scanned Torch Lake and slowly began to zoom in on the Jordan River Valley. Below stood a solitary figure…

When Ivy was fifteen, he became hooked on the writings of Ernest Hemingway. He read all his novels, interviews, articles and short stories. One day while in a small library in Clio he came across a small book containing the diaries, journals and otherwise private writings of Hemingway. Journals and diaries the writer had kept since he was a kid. The most fascinating story was that of a trip Hemingway and a friend had taken when both were fifteen years old. They left Chicago land by train all the way to Kalkaska, MI and hiked and fished their way across the great Northwest of Michigan including fly-fishing the Jordan. Ivy was able to talk his dad into letting him replicate the trip, well part of it. While staying in Petoskey, his father allowed him to bike to several of the locations on Hemingway's trail. He fished the brushy overgrowth of Horton's Creek, Horton's Bay, Walloon Lake and the Jordan River. It was while he was on the Jordan that Ivy clarified his vision for his future.

He saw himself going to an Ivy League school, majoring in archeology and spending the rest of his life on digs located in dozens of locations all over the world. It seemed a very doable plan, and Ivy felt confident in his ability to pull it off. This dream truly terrified Ivy because he had lost all control of that future. He had no future. He had nowhere to go that would ever allow him that future. He could escape his life but only through a combination of plastic surgery and elaborate country hopping and even then, he would always be on alert to someone, anyone, catching up to him. All hope was gone, and the reality of it burst out of a sequestered area of his mind. The hope and joy of the Jordan experience, all those years ago, gave stark contrast to his hellish future of today. His whole mind and body was enveloped in a casing called, "no hope". It terrified him in a manner he had never experienced. It was a holistic terror. He had a sudden urge to take flight, since there was nothing tangible to fight. He was irrevocably all alone. It was all he could do not to scream and run madly into the woods.

CAN'T BE HIM

"Can't be him," said Sheriff Roy.

"I don't hardly think so," said Cy.

"This poor guy lost his wife and daughters in an auto accident down at Twelve mile and Telegraph almost two years ago. I've talked to his Pastor and his doctor so no way he's the guy."

"Anybody else, Cy?"

"There's a man here from New York," Cy looking through his register. "He's here for a week. Yeah, right here, he's driving a '94 Bonneville. Plate number is BD7107."

"Is he here now?"

"I don't know. He's not from the city; he's from Clarence Center near Buffalo."

"From New York? Do you get a lot of New Yorkers here?"

"Oh yes. The whole of Northwest Michigan has a strong history going back to the first railroads. The railroads made some kind of land deal with the Methodists and Episcopalians. There is large settlement of Methodists up near Petoskey and one of Episcopals in Harbor Springs. They came for the pollen free air, the water and the fishing. Hemingway fished up around Petoskey and Walloon Lake, 'course he wasn't from New York but, anyway, yeah we get quite a few New Yorkers."

"Just the same, I am gonna run the plate and see where it came from. Thanks for the history lesson," Sheriff smiled. "And be careful, the guys looking to take him out are at the top of their 'craft.' They'll quietly kill anyone who gets in their way. You won't even know they were here."

"Thanks, Sheriff. I see anything I'll call you." CY felt a fear he had not experienced before. He knew this was real and wondered how in the hell he came to be in the mix.

AGENT WILLIAMS FROM DENVER TO MESICK

Agent Joe Williams jumped on the highway that would merge into Interstate 80, northeast of Denver, CO; the news of Ivy's identification pushing him all the way. The flights out of Denver were not available and he was too restless to wait. He had three days to get there, as his quarry would be there for another week, according to Ivy's accommodations at the Mesick Inn. If all went well, he could be done by Friday or Saturday. The rental he drove was a one way and he could just fly home. He wanted to take a week off and was sure it would be easy once he put Ivy under arrest. He had been asked to assist Officer Guy Veitengruber up in Michigan and his history with Ivy made him the right man for the job. Many complained about the drive across Nebraska but he liked the Old West feeling and the miles of open prairie. He imagined the massive herds of American Bison thundering across the Ogallala or the cattle that had been driven through here before the fences went up. He liked Omaha and its Middle American stockyards and great rib eye steaks with corn, green beans and salad at the truck stop outside of Lincoln. *Interstate 80, "the bowling alley" across Nebraska,*

Williams thought. He would be driving by his home in Chicago but decided not to stop. He would plow forward around the horn of Lake Michigan while the traffic was somewhat light. *Damn Chicago, hell to get into and hell to get out of; 'hell of a great town though,* he said to himself. He referred to it as a town because even though it was a huge city, it felt smaller, more intimate, and definitely friendlier than most large cities. He remembered the night he found himself at a local roadhouse in the far northwest suburbs. He sat and talked and played cards with a group of strangers as if they were lifelong friends. He had encountered the same attitudes smack in the middle of Chicago. *You almost never encounter people like that in New York*, he thought. But it troubled him that the taxes were ballooning and the socialist mindset of the northeast was taking hold.

Williams was six foot four, knotty muscles, and jet-black hair on his head, with little hair elsewhere. He was that rare combination of a black haired guy who was not going bald and hairless everywhere else. If he did not shave for a couple days his beard looked merely ruggedly handsome, not disheveled. He was a person who had developed analytical skills although his central personality was that of an expressive. The technicians from the New York State Police Crime Lab got along with him very well as he demonstrated his respect for them by learning from them. He took the time to learn from them. Others in the field simply got the results and politely said thanks. He would hang around and ask questions and often would ask for specific techs by name because of their expertise or speed. At forty-one, he had never married. *The work,* he told himself, *would not be conducive to family life.* Lately, a widow with two teenagers was giving him serious second thoughts. He took her thirteen-year-old son golfing outside Vale, and found himself falling for the kid. The boy was strong, smart and full of energy. He was also a polite kid and the hardened agent found himself wanting to be a dad. The widow's daughter of sixteen was as beautiful as her mother, naturally muted shades of blonde hair that shown like dew in the daytime sun. She had green eyes and a kind of smile that generates warmth and comfort. It had been a year now that he knew the widow, Shelly, well. He had seen her in good and bad situations. She was measured under pressure, was terrific, balanced mother and a person he liked and admired long before he loved her. Her son, Bob, and daughter, Pam, were far from interfering appendages to his relationship with their mother; they only added to the whole package. They were part of her and only made him love her more. He was not a rich man but he was very financially secure. Shelly was moderately well off, but worked hard as her role of prosecuting attorney and mother. Shelly was a devout Christian. Williams was too. They had not yet had intercourse but it was getting damn hard not to. He decided he would do it. He would ask her to marry him when he got back. He picked up his cell outside of Davenport and called.

"Shelly, what's up?"

"When will you be back, my secret agent man?" asked Shelly.

"In a few days. We either catch the bastard or he will get away. If we catch him, I will be right back. If we don't…Then I don't know."

"Listen, Shelly, I just wanted to call to say that this last year with you and the children has been so great."

"It has for me too. Do I hear a but coming?"

"No, no *buts* of any kind. I would like you and I to celebrate at Morton's when I get back."

"That sounds great, hon."

He loved it when she called him hon in that minor Western accent of hers.

"I also wanted to say that I will be in the birthplace of trout unlimited. I am going to stop in at the Fly Factory and buy Bob some stuff. Then on my way back I will stop and see if Tim will sign a DVD for Pam."

She felt warm all over, "They will love that. You know you don't have to do these things for them.

"I love them, and I would do it for them, even if I only knew them and not you."

Shelly began to cry, "…I don't want you to buy me anything. I just want you home in my arms as soon as possible."

He would not buy her anything except for a combination diamond and emerald engagement ring. He was confident she would accept. He would be right.

He decided to spend the night in Grand Haven, MI and head out early in the morning for Mesick. He picked up his cell and called Sherriff Wheeler.

"Sheriff Wheeler, sorry to call so late."

"No problem. Hey, the other guys from the Lansing office are already here. Do you really think you'll get a twofer out of this?"

"Yeah, I do. This Ivy has killed over thirty people that I am fairly confident about. The pieces of identification I have picked up since New York fifteen years ago is substantial. Did you get the artist sketch I sent you?"

"Yes, we got it. I intend to start showing it around in the morning," said Wheeler.

"Sheriff, thanks for all the help. I have been after this son of a bitch for a long time."

"No problem, Joe. I look forward to meeting you."

Williams checked into the Holiday Inn on Spring Lake. Spring Lake ran into Lake Michigan not far across the highway. Williams stopped to look at the lights around the water. There was no place he would rather be than Michigan, unless of course, it was with Shelly and the kids. He decided to drive to the party store and buy a bag of popcorn and two bottle of Moosehead. Back in his room, he turned on the TV. He then turned it off. He took out a copy of his file on Ivy. He took out a book he was reading on the private lives of ancient Pompeian's. He opened both beers and tore open the microwave popcorn that was already in the room, tossing the store bought stuff. He settled in with his book. He threw off the blanket and bed covering. He chugged down half a beer; it tasted clean and slightly bitter. He belched loudly like a teenager. *How could it ever be better than this?* He thought.

AGENT WILLIAMS REVIEWS HIS FILES

"Yeah, I spent the night in Spring Lake and drove the rest of this morning. So Sheriff Wheeler, we think he is there? Let's set up a sweep of the area, but keep it low key."

"Not sure I have the manpower you might want, but the locals and county will do all we can," said Sherriff Wheeler.

"Sheriff, we know your background and I am glad you're there. Captain Johns of Traverse City rounded up all the State troopers he could free up. Can't tell you how long I've wanted this son of a bitch. I knew his work in the northeast. It killed me to have to go to Chicago without catching him. I thought I lost the chance, but when the Director in Detroit asked me to be assigned to this I was on cloud nine. This Ivy bastard is a damn ghost. He gets in, out, and long gone before the body is found."

"I thought he worked in the northeast? What is he doing out here, especially in sparsely populated north of Michigan?" Asked Sherriff Wheeler.

"Well, the Intel is one of the targets who decided to leave New York City before he could be had. Seems he ripped off one of the Dons in New York. By the way, as far as I'm concerned, the bastards can kill each other off, but some of the hits Ivy pulled were on some poor sons a' bitches in the wrong place at the wrong time. On Long Island, a dockworker stumbled across a trafficking ring. He found some opium under a false stern. He called the State Police and customs, and for over a year this dockworker monitored who came in and out of port and found three ships using the same false holds. The guy was married for twenty-five years. I went to his anniversary. He had one boy in high school and his daughter was at Columbia with a science scholarship; really great people. Great family man…" Williams trailed off for a moment. He regained his composure. "He agreed to testify but someone on the docks found out and Ivy was sent in. He cut off the guy's balls and stuffed them in his mouth and duct taped them in, and shot him twice in the back of the head. It was a real SS kind of tactic. I couldn't sleep for months. I see the family from time to time; I owe them—we owe them. That guy was a bon a fide hero. We haven't had anyone from the docks cooperate with us since then. Too terrified."

"How do you know it was Ivy?"

"A snitch I worked with inside Stringini's group had Ivy shoot the snitch's brother in law."

"Where's the snitch now?"

"Gone. Ivy probably dumped him in a vat of acid at some tannery." Agent Williams pulled out his file on Ivy. He started with the photos of his victims, killed in a variety of ways.

"Do you know he did all of these?" Asked Sheriff Wheeler.

"I know he did, but I could never prove it."

"My God, this guy is a block of ice. Look at the way he used the necklace on this guy."

"How did you know it was a necklace?" Asked Williams.

"Well, he's burnt as hell and I believe those are steel belts around his upper body, or whatever's left of it."

"You're right, he was 'necklaced.' He was the owner of an auto parts distributorship who had borrowed money from Stringini to keep his company alive. Obviously, he didn't meet the terms of his loan."

"I want the bastard dead or alive."

"What does he look like?"

"The only picture I have of him is old, but he still looks remarkable young, fit. Here, it was when he was at Harvard. See? He's sitting next to another kid who got involved with syndicate drug trafficking," said Williams, holding up a photo.

"This went on at Harvard?" Asked Sherriff Wheeler.

"Yep. I guess he just wanted to keep up with the lifestyle of his rich friends or something, I could never figure it out."

"The story is, Ivy lost or stole a large stash of coke valued at over 500 Gs and his friends told him they would let him off if he took out the other kid in the picture. He did it. I don't know why…Fear? Self-preservation? Anyway, he killed the kid. Somehow from there he slipped into the life and became the ghost that he now is. I saw a picture of him only as recent as five years ago. I'm sorry I don't have it with me. He looks so much like he did when he was young it was hard to believe. Getting an image of the son of a bitch is almost impossible and the informants I get info from are scared to death to be caught taking his picture…'Seems Ivy got wind of the fact that one of Stringini's guys was tailing him, taking pictures, bugging one of his hotel rooms. Ivy found the guy, got all the images and shot the guy's balls off. He sent the guy back to Stringini to warn him not to tail him ever again. Oh yeah, he took the film, melted it down into a black mess, and shoved it up the shadow's ass. I'm not kidding."

"How did the guy ever get back to Stringini like this with the message?"

"Ivy loaded him into a small car, drove him to the emergency, pulled up next to the door, wearing a ski mask, and walked away. The hospital fixed him up and said he would have died if the remaining stub between his legs hadn't been prevented from bleeding further. It sure as hell worked because getting a current picture of him is impossible. My informants tell me he is very quiet, very well-mannered and gentlemanly; 'moves around a lot."

"What do his parents make of all this?"

"They were told of his drug activity and that he was missing. They still assume he must be dead or he would have turned up by now. Poor people. Nice folks too. God, I can't imagine what they have had to live with, and I can tell ya' if we locate the son of a bitch I hope we have to kill him and make sure they never find out. They don't need to know what a fucking monster he turned into," Williams continued. "He's an excellent physical mimic and changes aliases all the time; never the same one twice, not that I can find. His so-called disguises are simple: wigs, mustaches, and clothing. I worked with an informant who went on a couple hits with him and the guy tells me that he never saw him without some kind of disguise, but from what Guy Vietengruber says, he may not be wearing one right now. If Guy could recognize him, then we're as close as we have ever been. Oh yeah, a curious quirk here I discovered a few years ago. Ivy gets a lot of his companionship from very high priced call girls or from women he may meet when well outside of the northeast. A couple grand a night for these women, real lookers, like they came out of Vogue or something. I've interviewed nine of them and every one of them liked him. They found him caring, attentive to them, generous and a great conversationalist. There was one woman in particular I found out about, through a call girl working in Connecticut, who told me that her friend Alex was Ivy's exclusive girl for over two years."

"Exclusive?"

"Yeah, he kept her in a home in Simsbury, a big friggin' place. His deal was that she was not to be with anyone else as long as he paid the agreed upon income. Listen to this, he gave her a hundred thousand bucks cash every year, and paid for a full health and life insurance policy, the deed to the house and all expenses. He also paid her tuition to an acting school. She was good too; she eventually had small roles in Three Men and a Baby and Bull Durham, at least that's the two I remember. I interviewed her in her home in Manhattan. She is married now and has a little girl; her husband is in benefits and has carved out a niche in the entertainment industry. He writes specific policies for film work, plays and the people involved in them; a very nice man. Anyway, when I met her I asked her about Ivy and she was incredibly embarrassed that I knew. She told me she had already told her husband and he accepted her for what she is, not what she was. I know she wasn't bull shittin' me because half way through the interview he joined us and sat with his arm around her. She said Ivy was incredibly polite, sweet, and worked as an oilman out of west Texas and Kuwait. She said he told her he was not married, never had been and was just looking for some reliable companionship without all the strings attached. 'I knew he was lying, but at that time I didn't care. He was a fantastic meal ticket and was a very sweet person.' She said he was always taking her to places she wanted to see: Paris, London, Big Sur; he even took her to an archeological dig in Syria. Unlike the unpredictable creeps she would often meet, she thought Ivy was a real gentleman. 'He was the only man I ever received pleasure from, if you understand me,' she said. What really tipped me off, that this had to be Ivy, was that he took her to Tapawingo, MI all the time. He loved to go golfing in Northern Michigan. He'd just get on a plane and go at any time without notice. Well, he did give notice. She said he would call and ask if it were a good time to go there and if she had a conflict, he didn't press. Unbelievable, I know."

"The guy sounds like the perfect husband."

"Yeah, well, in a lot of ways he was."

"So how did she disconnect from him? Did things go wrong?"

"Nope. She got up one morning and on the kitchen island was an envelope with $700,000 in it, the deed to the house, and a ten-year paid off health insurance policy. She said, 'He left a short note saying I'm not the man I say I am and not good enough for you. Get the hell out of your business. Please accept this and continue to pursue your acting career.' She said he was gone. Just like that," Williams explained. "She asked me why I was asking about him and I told her what he was. She got up and threw up in the toilet. Her husband looked at me and said, 'I'm not surprised. Who the hell sets up a call girl like that? I'm not naïve. I know she was hoping he would marry her, and I do think the guy loved her too. Lucky for me they didn't.' She returned and said, 'you mean I was living with an assassin all that time? My God! What an ass I was…what a complete jerk.' I said to her, 'Look, don't beat yourself up. If there is any consolation Ivy treated you like no one else I have interviewed. His behavior toward you was a real anomaly. It sounds to me like the man loved you but knew you would not stay if you knew what he really was, correct?' She sat there for a while, '…Right.… I set up a group out of our church here for women who have fallen into the life. When I sold the house I used the money to establish the group. It's the only decent thing I did during those years. Believe me, Agent Williams, it's never worth the money to sell your soul and that's what prostitution is, not just selling your body, it's the loss of real honest human contact. You lose the ability to connect love and sex. Although, I must say, in his own way, Ivy was very good to me. I was very lucky.' I'm tellin' ya' Sheriff, I saw a horror in her eyes when I told her, 'You're lucky he didn't just kill you in your bed.' Believe me, she knows she is blessed to be alive. The guy has some semblance of humanity in 'em, but his victims would never know that. Ya' know Sheriff, sometimes I really get stuck on the evil issue; I mean here was a nice kid, smart kid, talented as hell. He gets the opportunity to go to Harvard and throws the whole damn thing away. Now that's odd enough, but to keep on killing, what is that, if not evil? That's about as conscious of a decision I've ever seen."

"I always believed anybody could go there. It's not that difficult to do. I believe if you can turn the faucet on, it gets easier and easier to just open up the valve all the way. I truly believe humans have the capacity to allow evil to run their lives, and by the time they do, they don't even think about it much anymore; it becomes a habit," said Sherriff Wheeler.

"I think your right, Sheriff. There has to be some kind of struggle going on inside him though. Man, was this woman beautiful. She remembered a time when she got up at night and he was on the couch quietly crying. She came up behind him and he turned and in one quick movement had her head in position to snap her neck. As soon as he realized it was she, he began to apologize profusely and kept crying all the while. She said he explained it by saying that he had learned the move as self-defense when in Kuwait as some of his fellow traders had been killed in their sleep. He said a man he had known for a long time had just died and it was finally getting to him. At the time she believed him. She said she mothered him to bed and when he had fallen asleep she came down to straighten out the couch; the pillow soaking wet."

"Holy shit. Sounds like the guy is conflicted but not enough to turn himself in. He feels trapped. Yeah, a real Judas," Sheriff Wheeler gave a mock shiver. "Damn, what a damn tragedy all the way around. Well, Agent Williams, I guess now is as good a time as any to put this thing to rest."

"Let me try to get a hold of Guy Vietengruber."

AN UNKNOWN CLOSE ENCOUNTER

The place was a cesspool, born of moral decline and a taste for tax dollars. Kirt hated to even go there, but his daughters wanted to see where the big ball dropped on New Year's Eve. The TV broadcasters avoided showing the Real Times Square with all its sex trade. They sanitized it for family viewing. Kirt and Beth laughed at the marquees at the "movie" theaters. "The Sperminator", "Debbie Does Everything", "Hammer and the Twins"; they were as stupid as they were disgusting and looked like they were written by some kids in a junior high locker room. They went there during the daylight, as the sunlight helped to sanitize the place, also avoided the hypnotic effect of all the lighting at night.

"What's a *spermamator*?" Julie, Bonnie's six-year-old sister, asked her.

"I don't know," said Bonnie, who at twelve had a pretty good idea; she was a little embarrassed to have been asked.

The answer seemed to satisfy her little sister Julie who said, "Oh…"

Kirt smiled at Bonnie and winked to indicate he appreciated the way she handled the question. "I'm glad the mayor is cleaning this place up," said Kirt.

"Why do you think they let it go on this long?" asked Beth.

"Money and graft, pay offs and tax revenue. Hell, that idiot Jimmy Breslin wrote a column decrying the clean up as somehow anti-New York. He likes the 'Honest grit' of the city. Great writer but a huge dumb ass," said Kirt. "Okay, you've seen the ball, now let's go eat."

"Is Hoss gonna meet us for lunch Dad?" Asked the girls.

"Yes, and afterward him and I are gonna go see a business partner of ours."

"Great!" Said the girls. "Then we can go shopping with mom."

"That's right, and save some money for me!"

"I love Hoss, Dad. Are we going to his house again after Christmas?" Said Julie.

"Yes we are and I'm sure Hoss can't wait to see you two again at lunch."

"Where we gonna eat, Dad?"

"Carnegie Deli!"

Both girls shouted with joy. They loved the giant PB&J made on Challah bread, the big fresh pickles and egg creams.

Beth whispered into Kirt's ear, "Let's go. I'm starved, my little sperminator."

Kirt smiled back. God he loved his family.

After lunch, Hoss and Kirt took a cab over to Brooklyn to see The Hermann's. They were a fourth generation freight forwarder that moved all of Hoss' products into Europe, Britain and the Far East. Rolf and Heinz Hermann were big Teutonic bastards of giant stature. They loved their business, and Kirt had worked with them for years. Today would be a sad reunion though, as Rolf had recently been murdered. It seems the boisterous Rolf had let his gambling get away from him. Normally he was in full control, but one night at a mob-arranged poker table Rolf got into hock for over two hundred thousand dollars. Nick Stringini, who owned these games in Manhattan, saw an opportunity to leverage the situation.

Stringini came to see Rolf at the Hermann's trucking terminal in the city. "Mr. Hermann, I understand you run a damn fine freight service. I would like to use your services. You see, with the interest on your debt beginning to eat you up I thought you might like a way to work it off," said Stringini.

"What did you have in mind?" Said Rolf.

"Well, I have shipments coming in from Yemen. You know, olive oil barrels, some dried fruit boxes, stuff like that. I would need you to receive them and make sure they get to the various customers we have around the country."

Rolf knew exactly what he meant. He wanted him to ship drugs, probably heroin wrapped in green bags that sank to the bottom of the olive oil or packed into the center of a box of dried fruit. In all generations of shipping, The Herrmann's had never shipped an illicit item in their life. They knew their competition did but they had fought off the temptation and sometimes lethal force by rejecting the attempts using the police and if need be their own internal "police".

"I'm afraid I would have to pass on that, Mr. Stringini. We are all full right now in those channels."

"Well Rolf, can I call you Rolf? If you don't do this for me, you will have to pay off that debt by next Saturday. I can't let an outstanding debt be left unpaid. It is very, very bad for business. People might start to think I'm an easy touch. I tell you what. I have a load coming in tomorrow night and you will take it or I will be forced to tell your brother to come and pick up your body."

Rolf was truly terrified and flagellating himself for his stupid behavior. He knew Stringini meant it and he did not want to reveal this to his brother Heinz. "I tell you what, I will take this one shipment and we are even, okay?"

Stringini leaned into Rolf, "That's a good start, but I will let you know when were even," he got up and turned to go. "The shipment should arrive tomorrow by 3:00 pm. The forwarding addresses will be brought to you before that. See to it that those end customers get their goods. Thanks, Rolf, a pleasure doing business with you. I can see why you are so highly thought of."

The Hermann's looked hulking, and physically they were, but they were worldly men and quite elite in their way. They spoke German, French and some Russian so as to better interface with their customers. What languages they did not speak they used a translator service to do for them.

"Just being around the languages keeps you sharp," Heinz often said.

"You get to know the language and you get to know the people," said Rolf.

"Maybe that's why I don't get you. I don't speak Kraut," Hoss would say affectionately to the brothers.

"I'm pretty sure nothing could get through that Neanderthal skull of yours anyway, Hoss," Heinz said as Hoss laughed in his infectious manner. His laughter started out like a tire leak until he simply burst out in a full laugh, sometimes causing his face to redden and tears to roll.

Rolf's own cowardice revolted him. He had allowed himself to be bullied and he could no longer stomach it. Of course there would never be a day when he would be square with Stringini. The Hermann's did not get bullied into shipping illicit cargo, never. Everyone knew they were clean, which is exactly why Stringini wanted to use him, and Rolf had given Stringini an opening. Rolf had made up his mind that he would go to the authorities if need be.

Rolf told Stringini, "No more shipments."

"Stringini stopped in to talk to Rolf at Hermie's, Hermann's trucking subsidiary. Rolf told him to go to hell and two days later he was pushed off the observation deck at Hermie's. It was an irrational move on Stringini's part because now he had fully lost the use of the delivery system. He would have to piece meal it back together with a variety of shippers instead. Back to square one. Rolf shut him down and had paid the ultimate price for it. The police investigating yielded no evidence of foul play and the death was ruled accidental due to intoxication.

"Hell," Heinz said. "It was the end of the day. He was always a little juiced and he never fell off no platform before. I just don't get it."

Kirt and Hoss just hung their heads.

"I can't believe he's gone," said Kirt. He began to weep.

"Son of a bitch!" Said Heinz, and he too hung his head and wept.

"Hey, hey if Rolf were here, he'd kick our butts. No more cryin', let's go hoist a few for Rolf and talk about the great memories he gave us," said Hoss.

"Sure, sure," said Kirt. "Jules?"

"Where else?" Said Heinz. "No reason to break tradition now."

The three of them spent the next few hours at Jules and then broke off and Hoss and Kirt returned to their hotel rooms.

"Sounds to me like somebody pushed him," said Hoss.

"I think so, too. Rolf was a big son of a bitch, shaped like a pear. I can't see him falling off that platform over a railing damn near as high as his chest. What I don't get is why the police said he did."

"Probably just too much of a case load and not enough evidence to prove it, or no witnesses willing to come forward. Damn it, Kirt. He was just out to the foundry last month. We were fishing for two days. Drank a shit load of that Bock beer of his. Just like that he's gone? Son of a bitch," said Hoss.

"Yeah, son of a bitch. Just like that," said Kirt.

MAGGIE AND HER LATE HUSBAND JOHN

Maggie and John grew up under the shadows of the white pines where the soil was acidic yet loamy and the soil outside the shadows was always sandy and the lawns were usually full of weeds and clump grass. When they were first married they put a lot of effort into growing grass on their back lawn and around the edges of the front lawn. With patience and consistent applications of topsoil and lime, John was able to nurture a lawn that was the envy of the neighborhood. John and Maggie installed their own sprinkler system that drew water from the stream that passed by the back of their yard. The rest of their property, some thirty-two acres, was left untouched and their self-named Mesick Burn (a feeder stream of the Manistee) was kept barrier free so that the occasional steelhead or King Salmon might find their way up the Burn. The only sign of human traffic was the various paths beaten down by their daughters and their friends. It was a piece of property as virgin as one could find since the feverish logging years of the 1890s had stripped this area. There were a myriad of native trees and plants, birches, various pines, cedars along the Burn, trillium, violets, willows, ferns, a few Oaks, and a single massive Sycamore their twin daughters used as a jungle gym. It was far from idyllic, but it was theirs and they had earned and built a life that was solid and a family full of love and encouragement. Wildlife was also abundant and necessitated that John built an open woven nine-foot fence with an outwardly angled barbed wire extension along the top. It enclosed their full acre back yard and kept the flowers, vegetables and grass from the whitetails, porcupines, raccoons, rabbits and ground hogs. Once in a while it became evident that a rabbit or ground hog had invaded under the perimeter, which required John's .22 caliber to be put to use. Actually, the girls now took turns plinking the intruders. Raccoons would stay pretty much around the Burn. The Burn was only about four to six feet wide and then widened considerably once past their backyard. The Burn's bottom was lined with sand and the most beautiful river rock in shades of brown, red, black, green and a number of other hues. The rocks near the edge of the stream were polished as smooth as if a rock hound had tumbled them, and Maggie and the girls used them to make jewelry over the years. It was the perfect environment for brook trout: isolated, quiet, ice cold, clear as vodka with many pools plunging ten to twenty feet.

Occasionally on very hot days, the family would plunge into one of these pools and John would whisper to Maggie, "I think the twins went back to where they came from."

Maggie had become proficient at catching the tasty brookies. She used a stealth-like approach coupled with a deft dappling technique using the short 4 weight bamboo her grandfather had given her and her own hand tied flies; wet and dry. Just one hundred feet or so away from their backyard, the Burn widened to about thirty feet, averaging three feet deep with frequent pools. The water was so clear that ten feet seemed like twelve inches. The shadow of the willows and birches did make it difficult to see into some these ofpools, and it was in these that the brookies would collect in uncommon numbers. Over the years, Maggie had caught a steady take of six to ten keeper brookies a week. The family never tired of eating brookies in sage infused butter with warm tender fiddleheads with asparagus and watercress salads or wine rehydrated dried cherries. Both Maggie and John had grown up eating brookies this way and the smell of pan roasted sage and browned butter carried with it deep emotional memories of their own particular childhoods.

It was an aroma embedded in the brains of most Mesickanians. Now their girls too were gaining the nurturing imprint. The aroma was somehow primal, yet also highly sophisticated, as not only the locals ate brookies this way so did the wealthy seasonal folks living in second homes or staying at the myriad of hunting, skiing, golf and fishing resorts and lodges. They came from Chicago, downstate Bloomfield Hills and other posh environments; New Yorkers had been coming for years, and folks from Indiana. Tom Watson, the accomplished golfer, had started coming to the Charlevoix, MI area with his parents. His parents came from Kansas to play the Belvedere Country Club, which was and is a terrific golf track laid out by a Scotsman named Willie Watson in 1927. Tom was still a member and came there whenever he could. The locals thrived on this traffic and loved the variety of people who came up, including these old moneyed folks as well as the average families who stayed in local hotels and campgrounds. For a while Maggie worked at Crystal Downs Country club. The club's course was designed and built by Alister McKenzie, the former WW1 camouflage expert who designed Augusta National, Pebble Beach, Cypress Point, Royal Melbourne, University of Michigan and Ohio State Scarlet courses.

Contracting McKenzie to build your course was not easy and is indicative of the kind of influence the wealthy of the area had exerted for over a hundred years. Crystal is considered one of the few must play courses on any golf addicts' list. Situated between Crystal Lake and Lake Michigan on the highlands above the shoreline of each the property, Downs, seems to have been prepared for exactly this purpose. The ground is sandy and the trees and plants are alternately full or scruffy, depending on the prevailing winds, which can blow very hard at times. In fact, McKenzie said he did not built Crystal but "God" built Crystal. "All I did was situate the tees and greens."

While at Crystal, Maggie was still in her early twenties and if not for the objection of her father she could have gone to New York or Chicago to become a model. She attracted a lot of attention. She was not, however, your "typical" model material as she was very bright, intuitively smart, moral and committed to her faith in Christ in a very healthy way. When she asked her father to consent to her working with the famous Ford Modeling Agency he said, in his typical homegrown manner, "Michelangelo was once asked why

Mary in his pieta was so young and beautiful in appearance for a woman in her early forties. Michelangelo replied, 'Don't you realize that chaste women remain beautiful much longer?'" The indirect condemnation of the modeling world was understood by Maggie and she then endeavored to build a business case for modeling while remaining chaste. All her research yielded little evidence that such could be accomplished. She decided to give up the idea and look for something more substantial. She decided to work her way toward a PhD in Ancient History. At Crystal, she was approached by a variety of men her own age and also those in their fifties looking for an infusion of their former youth. One man in particular was charmingly assertive. He was from Winnetka, IL and came from money he inherited from his great grandfather who was one of the original founders of Standard Oil, the company that had contracted with McKenzie to build the course. Maggie was in fact quite taken by him and his attentions. Brian was thirty-one and she was twenty-three. He had graduated from the University of Michigan and had become a cancer researcher working with a team at Northwestern and Ann Arbor's University of Michigan Health System. Brian was far from a shallow brat living off the fat of the family fortune. His family had a tradition of working at something every day, anything one could love and do well and that others could benefit from. He was an avid golfer. One evening after seeing Brian come off the eighteenth hole, she watched as he conversed with an older gentleman in his seventies that he had played with that day. He was kind, deferential and she noticed how he would always be there if the old guy seemed a little off balance. The older gentleman was retired from his steel business and just in time as the US Steel industry had fallen on very hard times. When Brian and Mr. Rooney entered the clubhouse restaurant she could hear Rooney quietly say to Brian, "Your father would be proud of you, Brian, for the solid man you have become." Brian was genuinely touched and flattered as he hugged Mr. Rooney with strength and tenderness. Maggie liked Brian and he caused her to begin to rethink her love for John whom she had known since she was a child. She knew she could pursue Brian and probably fit right into his world, mostly because he made sure his life consisted of good people, wealthy or not.

Brian was taken with Maggie's chaste life and her active mind that always seemed to be reading and acquiring new information about a broad number of subjects. She had even read about his work and had a darn good lay view of the mechanics of cancer that the team was trying to influence. She was highly seductive without trying to be. Her smile revealed a deep dimple on either side of her mouth. Her lips were naturally reddened with a fullness that was not gaudy in any way. Her green eyes were flecked with a metallic copper/brown, which matched her fair yet not too delicate skin. She was covered tastefully with freckles across her face, down to her shoulders and chest, and Brian correctly imagined, all over her breasts. He could tell from time to time that her nipples were large and he envisioned them to be surrounded by small erectile bumps. He had to stop himself from thinking about this so as not to be distracted by what she was saying and saying so well. He was deeply smitten and why shouldn't he be? Maggie liked him too but on some deeper level she just could not really commit. For one thing, he was devoutly Roman Catholic. She admired his integrity but knew she could never agree with that theology. But there was something more. Brian was way ahead of her intellectually and it intimidated her. He never belittled her with it but it made her feel awkward from time to time. He was worldly; she was not, having only left Mesick for other cities in

Michigan and a couple trips to Chicago. Her trips to Chicago land informed her of the Village of Winnetka where Brian was from. It was an old money village with massive homes and designed lawns. Many of the homes were located right on Lake Michigan. The Lake was maybe the only thing they really had in common. She worried about ever being accepted in his world, even though he would never have a problem regarding that. Brian was classically handsome. He was a tall, almost toe headed blonde with somewhat ruddy Irish skin. He was solidly athletic without looking over muscled. He seemed to have a perpetual tan that made all his features stand out including his deeply brown eyes. He inherited his father's radiant grin and gregarious laugh. He seemed to be only what you saw and nothing more, and his generosity was quietly legendary around the club. He had sponsored three students in Traverse City to attend Northwestern. The three were sons of a greens keeper at Crystal who was also being underwritten by Brian for an apprentice position with Tom Doak, the famous golf architect. Brian had adopted this family because his sister was best friends with the father's wife who had been killed in the line of duty as a police officer in Traverse City. In addition to his individual philanthropic work, he also chaired the

Energy Trust Scholarship, which gave scholarships to budding geologists working on oil and natural gas exploration, including the new theory that oil is a renewable resource generated by the earth's crust. Brian's golf swing was minimized to as few moving parts as possible. He was a scratch golfer and smoked three to four cigars every round. Several times Maggie had seen him coming down eighteen in the failing light and knew it was him from his cigar torch glow he used so often to keep his stogie lit in the Lake Michigan winds. He was not a cigar snob and smoked a variety, none being from Cuba. He drank vodka or tequila and preferred cheaper grades. "They have earthier flavor," he would say. The only real high-end luxury he fully indulged in was his numerous golf club memberships around the world and the weekly lunches he had brought in for his research team from Zingerman's in Ann Arbor or Morton's in Chicago. He was also funny as hell. One night Maggie had arranged to prepare Brian a meal of brookies, asparagus and baby potatoes with cherry pie and beer. She prepared the meal in the Crystal kitchen and they ate it on the porch in the early evening. "Terrific!" He earnestly said as his eyes looked up from time to time while he savored the meal. "Just terrific, Maggie," he said with his mouth full.

It was late summer and Maggie had used only local produce and brookies caught from the Betsie river headwaters.

"My God, Maggie, that was the best meal I have had in a very long time. Five stars, Freckles, five stars! You've got so many talents."

"It's just local peasant food, Brian. Not a big deal," said Maggie.

"Some upscale peasants," Brian replied with a big smile.

"I'm afraid that my tastes are pretty simple," she said.

"Any great chef will tell you simple is the genius ingredient in cooking."

Brian leaned over and kissed her on the cheek. Maggie leaned forward herself and kissed him on the mouth.

"Maggie, those lips of yours are incredible."

Maggie smiled, "Thank you, Brian."

After the meal, Maggie drove back home. She was unsettled, confused. Brian was a good man; he had everything she could ever want. *What about John?* She said to herself. Even though her love for John and his for her was not a fully settled thing, she felt unfaithful but she said to herself, *I have done nothing wrong. I have a right to make sure before I settle down with one man. What if John isn't the one? After all he is my first real love. What experience do I have with adult love, really? Maybe John's just safe, comfortable, familiar.*

She drove home to take a shower and settled into a book on the private lives of ancient Roman citizens. The small efficiency she rented consisted of a small bedroom, a bathroom with a walk-in shower, a kitchen and a living room. Nothing else. No patio, no garage, very simple; neat, cozy and clean. When she stepped out of the shower the phone was ringing.

"Hello?" She said.

"Maggie. Its John."

"John. How was your day?"

"Well, I picked up three new projects. The new bank on M31 and two new, big ass, huge, homes to be built on Sutton's Bay overlooking the West arm."

"That's fantastic, babe! I am so proud of you. Did you get the partner work with the architect in Bloomfield?"

"Not yet, but it looks very promising. Hey, Mag, how about meeting me at Boones for a drink?"

"That sounds good. Give me about an hour," said Maggie.

"How was your day, honey?" Asked John.

"Well, really well, but I am concerned about what I'm gonna do when the club closes for the winter," said Maggie.

"How would you like to finish your History major?"

"I don't have the money," she said a little embarrassed and frustrated.

"I do, at least I will when I nail down those three projects on Friday."

"I can't do that, John. I would feel like a mooch or a kept woman."

"I know, which is why I had our attorney draw up a loan where you can pay me back over a fifteen-year period after you get your degree."

Maggie was thrown for a moment. She hadn't considered that before. "Let's talk about it at Boones," her voice began to quaver as a few tears welled up. "That is very thoughtful, John."

"Maggie, I know you. You're no freeloader and I want to help you in a way that makes you comfortable and confident."

"I'll see you in a few," she said. He, too, was a very good man.

As Maggie drove to Boones she recalled her time with Brian. Her conflicted emotions continued to disturb her. When she arrived John was already sitting at the bar. She looked at him with as objective a view as she could, maybe doing a little comparison in her mind. *He is a gorgeous man,* she thought. *Who would have believed that the young pre-teen I met so many years ago would turn into this hunky son of a gun?* He was now six foot three, very dark brown hair, eyes as blue as the bay, strong, bright, funny and authentic. She envied him. With his parents' help and summer construction work, he had earned an architect's license from Lawrence Tech down state. He was accomplished in a way she felt she was not. With all of the opportunities he had to select another woman, he never had. She was not naive, he probably had dipped his toe in the water, but it was obvious to everyone and her that John wanted no other woman than Maggie. He was no longer a Jack pine bumpkin and sitting on the stool she could see how he would be at home anywhere but he wanted to be here in Northern Michigan. With the growth of Traverse City and the continued building of large second homes he was making a great living now. His Prairie style ranch mansion, built for a family from Bloomfield hills on the high bluffs of Arcadia overlooking Lake Michigan had caught the attention of the trades. "From the lake," said the writer from Architect's Digest, "The twenty thousand square foot Prairie Ranch seems almost cozy and appears to have grown naturally out of the solid soil above the bluff's face." In partnership with his childhood friend's landscape firm, the home did indeed look warm and inviting despite its massive square footage. This young genius who had such an eye for structure and beauty wanted no one else but Maggie, and had told her as much a few years ago when he said, "Maggie if ever there was a work of art, you are it."

She stood there, looking at him with pride. *Look at him,* she thought, *he is a stunner.* She felt a familiar feeling; a desire to give into temptation and allow him to deflower her tonight. But as before, she shook it off in some mental cold shower only a woman like her could summon up.

"Hey, sweet ass," she whispered in his ear.

John turned around and gave her a long open mouthed kiss. She instantly felt deeply loved and at home. "I just called the office and a message was left telling me that the Bloomfield builder wants me to design the new facilities and club house for the new golf course Jack Nicklaus is building in Acme. I can't believe this is happening like this all in the same damn week! Three years ago, I couldn't catch a cold and now I have enough work for the next three years. You've gotta let me float you that loan now, Maggie."

"Okay," said Maggie, surprising herself with the sudden decision.

"John, I can't believe this, I mean, I always knew you would do well, but not like this and not so early. What kind of building will you do for the course?"

"Well, I was thinking something ranch-like again that would blend into the rolling landscape, but I would have to add an elevator that would go up to a roof top restaurant overlooking the old orchards and the new course. They tell me Nicklaus wants to retain as many black cherry trees as possible so that they can be maintained and when they ripen the players can just drive up and grab a handful. Doesn't that sound great?"

"Where would I go?" Maggie blurted out indicating that she had not been completely listening and was wondering which school to attend. "What about us? How could we see each other? I hated it when you were at Lawrence."

"Well, what about U of M in Ann Arbor? You've only got two years left, and I will be going down state a couple times a month."

She looked at him with a gut filled satisfaction missing from earlier that day. "I will miss you. I will be happy for you, but I will miss you, John."

"I will come see you often. It's only two years. Hey, wait a minute… Maybe there is an accelerated program. Check it out."

"I will," she said with an upbeat note.

John's name was called and they were escorted from the bar to their table. At the table, John stood up in mock manner and said, "Oh, I forgot. We are not eating here tonight. I made other arrangements."

Maggie asked a little excitedly, "Where?"

"Well, at our dream house."

She instantly knew he was talking about: the Bay Harbor Inn. It was a beautiful old home converted into a restaurant looking out over the East bay. It was a little costly, but they liked to go there once in a while. Maggie said it would be her dream home because of its location. They left Boones and jumped into John's Chevy pickup. The passenger side was covered in drawings and documents.

"Still a slob, I see," laughed Maggie.

In his best Gary Cooper John said, "Yep!" He smiled.

John had arranged for them to sit near the front bay window. Even though it was dark the window looked out onto the front garden. It consisted of all kinds of sedum, mums and old gnarled pines and cedars, all of which were illuminated by tin barn lights, that casted soft light and shadow over them.

"Maggie," John said as they were sitting down. "I don't want to sound like a jerk, but what's up with this Brian at Crystal?"

"Morgan…" Maggie thought out loud. Morgan was a mutual friend and also a greens superintendent at Crystal.

"Yeah, Morgan. He wasn't spying or anything, he just mentioned he'd seen Brian giving you a lot of attention. Not that I blame him. Hell, Maggie, a guy would have to be half dead not to desire you. Damn it Maggie, I'm twenty-five and I'm still a virgin because of you."

"You're still a virgin?" Maggie said in a surprised manner.

"Yes, aren't you?" John said in a concerned voice.

"Yes, yes I am, but with all the time at college you never gave in? Didn't you want to?"

"No! And yes I did, but I wanted every shot at keeping it for you. To tell you the truth Maggie, I've been walking around with blue balls for a long time now." He smiled.

"So, what about Brian?" He was trying to appear calm but his burning jealousy was leaking through.

Not wanting to be painfully open, yet not wanting to lie, she said, "He's a great guy. I have been second guessing myself thinking that I might be making a mistake by sticking with the first man I ever loved."

"Hey, I get that. I've had those doubts, but I have met a lot of women in the last few years and no one does it for me like you. I ache when I can't see you, just like I did when I was fifteen. I wish I could say this *Brian guy* was just another rich jerk wanting to get into your pants, but Morgan says he's a class act. 'Says I'd like him.

Which in all honesty didn't make me feel better. I guess I'm scared and insecure, but for God's sake Maggie, what man wouldn't want you! You're the whole package and I can't blame the son of a bitch for seeing that."

She smiled and said, "John, I really liked Brian and he is a great person, but tonight when I walked into Boones and saw you sitting at the bar I felt fifteen again myself. I love you and I want all of you for as long as God sees fit to leave us on this earth." Her last words trailed off as she wiped an almost involuntary stream of tears from her face. Her makeup began to run and was all over the fine linen napkin. John welled up as well and wiped his eyes. He stood up slightly and leaned across the table to kiss her tenderly and passionately. An older couple sitting nearby smiled and quietly clapped when they were done.

Maggie said, "My face must look terrible."

"Not at all, Mag. I have never seen you more beautiful."

With that, Maggie started to cry again and got up to go to the restroom. When she returned her makeup was fresh and lightly applied. Her freckles were more apparent and it drove John wild with passion. He loved her damn freckles, always had. They ordered their meal, drank two bottles of wine, passed on dessert and walked out into the cool fall air under the barn lights, and sat down on a large cedar garden bench. With all of the old fashioned romance he had in him, John knelt down on one knee and asked, "Maggie, will you marry me?" He opened a box with a small, but tasteful engagement ring.

Maggie grabbed his face and kissed him as hard as she could. She wanted to melt into him. "Yes, John! Yes, I will. Now let's go neck," she said with a hardy laugh.

They were married the week before Christmas and their first child, a daughter, was born the following November. Before Maggie left Crystal, the members and staff gave her an envelope for her upcoming marriage. It was a very large sum of money, which they used toward the purchase of their new house. When they gave her the envelope, which Brian had contributed to generously, Brian was not present. He told Mr. Rooney that it would be a while before he could visit Crystal. He did survive though, and married a fellow researcher six years later.

The night Maggie accepted John's proposal, they did something they had never done before. They went to her apartment and explored every millimeter of each other's body without full consummation. They found substantial ways to provide each other with orgasmic relief. They slept in until 11:00 am, had breakfast, went swimming in Frankfort, and then played golf at Crystal, courtesy of the members who always provide them with an open invitation. They continued on for a week until they had to return to work. Each time they touched each other's naked skin they radiated heat and through various means continued to find satisfaction. While Maggie was in full release, John would stare at her face. Her image often returned to his mind for the rest of his life. They had twelve great years together before his death. He loved as well in those years as any man ever has. It took years before the beautiful and still young Maggie could give her heart to another man—another good man.

KIRT AND BETH

One of the symptoms, early symptoms, of Kirt's depression was something called racing thoughts. When he was thirty-seven, a shrink he went to see asked him if he had ever had racing thoughts. Kirt was elated to have someone know what racing thoughts were. No doctor up to that point had ever asked him

"Yes!" Kirt said. "When I was a young guy around twelve or thirteen, I would tell my parents what it was and they could not understand it. They took me to my family doctor, but he thought I was just high strung. I just kind of gutted it out when it would happen. My dad called me overly dramatic when I would try to explain it, but he had no idea what it was, not even the doctors. It was as though a fast-forward of everything I was hearing or thinking would run in my head. I learned to ride it out until it went away. It went away a few years later though."

"Yes," said the doctor. "We now know that this can be an early sign of synaptic problems in the brain."

It felt good to know that this phenomenon was understood. Up until the death of his ladies, Kirt never had another racing thought. One night after the funeral he came home and a narrative of his life began to race like before, through his head. It scared the hell out of him. He let it play out though and it went like this:

(Punctuation is reflective of his thoughts that night).

The Clio area still had a few one- room schools left then Kirt and Beth we went to them from kindergarten until sixth grade when they closed all the one rooms and consolidated the schools they consolidated the elementaries into just three and created a Middle School next to the high school Beth Rousseau was an extremely cute little girl with deep dimples and sky/marine blue eyes her hair was light brown and blonde with just about every shade of blonde you can think of it was naturally streaked in a very subtle way and the blondest of the streaks made the rest of her hair kind of shine in the summer her hair was incredible when she was older all the women would have killed to have her hair Kirt always thought it was special Kirt liked her right away not because she was beautiful but because she was so tough she was a tomboy and up to any physical challenge she had no problem putting a worm on a hook catching frogs and snakes or cutting off frog's legs for dinner she was fun and very loyal whenever Kirt and she or others got into trouble she would never rat out a friend never never never never (Kirt's mind was stuck like an old record player) they would go to each other's house to play and Kirt's parents fell in love with her in many ways she became the girl they never had Beth liked the dresses Kirt's mom would give her Beth loved beautiful clothes as much as she liked spearing frogs Kirt and Beth's parents became friends as adults often do when their children are close Beth's parents liked little Kirt too Beth's Dad gave Kirt a shortened 7 iron that he learned to hit over 75 yards Beth's Dad would let out the most joyous laugh every time Kirt nailed that 7 iron with both Kirt and Beth being only children it was special to have "back up parents" as Beth called them Beth was exposed to different traditions than her own and so was Kirt Kirt's family was Teutonic and Beth's was French so it was a potato pancakes and crepes kinda friendship…When Kirt was nine, Mr. Rousseau took Kirt to the Clio Country Club to play golf on a real adult golf course. Beth's parents loved the game, The Melding, as Mr. Rousseau called it. According to Mr. Rousseau, whenever he was playing particularly well and was in that wonderful place that all golfers know as in the zone, Mr. Rousseau said it was like melding with the creation. "Ye caint asplain it, little Kirtie, untiel yove experienced it," he would say in his rather excellent but imitative Scottish brogue.

(Kirt's mind began to make appropriate pauses, but still at a racing speed).

As time went on, Kirt too understood what it was to meld. "Its tha state ya seek evr tyme ye tread tha links" Kirt loved Mr. Rousseau because, like his father, he treated him with no deference to his age. They gave him a sense of confidence by their expectations of him. Beth's parents were considerably more well off than his own parents, but wore their wealth lightly and with dignity. They never felt compelled to speak of it or flaunt it. Because neither of Kirt's parents golfed, they were more than happy to have Mr. Rousseau take Kirt to the course. Actually, the golf course was only four miles down the road from where Kirt lived and a mile and a half way from Beth's house. Kirt could actually strap his clubs to his bicycle and ride to the course. Both of them lived in the country, meaning outside of the Clio city limits but within a few miles from town. The Clio area was a combination of General Motor's workers and farmers. Michigan has never lost its agricultural roots... Kirt's parents made an arrangement with the Rousseau's to pay them a monthly fee to have Kirt attached to Rousseau's membership and after a few years, Kirt's father tried his hand at the game and came to love it too, although he never joined the club. Kirt's father, like Mr. Roussea,u was touched by the way they treated each other's children. Kirt's father had the Rousseau's over often in the summer for his famous rib eye steak dinners with fresh vegetables from the garden. They were a tight group. In so many way,s Beth and Kirt felt like friends and family, which made it awkward when things took a romantic turn. Mr. Rousseau was a great teacher and Kirt became a very solid golfer. He grew as tall as he ever would, six foot two, by the age of eighteen. Beth also grew taller and topped out at five feet, ten inches by age nineteen. Beth's hair and eyes remained the same all her life, with the exception of a few gray hairs that were indistinguishable from some of the very blonde ones. Her lips also remained naturally full and rosy. She was so often outside that her skin was tanned and freckled. The sun brought out more freckles *than in the winter when they were more subdued. Her dimples seemed to deepen a bit as she aged. In her thirties she took to wearing a wide brim hat to "save her face", which did help, but Kirt missed the freckles that the sun would bring out.*

Somewhere around age fifteen everything changed for Kirt. One afternoon, Beth and Kirt were playing golf with Jane and Tom. On the fourth hole, a par 3, Kirt was sitting on the bench rather dejectedly having hit his shot twenty yards short of the elevated green with the pin placed just on the other side of the "buried elephant," a hump in the middle of the green. A bad place to be and he wasn't melding today. Jane and Beth were on the women's tees, and the guys were waiting for them to hit up to the elevated green. Now, don't misunderstand, it was not that Kirt had been blind to Beth's femininity but for some reason today as she took her long fluid swing, she cast a silhouette against the solid blue sky to which he was riveted. She was softly ropey from all her athletic endeavors with a flexibility that allowed her to make that languid and effective swing. As she finished her shot, Kirt focused on her calves and back muscles. For the first time he began to see her as a woman to be desired. Not only was she a great friend, but for him, from now on, she was his love. The emotion took him so fully that he looked around to see if he had telegraphed it in any way. By the looks on the faces of his friends he could see he had not. Never the less, it felt like if he looked Beth in the eyes she would be able to tell. How could he tell her, should he tell her? It troubled him greatly and it reflected in his game, which was a little off form even though he scored rather well.

Time passed and both of them dated others. Often they would compare notes on how the dates went. Every time he heard of how some guy had kissed her he cringed, but did not let on. Kirt began to accept that Beth probably just didn't love him the way he loved her. Of course their friendship remained strong and they continued to golf, fish, see an occasional movie and do homework together. One night they were fishing at a large gravel pit not far from where they lived. They went to fish for crappie and largemouth bass. The Michigan Hex, a very large Mayfly, often mistakenly called the Michigan Caddis or the "fish fly," was beginning to hatch. The large winged yellowish/brown mayfly was a feast for the fish. Folks from all over the world would come to the Au Sable and Manistee rivers just to fish during the hatch. Although mayflies were well-known for satisfying trout, they were also for the warm water species. The gravel pits had rather clean water, and were fed by clean, clear springs and had sandy bottoms where the Hex would thrive. Even though the two of them couldn't go up north to the blue ribbon trout streams, they did take advantage of the hatch in this gorgeous gravel pit. They were hauling in the crappie, and the large mouths were slamming Kirt's self-tied flies. Neither one of them wanted to quit, but it was a very black, moonless night. Wearing the mosquito netting was starting to get irritating.

"Son's a' bitches," Kirt said as one of the loudest buzzing skeeters landed on his mesh near his ear.

"Damned mosquito!" Beth laughed at his irritation and said, "One more cast."

She gingerly moved forward to more easily cast to the crappie in deeper water just beyond the drop off. She went too far and plunged in over her head. Kirt was a little panicked for her safety. He threw his rod onto the bank and ripped off his waders as fast as possible. He jumped in after her but she seemed to be handling it well herself. Just to be sure, he picked her up and carried her to the shore. "I'm fine, Kirt. Really, thanks for being there though." As he put her down on the shore he brushed his right hand across her breast. She looked at him and smiled. He thought he saw a hint of pleasure, but thought it was probably wishful thinking. She was not wearing a bra, which was the fashion then, but Beth always wore a bra.

"I didn't wear a bra tonight because I thought with the waders and netting it would be too hot. You know me. I don't like that hippie look."

"I figured as much," said Kirt.

Her breast was cold from the spring water and even as she lay on the ground it was obvious that they were firm. Kirt had felt breasts before in a more direct manner, but this was *Beth's* breast. It was far more than sexual for him; it felt like touching her on a level he was unable to describe.

"Let's go to my house and clean these fish. We can keep some for the next few days and freeze the rest," directed Kirt.

"Sounds good," said Beth.

Under the waders and netting she was wearing a t-shirt, shorts and sandals. She asked Kirt to stop at the gas station so she could go into the bathroom and put on a bra. Looking at her breast with their nipples at attention he could easily imagine her naked. He glanced at her as they were driving down the road toward the gas station and he could see the little girl in her face. He knew her so well but not enough yet. She ran off to put on her bra. Kirt wished he had told her not to bother but he kept his mouth shut. When they arrived at his home they took the fish out back to the galvanized table his dad had made for the purposed of cleaning fish. Also at the table was a hose used to wash off the table when you were done. Kirt watched as the graceful hands, that he had once seen hold an open children's book, deftly cleaned the fish. The tomboy he knew was still a tomboy with some wonderful feminine additions.

"Hey, how did you do?" Kirt's father asked Beth.

"Great, thanks. We kept about thirty crappies. We must have caught at least that many large mouths. We threw those back. The large mouths were attacking the duns and spinners."

"Beth, before you go make sure to see Cheryl. She finished sewing that costume for you," said Kirt's father.

"Already? She's a sweetheart."

Kirt was conspicuously quiet and his father did not press the issue. After they cleaned the fish, the three of them sat on the patio and talked for a while. Beth got up and went to the house to get the costume and then yelled good night to all.

Kirt's father looked at him and said, "Alright son, what's up?"

Not wanting to talk about it Kirt mumbled, "Oh not much, nothing."

"No something is wrong. What is it?"

Kirt wished his Dad world let it go but he knew he wouldn't. "Dad, I am really screwed up. I'm scared."

"About what?"

"Beth."

"What, is she okay?"

"Yes, she's fantastic, absolutely fantastic. She's incredible. I, I…I love her."

"Have you told her, son?"

"No."

"How long have you felt this way?"

"Over two years."

"Two years! Son, that's gotta be torture. You have to tell her."

"What if she doesn't feel the same way about me?"

"Son, life is all about taking calculated risks. You have everything to gain if she feels the same way, but she may not. Believe me, you can deal with that too."

"I thought you would tell me I was too young to know what love is."

"No! Not you, son, and not in this situation. You're a maturing young man and you have been best friends with Beth since you were little. She was a great kid then and a great young woman now. I'm not at all surprised this happened."

"You're not?"

"No, not at all."

"You two know everything about each other warts and all. She is exactly who she is and there is no guessing what you would be getting into. Can we pray about it?" The two of them prayed to give Kirt the eyes to see an opportunity to tell her how much he loved her, and the strength to deal with whatever answer she gave.

"Thanks, Dad," said Kirt.

"Son, I do know what you're going through, and it's wonderful and gut wrenching at the same time. You feel elated and you want to throw up too," he smiled.

"Yeah, I love her so much it actually hurts. I never knew what that meant until lately. It hurts. I'm so scared I will lose her, scare her off."

"I know. You be ready and when the opportunity happens tell her, don't pussy foot around let her know everything."

On the following Friday afternoon, Kirt and Beth played eighteen at Clio Country Club (CCC). Kirt was on top of his game and so was Beth. At the turn Kirt had a thirtyseven and Beth had a thirty-eight. Neither one of them talked about scores, but they knew they were competing with each other. On the par four number ten, Kirt pulled his drive and had no other shot but to chip thirty yards back into the fairway. He then hit his third shot just right off the green across the creek. He stubbed his chip shot and two putted. Beth pared the hole so she was now one stroke ahead. By the time they reached the long par four eighteenth, Beth was still one stroke ahead. Kirt then blurted out, "Okay, I know you're one up on me!"

"Oh really? I wasn't aware," she said mockingly. Kirt stepped up to the tee and struck a melding shot that went three hundred and ten yards with the help of the dry ground. He had a second shot of only a hundred and thirty yards. Beth hit a solid drive and landed only sixty yards or so behind Kirt. Beth then took out a four wood and floated a beautiful shot twenty feet from the pin. "Beautiful,"said Kirt. He then stepped up to his shot armed with a 9 iron. He hit the ball solidly. It flew directly online, bounced twice and dropped into the hole. Kirt, in a self-parody, dropped to his knees with his hands on either side of his head saying, "It can't be so!" When he stood up he was giddy as he grabbed Beth's bag and slung it over his left shoulder handing Beth her putter. Beth missed and made a par. Kirt had beaten her by one shot. As they walked toward the clubhouse, they good-naturedly ribbed each other. The fall sky was full of the aroma of burning leaves and freshly mowed grass. Beth tipped her head back and laughed saying, "You're a lucky S.O.B."

"Just as I envisioned it. Did you see the little kick it took off that dry patch in front of the green?" Kirt said with a faux serious face.

"Ya, like I said, lucky S.O.B..."

He went into the building with her while she cleaned her spikes, changed into her sandals and stored her clubs. They sat down at the grill and ate grilled cheese and fresh cucumbers and tomatoes.

"Thank Hal for the veggies, Julie. They're terrific!" Kirt said to the cook. The members often brought in excess garden vegetables for everyone to eat. It was here that Kirt first fell in love with gazpacho, fresh, right out of someone's garden. At eighteen years of age, both of them had voracious appetites so one grilled cheese was not enough and neither was one plate of tomatoes and cucumbers. Kirt then asked Julie if they had any fresh mozzarella, which they did, so he made a stack of beefsteaks and mozzarella and poured Italian dressing over it. The two of them ate it up as fast as they could prepare it. Kirt paused a couple of times to watch this medium built, soft and ropey young women, with perfectly streaked hair, deep dimples and marine/sky blue eyes, as she pounded down enough food to feed three women. She had an appetite for all of life and he loved to watch her eat like this. He thought to himself, *I have to tell her tonight.* They ate fairly quickly and then joined the conversations in the room when Beth shouted out, "Kirt got an eagle on eighteen tonight!" Kirt was surprised that he felt a little embarrassed, but accepted everyone's congratulations. Of course, like all golfers, it was demanded that he give the details. By the time they left it was truly dark. Kirt stepped outside, picked up his bag and started to walk across the gravel parking lot. Clio Country Club (CCC) at that time was a bare bones operation. The emphasis was on the golf. There were no swimming pools, no tennis courts; just golf and a simple clubhouse. CCC was a player's course and its members were all solid golfers. A gravel parking lot was reflective of the club's modesty. Hell, after hiring an architect, the members all helped to build the layout starting with the first nine and then a few years later they finished the other nine. The course followed the natural hills, contours and creek. The wind swept across, mostly from the west, and could change the way you played in a dramatic manner. There were few trees, but where there were trees, they definitely came into play. There was also a fair amount of sand, and the creek could jump up and bite. It was a solid course, members consisting of blue-collar workers, merchants and small town professionals who joined forces to build something they could call their own. Kirt loved the sound of his metal spikes against the gravel in the calm quiet of a warm summer night. The smallest sounds were heightened and crisp. He put his clubs and shoes in the trunk and walked back to Beth. Beth stood under the light of one of the several mercury pole lamps around the parking lot. The word "luminous" came to his mind as he looked at her in the strange mercury light. She looked at Kirt, "I better get home. We're playing Flushing tomorrow and I want to be rested."

"Match play?" said Kirt.

"Yeah," she said, a little tired.

"You play like you did tonight, and you'll have no trouble."

"I hope I didn't use it all up tonight."

"No, you're amazing; you won't run out of steam."

"Thanks, Kirt."

Then Kirt said exactly what he had rehearsed all week. He felt his throat constrict, his carotids were pounding in his ear. He took her hand and she felt an uncharacteristic clamminess in his palms.

"What is it Kirt?" She said thinking he had bad news.

"Beth. We have been friends forever, since we were little. Your friendship means more to me than anything else in my life, which is why I don't want to lose it by telling you this."

"What, Kirt? You're scaring me."

"Beth, I love you."

"I love you too."

"No Beth, I mean I *really* love you. For the last couple of years, I've held this in. Every time you went on a date I got sick to my stomach. Thinking of someone else kissing you made me nuts. Somewhere along the line I woke up and realized you are the most desirable, intelligent, sweet woman I have ever seen. I love you so much Beth. I wish I had the right words to tell you."

Beth stood there with a confused look on her face. She didn't know how to take this. She did not know what to say. She looked at Kirt's eyes and could see moisture and earnestness there. He was deadly serious.

"Kirt... I don't know what to say...I never really thought of us like that."

"Never?"

"Well, a couple of times the thought crossed my mind, but we have been friends for so long I assumed that would not happen."

"Do me a favor, Beth."

Almost afraid to ask, she eked out, "What?"

"Let me kiss you," the words flowed so naturally from his mouth it surprised him.

Feeling a little off guard Beth said, "Okay."

Kirt put his right arm around the small of her back, and his left around her shoulder. Then he slowly brought both hands up to the sides of her face and deliberately placed an open mouth kiss on those full lips. He thought was going to pass out. That kiss was more impressive than he had imagined. Beth kissed back with just the right amount of pressure and as their tongues touched, Kirt could taste the Italian dressing and the fullness of her lips. He did not want to stop, but felt he might completely frighten her off if he did not. He stopped kissing her and pulled her close to him in a firm but gentle embrace. Something was happening to Beth, but she was so confused she did not know what it was. Several weeks earlier she had allowed a date to hold her breast in his hand over her sweater. It was not as satisfying as she was told it would be.

She gently pushed away from Kirt, "Kirt. Please, hold my breast."

Kirt thought his legs would give out, but he placed his right hand over her right breast over the sweatshirt she had been wearing all day. The sweatshirt warm, warmed from her body. This was not the first breast he had held but like at the gravel pit, it was Beth's breast. It filled his hand and was firm and slightly pliant. He could tell her nipples were reaching up to meet his hand. They were stiff and he knew all the tissue around them was gathering up too. Kirt looked at her and said,

"You are so wonderful, Beth. You feel so wonderful."

Beth very gently pulled his hand away, and somewhat befuddled said, "I'm gonna have to think about this, Kirt…I don't know; I need to think." She started to cry, "I'm sorry if I disappoint you, Kirt, but I need time."

"You can't disappoint me, Beth. You're my best friend and I couldn't go on like this without being honest. You wouldn't want that, would you?"

"No, no Kirt. You're so sweet, I love that you told me. I just…"

"I know, Beth. It's a lot to take in. Go home and think about it. You tell me what you think when you're ready."

"Does anyone else know about this?"

"No, just my Dad. I had to tell someone."

"And you felt this way for over two years?"

"Yes…"

"Why didn't you tell me earlier?"

"I thought if you didn't feel the same I would lose you completely. But I can't live like that anymore."

"What happened to make you start feeling like this?"

"You happened. You grew into the most appealing woman; strong, beautiful, smart, and wonderful. What can I say? I fell in love with my best friend."

"Oh, Kirt," she hugged him and ran off to her car.

His mind began to race at a higher speed and all appropriate pausing was lost. *Why did she want me to touch her?* Kirt thought. *Did she like it? Was I too eager, too rough, too soft?"* He ruminated as he drove home.

They didn't talk with each other all week. Kirt did not want to reach out to her. He wanted her to call him. Kirt went to school to meet with his independent studies teachers Kirt had met all of his graduation requirements but for four more classes he had arranged to do two independent study courses each semester this way he would go to school only occasionally and work full time at a local factory that made corrugated boxes for the auto industry he intended to use the money when at college when he left the school that morning he ran into Beth and several of their friends she acted as though nothing had happened which bothered him he did not know what to think was she put off, was she ignoring the subject as he turned to leave he felt her tug at his arm—

"Can you meet me tonight around 7:00 pm at Clio Country Club? I want to talk about last Friday night… Will you meet me?" Said Beth.

"Yeah, yeah. Sure," Kirt said as Beth smiled a non-committal smile.

"I'll see you there," said Beth.

The world around him receded into the background his stomach began to churn his mouth was bone dry and his heart was pounding he walked away from the school as fast as he could when he got to his Chevy Bellaire with its reliable 283 engine Cindy Powers knocked on his window he rolled down his window and said, 'Hi, Cindy!" At that she leaned into his window and planted a big sloppy kiss on him he could taste the marijuana on her mouth she was high and ready for action—Kirt could swear he was tasting that marijuana right now any other time this rowdy beauty with her well filled tube top and her short shorts would have left an impression on him but not now he wanted her to go away in her best throaty voice she whimpered in his ear—

"Hey Kirt. Ya' wanna do it?"

Kirt looked at her and said, "What? Oh thanks Cindy, but I'm late for work."

He lied he said it like he was turning down an offer for coffee he drove into town and went to a phone booth and called the box factory telling them he was sick and would not make it today in a way he was telling the truth he had never missed work before so the boss didn't think twice about it—

"Get better, Kid. We'll miss you," was all that his boss said.

It was just as well in his state of mind he might have lost a finger or something in the box slitter blades his stomach was a mess he went into the drug store and bought a Vernor's ginger ale everyone said it would settle your stomach and it did seem to help-What did she want to talk about? Was she preparing to let me down easy? Is she in love with me too?

His thoughts kept repeating. He couldn't calm down. He felt he would pass out—

Please God please make this stop!

Kirt prayed as the story continued to race forward. He drove over to Redeemer Lutheran Church. Maybe he could catch Pastor C. When he walked into the church office, Carol the office manager said, "Kirt. What's up?"

"I need to see Pastor. It's kind of important," said Kirt, frantically.

"He won't be back for a half hour or so. He has been at the hospital all morning. Mrs. Swain passed away and he has been with the family," said Carol.

"Oh, I didn't know. Jim will be crushed," said Kirt. Jim was Carol's son. "Well, okay. I'll wait outside."

Kirt circled around the grounds praying. As he walked, he compulsively repeated, as though God had not heard him the first time, "Help me handle whatever happens." He walked very little, but his panicked state caused him to sweat. He did not want to sweat, so he lay down on the long oak bench outside the main entrance. He and his Dad had built the bench. It felt familiar lying down on it. He took some deliberate deep breaths as he had been taught to do during a tense period of a basketball game or golf match. It helped. Kirt sat up and took another couple of deep breaths. He was able to relax. He started to fade off into sleep, when suddenly Pastor Craemer touched him on the shoulder.

"Pastor C! Sorry. I guess I was starting to nap," said Kirt.

"It's a comfortable bench. Come on in," said Pastor.

Kirt sat down where everyone sat when they went to see the Pastor. Pastor C was an extremely approachable man. His intellect and theological knowledge, preaching and counseling skills made it easy for him to work with just about anyone. When you talked with him, you knew he was giving you all the attention you needed. Kirt loved this man sometimes more than his own father, who also loved Pastor C very much.

"What's up, Kirt, huh?"

Pauses in Kirt's thoughts began to occur—Pastor was from the Toronto area and often used the word "huh" instead of his native "eh" so as to sound more American. It was an endearing affectation that he probably wasn't even aware of.

"I'm waiting for an answer from Beth. She is going to meet with me tonight at 7:00 pm over at the country club. It's only 1:00 pm. I don't know if I can wait that long."

"Wait for what, Kirt?" Asked Pastor C.

"Last Friday, I told Beth I loved her, and she looked confused and stunned. I told her to think about it and give me an answer. She kissed me. The first time I saw her all week was today when she asked me if I wanted to meet tonight. What if she doesn't feel the same way I do?"

Pastor C sat forward and put his hand on Kirt's shoulder, "Wow. What a load your carrying, Kirt." The empathy in his voice moved Kirt into tears. He didn't want to cry, but felt good to know Pastor understood. Pastor grabbed the Kleenex and gave it to Kirt. Wiping his eyes, he continued to tell Pastor the whole history of his love for Beth.

"Look, Kirt, I watched you two grow up. She is a wonderful young woman. I would normally say there are other fish in the sea, but that's B.S in your case. Whatever she decides, you will eventually be okay. I know your love for her is pretty, deeply entrenched. I have to tell you, if she decides she does not share the same feelings you have for her, you will go through hell for a while. If that happens, come back and see me right away so we can talk. I know a little bit about heartbreak and yours will be very tough."

"But what do I do until tonight?"

"Go do something physical. Take a long shower and make sure you eat. Call me when you get the word tonight."

"I will…" said Kirt.

"No, Kirt. You call me, you understand? I don't care what time it is, call me. In fact, call me no matter what the outcome, Okay?"

"Yeah, I will."

Pastor C had seen enough suicide over such circumstances and was doing all he could to help prevent any irrational decisions Kirt might make, even though he wasn't too concerned about Kirt. He was a solid young man but even strong men can break.

"Let's pray, Kirt: Lord, only you know the depths of emotion Kirt is feeling. The anxiety of not knowing is killing him. Remind him how much you love him as he waits for whatever answer the good Beth will give him. And Lord, please give Beth the right words to convey whatever she has to say tonight. In Christ's name: Amen. Oh Lord, I almost forgot. Give Kirt the ability to handle whatever the outcome tonight and in the days to come."

Kirt felt more relaxed and hugged Pastor, "Thanks, Pastor C."

You betcha', Kirt. You know I love you. You hang in there."

Kirt went back to his car and decided to drive into north Flint to the Balkan bakery. On the way he listened to Mountain at full volume drinking a large iced tea as he went. Once at the bakery he bought two slabs of pie, one cherry and one apple, they were cut square from a large rectangular pan. They were heavy with fruit. He then drove further into Flint to Angelo's Coney Island and ordered four Coney dogs, some fries and a large chocolate malt. The Coney's were the kind you could only find in Flint, and the best of them was at Angelo's. The meat sauce was comprised of some kind of organ meats, hearts, tongue who knew. It was ground up fine and seasoned in a manner that seemed peculiar to the Greeks of the area. Whatever was in the sauce he loved it topped with sweet onions and mustard. Angelo's was Flint's true blue collar gourmet, and everyone came for the Coney's. Their malts were loaded with malt and thick as a brick. It was the gathering place of line workers and professionals, a kind of egalitarian eatery. Politicians liked to frequent the place when they were up for reelection. Kirt smiled to himself when he remembered his Uncle Joe's confrontations with the local democrat congressman. One day, his Uncle came to Angelo's with him and his dad and Congressman Kilborn was sitting at the counter acting like "one of the people". Uncle Joe took one look at Kilborn and said as loud as he could, "Holy shit! Does it stink in here Angelo? Where's that comin' from?" Then he mock-sniffed around the place until he came right up behind Kilborn, "Here's your source, Angelo! Somebody scraped their shoe off on this stool!" Kirt's dad was embarrassed, a lot of people laughed out loud. Kilborn looked non-pulsed. A couple of line workers came over to the booth and said to Uncle Joe, "Hey, smart ass! That was just plain rude." Uncle Joe jumped up, "No! Rude is picking your constituents pockets and pretending that you're doing them a favor. That's friggin' rude, that's criminal!" The two men argued with Uncle Joe for a few more minutes, which were then invited to pull up a chair and talk for a while. They did. They found out that Uncle Joe was not the rube they thought he was. He bought them a couple Cokes and had them thinking differently before they left. He was coarse, but hard to hate for very long. Uncle Joe went on to lead a team of blue-collar United Automobile Workers (UAW) folks from Macomb County, which became known as the Reagan democrats. These thoughts took Kirt's mind off his concerns for a few minutes just thinking about *lovable* Uncle Joseph.

Like most young athletic men, Kirt left Angelo's full, but not stuffed. Returning to his car he drove about fifteen miles east until he reached a small gravel road. Down the road was a substantial farm. It was his great Uncle Lee's. He drove down a tractor path off the road until he reached the large farm pond on the north side of the property. Black Angus cattle were feeding in the adjacent pasture where his Uncle had pumped water from the spring fed pond into the troughs on the other side of the fence. "Walkin' beef," as his uncle would call them. Kirt's dad said Uncle Lee was not really a cattle rancher or farmer but he played at it. Uncle Lee had made most of his money during the depression and thereafter when he used the cash he had on hand to buy property. As the years went by, Uncle Lee would sell a chunk of property and live off of it until he needed more, and would sell off another chunk. Uncle Lee had over four hundred acres, and by the time he died, he had nothing. He even donated property to Big Brothers and Mott Community College. Kirt loved Uncle Lee because he was a maverick and treated boys like men. He always found the farm peaceful even when he was working his butt off feeding cattle or cleaning the barn.

Kirt removed the waxed paper from his slab pie and inhaled each as he parked under the large willow on the north side of the pond. He got out of his car and opened his trunk, reaching for his "junky fly rod", a ten-foot yellow Eagle Claw 7 weight. He liked to use this set up for casting big flies, and this pond contained some massive largemouth bass that required some big bugs. Kirt took out a large box of bass flies, some as long as six inches. It contained streamers, Mickey fins, some deer hair mice and frogs and an assortment of noisy surface lures that resembled many things and imitated nothing in particular. He made a few casts into the westerly wind and the Eagle Claw punched through it beautifully. He made some deep probing casts with a Mickey fin, but no luck. Inside he felt incredibly irritated and angry, and he let out a loud comment, "Son of a bitch, Beth! What is so dammed hard? Yes or no, damn it!"

Even as he said the words he felt the same aching love for her. He shoved his gear into the trunk in a sloppy manner then slammed the truck lid down. Before he got back to the car door he turned around, opened the trunk, and repacked everything neatly and shut the trunk lid again. He hated a mess. He drove down the path, throwing gravel and picking up speed as he went. As he left the trail, he pulled right out in front of a county road truck. The driver of the truck yelled a string of obscenities and offered him the middle finger with his left hand as far out the window as he could reach. Kirt furiously slowed down and made a quick U-turn to the driver of the truck. He waved at the driver and gestured for him to stop. The truck driver pulled over. Kirt got out of his car and walked toward the driver's side of the truck. As he walked up he yelled, "I'm so sorry," repeatedly. When he reached the truck, the driver had already gotten out.

"What the fuck, kid? What were you thinking?"

"I wasn't..." said Kirt. "I've had a lousy week, and I just wasn't thinking." He began to weep as he apologized again.

"Okay, kid. I get it. I appreciate you coming back here. Hey, aren't you Kirt Reinhart?"

"Yeah. How did you know?"

"I saw you at the Big Nine finals at Davison Country Club when you made those three birdies in a row and that eagle on the par five. I remember telling my little boy, 'There's a class act, no arrogance, no young hot shot B.S.,' " said the truck driver.

"Thanks," Kirt said, blowing his nose.

"Look, Kirt. I don't know what's eatin' ya', but I'd like to see you play again. I don't wanna read about you in the paper havin' wrapped your car around a tree or into another vehicle and how badly your parents are missing you. You got it? You have to focus on the road when you're driving in spite of what you may be feeling, or else get off the road. I'm gonna make an assumption from your behavior on the course that this is not typical for you. Go take your frustration out on some golf balls. Go hit the shit out of 'em," the driver said while placing his hand on Kirt's shoulder with a smile.

This man was hitting Kirt with a velvet-covered brick. Kirt got back into his car and tried to stop the pounding of his heart. His mouth was as dry as the road his was driving on.

Kirt pulled into a party store and bought a six-pack of six-ounce cokes and a bag of ice. He put the bottles inside the bag and set them on the floor. He then drove until he reached Clio Country Club. He pulled over to the south side of the lot, grabbed the coke and ice and opened his trunk. He took out a two iron and a bag of shag balls. He intended to practice a shot that was difficult for him but also perfect for hitting the ball around corners, doglegs, to the right. The tenth hole at the country club was a 347-yard dogleg to the right, and if you could fade a 230-yard shot off the tee, you were left with a perfect shot to the elevated green on the other side of the creek. Kirt had the ability to fire a two iron at least 230 yards; especially since the tee shot was downhill.

Kirt put twenty tees in a row into the ground just slightly above the grass, just enough to allow clean contact with the ball. He then took his 2 iron and positioned his feet and hands appropriately. Several shots in a row went bullet straight through the dogleg and out of bounds and into the fence along Field road. A few of his shots went over the fence onto the gravel road and bounced high into the air landing who knows where. Finally, he began to hit some correctly. He wanted to feel confident that he could hit the shot correctly at least eighty percent off the time. He stepped aside when a group was making the turn and needed the tee.

"Hey, Kirt. What's up?" Said Doctor Bruckner.

"Hey, Doctor Bruckner. I've been practicing off ten here, and I just wanted to warn you to make sure you know which ball you're playing with. I haven't shagged them yet. I didn't think there would be any folks out here tonight because of the Football game," said Kirt.

"No problem," said the jovial Doctor. "I'm not sure we will make it out as far as you anyway," he said in mock modesty and with a wink that only some can pull off and still be perceived as genuine.

Kirt knew darn well that any one of the "seniors" in this foursome could easily reach that corner. While Kirt and the guys were talking, a couple of young helpers, Jacob Brown and Danny Barnes, came bounding up the fairway. They jumped the field road fence and were running toward them. They were closely watching Kirt and already started to pick up most of his balls. Their pockets were stuffed, front to back.

"Well, there we go, Kirt. Jakey and Danny are on the job," said Doctor Bruckner.

Kirt watched as Doc watched the boys come up. Doc was a wonderful GP and Obstetrician, and probably delivered half of the folks born in Clio over the last forty years. Doctor Bruckner had a smile and a manner that instantly created trust, and his care over time confirmed that trust was well placed. Kirt smiled and watched as the two young boys run up the left side of the fairway with his practice balls in their pockets. Kirt had often paid the boys to shag balls for him. They were best buddies, neighbors and both were twelve years old and *seriously* going on thirteen. They were what used to be called, "all boy": full of energy with only two settings: on or off. Jacob and Danny were either awake and active, or sleeping and dead to the world. Kirt really liked them. "They are like a couple of chipmunks," he'd say about them. "They chatter all day and never stand still." The boys were also quite polite and not just when trying to impress adults.

"Hey, Kirt! Ya' need a couple a shaggers?" Asked Jacob and Danny.

Kirt smiled and laughed to himself as the boys came closer, "Guys, let's let the Doc's group get off first. You guys want a grape drink?"

"Yeah, Kirt! But we ain't got no money," said Jacob, the usual spokesman.

Kirt could not stop smiling, "You haven't got any money? Here, take this," handing them a few dollars. "And bring me back a couple hotdogs with mustard and onions. You guys want a dog too?"

"Nah, we just ate a couple of boxes of thin mint cookies from Jake's freezer," said Danny. The boys ran off to the clubhouse grill and were back in minutes with the drinks and Kirt's hot dogs.

"Okay, guys. I'll hit these down. I've got about thirty, no exactly thirty here I'm gonna tee up. I'll give you a twenty-five cents each for the balls, and twenty-five cents any other ball you can find down there in the creek and in the weeds along the fence," Kirt proposed.

The boys looked eager and ran down to the dogleg with the drinks in their hands. It was about 6:00 pm, and the last warm gusts of late summer were blowing across the fairway from the west. There's no other tree in the world whose leaves truly rustle like the poplar. Kirt could hear the rustle, and felt relaxed by their soothing, comforting sound. There were dozens of the poplars off to the left of the fairway. There were also called cottonwoods by the locals. Their cottony molt, which they shed every summer, turned the grass white as well as cars and buildings. The whitish cottony substance would decompose, and for a while left a brownish mess until they completely rot into the ground. Kirt hated when the cotton covered a lake or a favorite stream. It stuck to the fly line like glue, and was a pain in the ass to remove. He loved the sound they made though, and sometimes when heading back to a lake or stream he would come across a massive grove of them. These groves could cover acres with hundreds, if not thousands, of cotton reacting to every breeze; the collective rustle was incredible to hear. Although it could be extremely loud, it was never caustic; always soothing. It sounded to him like hundreds of mother's comforting their children saying that everything would be all right. Kirt began to hit each shot, taking a couple of minutes between each one. The boys didn't miss one. The "chipmunks" brought the balls back and Kirt had them retrieve another thirty. Once again, he set them up methodically, but this time taking less time between each shot. Toward the end of the line, Kirt was grooving in a nice willful fade to the right hand dogleg. It kept his mind off of meeting Beth, and was more soothing than he thought it would be. The boys came bounding back up the fairway with all of his balls and a couple dozen brand new ones that others had lost. Kirt paid the boys what he owed them and said, "Refills guys?"

"Yeah, Kirt! The big ones?" They asked.

"Sure! Make it three more big ones, one for me too." Kirt handed them a five-dollar bill, and walked over to the bench near the tee and sat down. Within moments, the boys were back.

"Here's the change, Kirt," said Danny.

"You guys keep it."

"Alright, Thanks!" They said in unison.

"No problem, guys. I think these new balls you brought me aren't older than a week or so. They are still pretty white. You two should shag as many of these as you can and ask Mr. Hipple if you could sell them in his front yard. He's so close to the course, I bet you'd sell 'em all," Kirt suggested.

"You think so, Kirt? Really?"

"Yeah, I know so! And if I were you guys, I'd pick up all the beer and pop bottles and cans too."

"That's a good idea, Kirt. I knew it was a good idea, but I guess I was just too lazy to go get 'em," said Jacob.

"Hey, Kirt. Do you think they would give us a quarter for every ball?" Danny asked.

"Yeah, but you gotta clean them up and separate the best from the rest."

"Do you think we could get enough to buy a three speed bike?" Jacob asked.

"How much do they cost guys?"

"About sixty smackers! At least that's what the metal flake green one costs that I want."

"So you guys would need a hundred and twenty dollars."

"Yeah, I guess so," said Jacob.

"Well, figure it out backwards. You'd need four balls for every one dollar. So what is that? How many balls would you need to sell to make a hundred and twenty?"

Beth pulled into the Clio Country Club driveway, causing the gravel to crunch and pop under the weight of the heavy Electra 225. While her parents were out of town she decided to have her own car tuned up and generally prepped for winter. So she was driving their car tonight with all the windows down. She noticed the different sound the big Buick made on the gravel from her smaller Chevette. She was so anxious to talk to Kirt, she hardly noticed as two White-Tailed Deer leapt in front of her car. She jammed on the brakes just as they both cleared her left front bumper. Startled, she sat there for a few moments to settle down. She hated the sheer numbers of these animals; they jumped in front of cars, ate everyone's gardens and plants, and were an all around nuisance. As beautiful as they were, she did enjoy seeing their bodies draped across the hood of some hunter's car. The upcoming hunting season would thin the herd for another year and yet their numbers kept growing. She couldn't understand why people went up north to hunt when they could sit on their back porch and pick them off. Beth didn't know what was worse, the deer herds or the massive amount of goose crap around the ponds on the golf course, or the way they fouled the swimming holes in the area. Normally she did not dwell on the subject, but this sudden miss pissed her off. She wanted them better managed and not eradicated because she loved to see them in the wild. Because of all the farms and the limited hunting in the area, the animals were thriving beyond reason. To help calm herself, she remembered the time she found a fawn in her field behind her house. The animal had been wounded somehow in the hindquarters. She and her dad took the fawn to the vet and she nursed it back to health until it was ready to be released. Summer, the name she gave the fawn, continued to hang around the house for a long time until she was likely mated and she left the area. Summer had beautiful eyes, and Beth would sleep with the fawn in the old chicken coop. Summer would lay her head on Beth's chest and fall asleep. The warmth of Summer's body kept Beth so warm that she only needed a blanket over her feet to sleep. Once Beth learned to drive, some of the romance wore off. Kirt loved to hunt and so did she, but neither one of them shot deer because they did not like venison. Their hunting was confined to upland birds.

Continuing down the long driveway, she reached the last curve before entering the parking lot. She looked to her left and noticed Kirt and the two boys on the bench talking and laughing. She slowed down so that the car was in a position where the gap between the large spruce trees was in alignment with the driver's window and both ends of the car were hidden by the pines. The light was fading and the last warm days were almost over. The air was dry, thin and clear. She could hear them talking but unable to make out the words. She heard inflections and changes in tone and lots of laughter. The difference between the deeper timber of Kirt's voice and the boy's still boyish voices was distinct. *He's such a sweetheart,* she said to herself. *Oh man. Those boys are in heaven right now. Kirt is being so nice to them. I don't think he knows how much it means to those boys for him to give them this kind of attention.* She thought of so many young men who would not give these boys the time of day. *God bless him. Thankfully he's not like most guys.* She sat for ten minutes or so and listened to the drifting laughter. She found it very comforting and very cheery. Finally, she pulled around the corner and drove into the parking lot. Kirt's attention was then diverted to the Electra 225 and he started to ignore it until he saw Beth step out. It was obvious Kirt was now paying attention.

"Wooooo! Who's that, Kirt? Your old lady?" Said Jacob, trying to sound hip.

"Jacob, that's no way to describe a woman. No, she's not my 'old Lady,' she's my friend."

"That's just Beth," said Danny.

"Just Beth? She is smoking! Said Jacob.

Kirt looked at Jacob and started laughing as he tried out this new word, "She's smoking, alright."

"Hey, guys. Looks like trouble over here to me," said Beth.

"Oh nothing much," said Jacob. "We're just commenting on how much steam you make coming across the gravel."

"Jake!" Kirt said sternly, while trying not to laugh.

"Oh! I see somebody's been watching too much TV," said Beth.

"Were just jokin' with you, Beth," said Jacob.

"Well, Okay, and thank you for the compliment. But if I were you guys, I'd be keeping my eye on Janie Biglow. She'll be smoking before you know it."

"Really? Ya' really think so?" Said Danny, not quite getting it.

"Yes, I do, and if you're not paying attention some other guy will be," she said smiling.

"Hey, Beth. Us guys were just planning a business where Danny and I pick up all the golf balls and beer and pop cans and sell them in Mr. Hipple's yard," Jacob explained. "Ya' think that would work?"

"You bet I do! I know it will… Ya' know why?"

"No," said the boys.

"Because Kirt and I used to do that every summer, and we cleaned up. We always had extra money. We bought a Go-kart one summer."

"You never told us that, Kirt!" Said Danny.

"No, I didn't," Kirt said smiling.

"So you guys, I mean you and Beth, did that every summer?" Jacob asked.

"Yes! We did when we were eleven, twelve, thirteen, fourteen, and fifteen. We would pick up some part time work."

"Soo, Kirt, my man, you were close enough to pay attention when she started to smoke," Jacob laughed at his own joke and the rest joined in.

"You guys are gonna be a couple of heartbreakers," said Beth. She leaned over and gave each a kiss on the forehead. "You two better get home, it's getting dark."

"Yeah, we better," they said, and ran off down the fairway toward home, joking and laughing as they went.

"Listen to them," Beth said. "The little buggers! Those boys love you, Kirt."

"Yeah, they're good kids…I guess I'm pretty attached to them, too."

Beth sat down next to him on the bench. "Kirt, I've thought a lot about what you said last Friday. I've been thinking about almost nothing else. I know I probably seemed strange to you last week, asking you to touch me, and then running off. It's just that I have always seen you as my best friend, not my lover. Over the last few years my friends have asked me if we were together but it didn't seem right somehow. There were times when I could look at you and feel, well, feel something beyond friendship, but I didn't know how that would work, or if it should. I have thought about you as more of a friend, but I always put those other ideas aside thinking I maybe shouldn't go there."

"Beth, it's not about having the right or even if it was, you do have the right."

"I know I do. I guess I had heard how a woman finds her husband at an older age after they have had time to look around to meet other people, ya' know?"

"Yes, I do. Like, if I were to hook up with the first woman I ever fell for, I might miss out on a better one down the road. I do think, in most cases, that's true. But for me, I'va always wanted a beautiful woman, a kind and generous woman, a strong and confident woman, a smart and adventurous woman… If I wait any longer to find what I want, I will miss the fact that you're already here. I got lucky, Beth. I found my special woman now."

Tearing up Beth said, "Did you just make that up?"

"Make up what? Damn it, Beth. That's how I feel about us."

Beth leaned over and kissed him like he had never been kissed. He did not want it to end. He was trying to remember every element of the kiss so he could recreate it in his mind later.

"Let me stay like this," he streamed out a prayer.

"I love the fact that all of this just rolled off of your lips, your gorgeous, irresistible lips." She continued to kiss him and then pulled his head back. "I love you, Kirt. I got lucky early too."

Kirt's eyes began to float upward and he passed out falling backwards on to the bench. Beth struggled to make sure he did not hit his head on the way down. She moved off the bench and put his feet up on the armrest. She pulled off her sweatshirt, folded it and put it under his feet. Under the sweatshirt she wore a sports top with light support built in. Her bare arms and shoulders looked lean and strong. Her breasts firm and of moderate size. She leaned back and let out a yell. The muscles in her neck and down her back strained to heighten her voice. Two men ran out of the clubhouse to see what was wrong.

"Oh, Doctor Bruckner! I'm so glad you're here. Kirt just passed out."

"Were you two eating anything, Beth?"

"No, we were just talking and he passed out."

"Good you elevated his feet."

"Just like you taught us."

"Somebody actually paid attention," he smiled.

"Hey, Bud. Go into the locker room and bring me my bag," said Doctor Bruckner.

Bud ran off and was back very quickly. "Here ya' go, Doc."

Dr Bruckner pulled out a capsule of smelling salts and passed it under Kirt's nose. Kirt sputtered and woke up with a confused look in his eyes. "What did you say, Beth?" He fumbled out the words.

"You passed out and Doctor Bruckner brought you back."

"Why the hell would I pass out? I'm not sick."

"We're you two fighting or something? Arguing?" Doctor Bruckner asked.

"No, no. We were just talking," said Beth.

"About what?" Doc persisted.

A little embarrassed and in a softer tone Beth said, "We were talking about how we feel about each other…"

"Oh? How so? How *do* you feel about each other?"

"Hey Doc, that's a little personal isn't it?" Said Kirt.

"It's necessary that I know, Kirt."

"We love each other!" Beth blurted out.

The story of his early life with Beth began to slow down, not as raced as before. Kirt let the story run its course.

"Was this the first time you two shared this?" Doctor Bruckner asked.

"Well, not really. Kirt told me how much he loved me last Friday, and I just had to think about it for a while. I just told him tonight that I love him too," said Beth.

Uncharacteristically Doc said, "Holy shit! A whole week of anxiety released in one night, eh Kirt?" Doc was laughing slightly, "Look. Your mind had your body in a knot all week, and from what I have observed over the last year or so, you've been pining over this lovely young lady for longer than a week. Everything just needed to snap into place again. I doubt there is anything else going on here but that. Stop by the office tomorrow and we can double check, but you're a horse, for cryin' out loud! Odds are very high it's just a case of anxiety."

"Wait, you've seen this before Doc?" Kirt asked.

"Oh, hell yes. I've seen brides and grooms pass out, fathers at the sight of their newborns, parents at their child's wedding. It happens, and it just happened to you." Doctor Bruckner smiled a comforting smile, and looked at the two of them. "About damn time, too. I was wondering how long before you two came together. You two are slow. I told my wife Jamie how much I loved her when I was fifteen. We've been married thirty-five years now, and together for forty-five. Good for you two, good for you." Doc kissed Beth on the cheek and gave Kirt a one-armed hug around the neck, and walked toward the clubhouse.

Beth helped Kirt to a stand, "You really do love me, don't you?" She smiled, her dimples appearing.

"What's next? What do we do now?" Said Kirt.

"We keep going on as we always have, but we add romance and some physical stuff," she said with a lilt. "If you get into that big Buick with me we can get started right now!"

"I don't want to be too forward, Beth, but would it be alright if I hold your breast again?"

"You better," she said. "And not over my sweatshirt this time."

"You smell great, Beth. What are you wearing?"

"Nothing. I just took a quick shower before I came over."

"We should bottle it and sell it at Saks. On second thought, no, it's all mine," and he kissed her on her freckled cheek. They walked to the car with their arms around each other.

~

Kirt's narration in his mind of their story slowed to a normal pace. He felt more peaceful. He decided the little reduction in medication he self-prescribed was never going to work. He took his medication as directed by his physician and went to sleep; deep and restful sleep. Never again did he ever experience racing thoughts. He was deeply thankful for it.

AGENT WILLIAMS

Agent Williams was able to get some Intel from his friends in New York City. The guy Ivy and Vincent were trying to hit had held back an estimated one to three million dollars over the last twenty years. His name was Nicholas Petro. He was not a made guy. He collected the monies from two heroin and crack traffic channels in the Northeast and the upper Midwest. His job was to confirm the numbers going out and coming in. He then would take the profits to Michael way out on Long Island. Stringini cut Nick in at two percent, which usually netted Nick about two thousand twice a month. Nick wasn't getting wealthy, but he had a great lifestyle and of course no taxes. Stringini trusted him completely. Even let him stay overnight at his house. He let him play golf with him too. Stringini was a member at Shinnecock Hills Golf Club and Nick relished the days he spent there. Stringini's kids loved Nick, and pressed him often to cook lamb over an open fire pit in the style of his Greek ancestors. One time the kid's pet, Brittany, had gone way down onto the shore and they couldn't find him. Stringini looked at Nick and said, "Are you sure you're cookin' lamb over there?" They still think it's funny. However, Nick was holding back about another one percent or less each pick up. He figured the small amount would not be noticed and besides, who would Stringini believe? Nick or some schmuck down the line who Nick would blame for the shortfall? There were always screw-ups he could blame if he needed to. He got away with it for a long time.

He kept the money in three different banks in three different safety deposits under three different names. He planned on disappearing with the money when he reached forty. What happened was one of the distributors got to talking with the others and starting keeping his own records regarding what they gave Nick collectively. This distributor was tight with Stringini's accountant and let him know what the totals were. They never matched but the accountant allowed for a little fudging down the line so he was not too alarmed. After several years of consistent shortfall, he decided he'd better approach with the information no matter how small the amount. Stringini confronted Nick and Nick swore on his kids that he wasn't doing it.

"You know me Mr. S, I wouldn't do that. Somebody down the line is skimmin' a little or maybe they are all skimmin' a little. Never more than a few bucks, which you told me not to worry about. Probably party money, a little celebratin' goin on." Stringini asked Nick for his books anyway. Stringini told Nick and the accountant that it was probably a few bucks all the guys were takin', which didn't concern him too much. On the side, Stringini told the accountant to continue to double-check each entry the guys in the field said they were giving Nick. Nick spent that day playing eighteen with Mr. S. He rested well and in the morning left the Stringini's home, stopping on his way at every safety deposit box and put his get-out-of-town plan into action.

Two weeks later, Stringini figured out what was happening and started to cry like a little baby. The betrayal was felt deeply. His kids were devastated that Nick would turn on their daddy. Stringini was as genuinely hurt as that kind of animal can be. He called Ivy and the hunt was on. Nick figured that anyone looking for him would figure him to be outside the country by now. He bought a used Mercedes under an assumed name and headed west, stopping at small hotels in small towns and paying for everything in cash. He dumped his used Mercedes, bought another used car, dumped that, and bought the Bonneville in Clarence Center. He had a stack of forged papers and passports designed just for this situation. He was quite confident he had eluded them.

CAL DROPS HIS PRIDE

Cal hobbled from the kitchen into the living room.

"Did you see the message that Guy called?" Cal's wife asked.

"Yeah, so what?" He said.

"Damn it, Cal! You call him and get over this right now. I won't let you sit there and wallow in self-pity. Holding a grudge against your best friend."

"My best friend…" He was not allowed to talk as she interrupted.

"Yes, your best friend, who shot off your left nut and put the bullet in your thigh. You still have one nut left. You have little pain there and your leg is recovering nicely. Your equipment is working great, even when you are not fully recovered," she smiled. "And all will be well."

"You really think my wedding tackle is working well?" It was a question borne of insecurity.

"Yes, I do. Great as ever! So shut off the incessant whining and call Guy."

"He knows better than to fire a weapon when someone could get hit in a cross fire," said Cal.

"He screwed up, everyone does. You guys caught the bastards, received commendations and you're still alive. I don't care if it hadn't been a tense situation, but it was. *Everyone* screws up, Cal, even you. He didn't do it without cause. He was afraid the Yemenite might set off a bomb and blow *you* and the drugs all over the parking lot, so give it up." Except for the smile regarding his sexual prowess, her face remained full of blood; the veins in her neck and forehead ballooning. She was pissed and disappointed. Her disappointment in his character hurt more than her anger.

"Okay, I'll call him. Where is he anyway?"

"Up north. Traverse I think."

Cal called Guy and Guy answered. "Guy, we need to talk about this."

"Great, I was hoping you would call."

"Why didn't you call me?"

"I thought you made it clear you didn't want to speak with me, so I was just honoring your wish."

"Yeah, well, I'm ready to talk again."

"Good."

"I'm sorry, Guy. I should have forgiven you sooner, I was so pissed. But I do understand how the accident could have happened." This was the first acknowledgement from Cal that it was an accident, and Guy felt relieved.

"I'm so glad to hear you say that, Cal. Damn I miss you guys."

"What are you doing up there by yourself anyway?" Cal asked.

"I just needed time to be alone without any outside voices to distract me."

"So are you ready to come back yet?

"Well…" Guy told him the whole Ivy story, and Cal sat mesmerized.

"You gotta be shittin' me, Guy. Only *you* could stumble across something like this," Cal laughed.

"You get that son of a bitch and get your ass home. I miss you too."

"I will. Give Connie and the kids a kiss for me."

Cal hung up.

"How did it go?" Asked Connie.

"Good. Let me tell you what he stumbled across."

"What did he say?"

He didn't get away with it. Connie needed word for word details before she was satisfied. He gave her the blow by blow. Then he told her about Ivy.

"Only Guy," she said, and left the room laughing.

Cal called Guy again.

"Hey you need any help?"

"No, the office is sending some agent who has experience with Ivy. He's from New York City, now in Chicago. So he is on his way up right now. I already got some help from the lab."

"Okay. If you need me just call."

"I will. Thanks, Cal."

"Hey, Guy. Try to have some fun up there, okay?"

"Yep." He hung up.

Cal lied back in his lounger, feeling much more at peace. He sipped on his Jameson's and fell asleep. Connie walked by, smiled and put an afghan over him. He looked relaxed and sexy again with the load lifted. She intended to take his last nut on another trial run later. She laid a note on top of his glass that read,

When you wake up come and get me, you sexy bastard!

I'm the one lying starkers on the bed.

ANOTHER STRIKE AT WALMART

The Walmart outside of town was the new town square. Everyone in Mesick gathered there to buy their goods and talk with friends. There were about fifteen handicap spots located directly in front of the entry doors. About twenty yards from the entry was a large garage door where large items were picked up or dropped off. This particular evening there were at least three cars parked in the handicapped area, and one in front of the pick- up door. None of the vehicle's owners were handicapped. Twenty minutes prior, a man in wrap- around sunglasses and a hoodie removed the valve stems of all four tires of all four vehicles. The man removed his hood and glasses; sat in his car several feet away, watching as one by one, the drivers entered their vehicles. The resulting frustration and coarse verbal outbursts caused the valve stem vigilante to bust with laughter. The laughter was too difficult to contain and everyone who saw the violators' situation were also laughing out loud. Vinny from the Mesick Inn walked into the store when he asked, "What's so funny?" Someone informed him and he too stopped to watch.

"I bet its Andy!"

"No, he wouldn't do that."

"Oh yeah? He is the only tow for miles and he gets seventy bucks every time he comes out to inflate these tires."

"He's too honest."

"Who is it then?"

The speculations continued. Vinny was laughing so hard at one of the valve stem vigilante's victims. The victim ran up to him shaking his fist, saying "This ain't funny, asshole!"

Vinny looked at the victim, "Yeah, yeah it is," and walked away. "Serves you right, you jerk!"

The sentiment expressed was exactly how the town felt about their valve stem vigilante. It was "community policing". It deterred folks from illegal parking, raised a few dollars for the towing truck and all at no cost to the town. Except for the few dollars the violators needed to spend in tow fees; no one got hurt. Vinny had stopped in to pick up a few items for Ivy. He grabbed a bag of squirrel nut chews, Ivy's favorite, a copy of the National Review and the

American Standard and a package of turkey jerky. As he exited, he saw the crowd pointing and laughing at the victims of the valve stem vigilante. Asking what had happened he received the whole story from an old river guide.

Bunch of rubes, thought Vinny. *Ivy, let's just get the job done and get the hell out of here.*

THE BIRTH OF THE VIGILANTE

It pissed him off. It gave him the idea. There at the end of the lane was a Mercedes parked in the "no parking zone" just off the parking line nearest the entrance to Hudson's at Somerset mall. The car blocked half of the open lane, allowing for only one car at a time to pass. He was in a hurry, and just needed to pick up an altered suit that he purchased a week ago. He allowed car after car to pass through the narrow opening as he sat, stewing in his accumulated anger. "Shit!" He said. He parked his car at the far end of the lot and stomped his way into the store office.

"I want to speak to the security manager."

"What is the nature of your concern, sir?" Asked a helpful and beautiful young black woman with British diction.

Good strategy, he thought. *Put the pretty lady up front to defuse the angry customer.*

He played along. Looking at her name plate he said, "Julie, there is a car parked in the 'no parking zone' at the end of the parking lane by the front door off of Big Beaver. It's blocking all the traffic. It could cause an accident."

Julie smiled and her deep brown eyes lit up, "A racing green Mercedes?"

"Yes!"

Julie picked up a radio and called for James, the manager, to come to the front desk, "Check the fourteenth lot camera, our Mercedes is there again."

"You know who this is, Julie?" he said.

"Yes, it's a VIP customer who thinks a little too highly of herself."

"Okay, well thanks."

Something didn't seem right to him so he walked back out to the parking lot, got in his car and found a parking space across from where the Mercedes sat. After a half hour or so he saw an attractive middle-aged white woman walking toward the Mercedes. She got in and drove off.

What the hell was that? He thought. *Didn't anyone chastise her or was she just done shopping?* He got out and went back into the store and headed for the manager's office.

"Did you find her?" He asked James the manager.

"No," he said.

"Did you wait for her to go back to her car?"

"No," James said. "I don't' have time to wait."

"But you do have time to sit here and talk to Julie, right?"

James looked a little embarrassed but said, "It's none of your damned business what I do with my time."

"James, you're either afraid to confront her or a lazy idiot, but she just drove off and she will be back again parking in 'no parking zones' as long as no one here does anything."

It didn't penetrate the entitled mind of James, not even an inch. As he drove away, he began to think of ways he could deliver a little justice to people like this without physically hurting them or doing any property damage. He considered piercing tires, but that was too destructive, putting stickers on their windshields, but that imposed no hardship on the offender. He simply had enough. He now understood what, "Being so mad you can't see straight," meant. This was just one of hundreds of such parking violations he had witnessed over the last few years. He had witnessed people parking in handicapped spots over the last few years. People with handicapped signs hanging from their windshields, who were obviously not handicapped, but parking in handicapped spots anyway, people double parking, cars parked at the ends of lanes at the movie theatre, restaurants, and the mall, people parking on the grass near the front door of events or stores. No one ever seemed to be ticketed or towed away as far as he could see. This was his new mission, to put a hurt on the violators without damaging their person or property. He settled on the idea of pulling valve stems out of their tires. Pulling out the stems would deflate the tires quickly. He would need to pull at least two stems per vehicle because if you only pulled one they could use their spare and drive off. If you pull two or three or even four they would have to call road service, pay a fee and lose time. His goal was four but he often settled for two. If word got out that this was happening to violators, maybe the violations would stop their arrogant behavior.

As his pulling prowess became more refined, he was able to pull a couple under sixty seconds. He always wore gloves, an oversized hoodie and black wrap-around sunglasses in the daytime. He enjoyed the minor justice and it soon became a game that he enjoyed maybe a little too much. He would drive around town looking for violators. The best part of the game was when he would sit some distance away and watch for the violator return to their car. Their reaction was always some form of anger and when they spotted the pulled stems sitting by the tires they really became apoplectic. Most of them didn't even know what a valve stem was so they remained puzzled. He found it funny as hell. When road service would show up to replace the stems and blowup the tires, they were embarrassed, as it was obvious the valve stem vigilante caught them. Some of them looked embarrassed when road service showed up, but others continued to rant and rave. He figured it was all helpful and good entertainment. He is still active and is even spawning copycats, which also makes him happy.

TRAILING NICK

"The trace on that car says it's legitimate; bought by a guy named Carol Garsen from Clarence Center, New York," said the researcher.

"Where did he buy it?" Asked Sheriff Williams.

"At a Buick dealership near there. He bought it three weeks ago."

"I know what your thinking, and I already have a guy checking on the description of the buyer."

"Great, thanks."

Sheriff Williams hung up and called Cy.

"Cy, Sheriff Williams. Good…Well, thanks. Hey Cy, what does that guy look like? Yeah, the guy we were talking about, from New York."

"He's clean shaven, whole head shaven like they do now. About 5'11" with a small pot belly. Oh yeah, he's got some pretty big hands," said Cy.

"Big hands, how so?"

"Yeah, really big, like twice the size of a normal guy. He reminded me of Stanley Tucci, you know that great actor we saw in that restaurant movie? What was that? Oh yeah, Big Night."

"Oh yeah, he's great. Well that's a pretty good picture. Thanks, Cy," said Sheriff Williams.

Sheriff got off the phone, and called the researcher back. "The Buick Salesman says the guy looked like Stanley Tucci with big hands," said the researcher.

"That's the way Cy described him too," said Sheriff Williams. "It could be Nick. He could have shaved his head."

Big hands? To himself, the Sheriff pondered. *This Garsen could be an alias. This Nick is supposed to be in great shape though, no pot belly. Could have a fake belly like those actresses playing pregnant. He's got to be pretty convincing to have fooled for so long.*

NICK'S GETAWAY PLAN

"That's right, Jim Phillips, 1178 Nighingale Lane, Bloomfield, Michigan…Okay. Traverse City, Northwest flight 131 to Houghton, Michigan and then to Bangor, Maine. Thank you." Nick hung up the phone.

He was only three days away from total freedom. Along the way west he had wired his money from several banks to a Costa Rican bank and kept a hundred thousand in his pocket. He intended to fly from Bangor under another alias to Los Angeles and then under another to San Jose, Costa Rica. He had purchased some property along the coast and he planned on growing fruit and settle down. He wouldn't make it, of course. Ivy never missed his mark.

~

"Vinny! What did you find out?" Ivy asked.

"Where the hell are you, Ivy? I've been lookin' all over for ya'."

"It's a long story, Vinny. I've been in a hospital and now I've got this FBI agent, an old high school friend…"

"A what?"

"He's a guy I went to high school with. He recognized me. Like I said, long story. I'll fill you in later. What did you find out?"

"Nick's been stayin' at the Lodge across the road. Ya' know the one by the river, that fishing lodge? Ya' won't believe it but the son of a bitch is still using the 'Carol' look and shaved his head, all of it. He's wearin', 'swear ta' God…" Vinny was bending over trying to prevent laughing. "He's got a fake pot belly! Funniest damn thing. He looks like that Tucci guy, ya know that actor from that restaurant movie? The one with the other Italian looking guy you said was really a camel jockey, Lebanese guy? 'Looks a lot like 'em but those big meat hooks gave 'em away."

"Where is he now?"

"I saw him last night at that friggin' Walmart. He bought one of those throwaway cell phones. I tried to follow him out the store, but there was this outbreak a rubes."

"What?"

"Ya' know, a bunch of those rubes you call Jack Pine savages? That valve stem vigilante guy was entertaining them all. I'm telling ya' Ivy, ya' gotta get us outta here. They got no good food here and the main entertainment is some crazy son of a bitch letting the air outta people's tires."

Ivy starting laughing again as he thought about the guy in the truck with the air out of his tires.

"Is he still driving the Bonneville?"

"I guess, but the car ain't over at the fishing place."

"Keep an eye out. I'm sure he'll come back. I'll be there in about an hour or so."

"Okay, Ivy."

Ivy hung up and pulled out a list of names, alias's and fakes IDs that Herbie had made for Nick. Herbie gave Ivy the list just before Ivy slit his throat.

He's gonna make a break out of the country soon, Ivy thought to himself. *I better get this over with today.* He picked up his cell and called Vincent back.

"Vinny. We are going to have to get this done today, in the daytime. When he comes back we need to be there to greet him. Go break in and I'll be there soon. Do you have the hot shot?"

"Yeah, should I just give it to 'em then if he comes back before you get here?"

"No. Stringini wants me to play the video for him before he goes out. Stringini was really pissed and wants Nick to know it."

"What video?"

"The one he gave me."

"'Ya' didn't tell me about that," said Vinny.

"I know…"

As Ivy drove back to the Feather and Hook, he began to consider his options. *Probably the best thing would be a couples of needles in the jugular, let him bleed out slowly while the video is playing. Have to tape his mouth shut. Damn Stringini and his stupid demands. If I could just go in and get out without all this vengeance crap. I hate this kind of hit.*

Ivy preferred to do it quietly and as painless as possible. He opened his bag and checked to make sure the camera was there. While all this was going down, Stringini wanted a video made. This demand also concerned Ivy because the job would be on tape and could, no matter how careful he was, provide his image. Anybody could get a hold of it, but Mr. S promised he would watch it and incinerate it. He had no choice but to trust him. To Stringini, Ivy was just another flunky. *Damn*, he hated this.

~

Guy didn't know what to do. Should he involve the agency officially in this now? He mulled it over and thought he had better call it in. He called his boss in Detroit who promptly told him what was going on with Agent Williams from Chicago and his past experience with Ivy in New York. He also told him of the Sheriff's involvement.

Ivy pulled into the bank parking lot a couple of blocks away from the Feathered Hook. With his LL Bean attire and his backpack he hoped to blend in. He walked up to the small cabin number eleven. The door was open. Vincent was sitting there with latex gloves on.

"What the hell, Vinny! Put these on," Ivy handed him a pair of leather gloves. "Did anybody see you with those latex on?"

"No, nobody saw me. I put 'em on inside, like ya' taught me."

"Those latex say, 'hey, look at me! I'm some kind of killer!' Stop using the damn things. Wear leather. Besides, you know how easily those things tear?"

"I tell ya' nobody saw me," said Vinny.

"What is it with you and the latex, huh? You got some kind of fetish I should know about? Those things bring you fond memories of your proctology visits?"

"Okay, okay! I won't use 'em anymore." To himself, Vinny muttered, "Proctology visits."

"Hey, Ivy. What's up with the camera?"

Ivy set the camera up on a tripod. He positioned one of the metal-framed kitchen table chairs in front of the camera. He looked into the viewfinder to make sure there were no reflections of himself that might show up. He even duct taped the frame of the chair to prevent reflections. He did the same on any other reflective surface around or behind the chair. Then he took out the tape recorder and put it into a portable player. Next he pulled out a copy of Biblical Archeology from the backpack, threw Vinny a bottle of Pinch and sat down to wait for Nick.

FINDING NICK

"Are you sure?" Said Cy.

"Yes, I saw a man go into eleven and he was not Carol."

"What did he look like?"

"He had on khakis, flannel shirt and a backpack."

"How did he get in?"

"He just opened the door and walked in."

"Maybe Carol gave him a key or something?"

"No he didn't use a key, he just opened the door and walked in."

Cy picked up the phone and called Sheriff Wheeler. He explained the situation about the guy in eleven. The Sheriff told him to stay away from the cabin.

Sheriff Wheeler turned around and said to Williams, "Somebody's in Nick's cabin, and it ain't him. He just walked in, didn't use a key."

"What did he look like?"

"Cy said he was wearing Khakis, had blonde hair…"

"That's him, that's Ivy. He's gonna take Nick out today. We gotta get over there now."

Parking on the north side of the bank parking lot, Guy watched as Ivy walked back to the Lodge. He walked down the hill a little bit. The hill was a ridge that followed the river that flowed behind the lodge. Carefully, Guy moved just below the ridge, tracking Ivy as he went. From the back of the cabins, Guy could watch between the open spaces between the cabins to help him determine which Ivy had entered. When he was sure Ivy had entered eleven, he got down and crawled to the back door of the cabin. All of the blinds were drawn. He searched the back wall to see if he could find some opening in the old logs. He couldn't. Going around to the side he noticed a ventilation screen for the crawl space below the cabin. As quietly as he could, he pulled back the crawl space vent. It was ugly in there; spiders, varmints, who knew what. He crawled in, pulling the screen up as he went and then turned over on his back. Luckily the ground was almost pure sand. It was typical North Michigan sandy soil with almost no vegetation growing. Scooting along on his back, his face brushed into spider webs, one after another. Where the back door met the floor there was a gap, a small gap between the threshold and the floor. A stream of light shone down into the crawl space. He could see movement of light up through the floor and he was able to hear a few comments, but for the most part Ivy and his toady did not talk. He decided to take a riskier approach. He carefully pulled on a strip of wood coming off one of the logs that comprised the floor. The strip pulled off easily and Guy carefully threaded the strip up through the hole. If they noticed, he was in serious trouble here on his back like this. Guy threaded the strip behind the curtain on the back of the door. He pulled the strip to the right, hoping he could part the curtain enough to see what was going on from a better vantage point outside. He was able to make a gap of about one inch. Going back to the crawl space opening, he turned over on his belly. Quickly, he moved around to the back door. He could just barely see a camera on a tripod. To the side of the camera and slightly in front of it, he could see the outstretched legs of Ivy. Straight across he could see the front door. To his left he could see Vinny falling asleep in his overstuffed chair.

The camera, he thought. *Proof of the hit?* He waited over two hours. Whoever they were waiting for, obviously Ivy had no idea when he would return.

~

"When is this guy gonna come back?" Sheriff Williams said to agent Williams. The Sheriff and the agent had positioned themselves in a motor home parked across the street from the lodge. Sheriff picked up his phone to check. "Has anyone seen the Bonneville? No One? It's a rugged area he could be almost anywhere. Make sure the park rangers are aware of this. Hell, he could hide in the parks for a long time."

~

Nick decided his luck was not good. He picked up his chips and went to the window to cash out. The Turtle Bay Casino in Traverse City was a big draw on down state and local silver backs. Week after week, they came to blow some portion of their retirement income or the social security check. It was a social security magnet. Most of the population worked and paid social security taxes, which were then divided among the blue hairs and finally into the hands of some Indian tribe, or at least a tribe member fronting for a bunch of down state Anglos who were cashing in. Nick had frequented these Indian Casinos back in upstate New York and this one was not different. It was unbelievable how these otherwise intelligent people would throw away the social security checks their children and grandchildren were forced to pay them. He lost over five thousand and that was more than enough. He could play poker fairly well against even the pros in Atlantic City, but these amateurs were killing him; too unpredictable. He bought a corned beef sandwich and walked back to his car. The Bonney was parked under a stand of pines at the side of the lot. He pulled out onto M-72 and then down US-31 South on his way back to the lodge. Tomorrow morning, he was out of here. He loved the west bay in Traverse, the water reminded him of the Caribbean, shades of green and blue with the sound of gulls in the air. He felt peaceful and proud of himself. That son of a bitch Stringini wouldn't get another dime from him. *Imagine,* he thought. *I'm handling millions of dollars, risking my ass and the freakin' grease ball gives me a lousy two percent, while he lives like the king of Shinnecock.* He'd miss the kids though. It wasn't their fault their parents were pricks. *Oh well,* Nick thought. *I'll find myself some Chilean hottie and have a couple of my own. Yeah, Randy Carlisle, my new character, was gonna live it up in San Jose.* He planned on growing berries for export to the states. He had already purchased the land for two hundred and fifty thousand, a fraction of its value in the states. The land had sat there unclaimed by anyone for over seven years, and so the Costa Rican government sold it via auction. He was right about the value. The Del Monte Corporation bought the land for 3.5 million long after he was gone.

He finished off the sandwich before he hit Beulah. Remembering how good the cherry pie was at the Cherry Hut, he stopped and bought two more. He scarfed down an entire pie right there in the parking lot. He was uncomfortably full and lovin' it. On his way to the lodge, he stopped fast to avoid a whiyetail. The other cherry pie flew off the seat and splattered all over the dashboard and inside the front window. Nick was pissed, but then started to laugh. What the hell did he care? Trash the whole car for all he cared. He laughed so hard he had to stop the car for a few minutes. Life was getting pretty damn good.

THE MEETING

"Hey, Nick… Nice to see ya'," Vinny said as Nick tried to retreat from the cabin. Ivy hit him at the base of the head with a wine bottle. When Nick came to, he was duct taped and zip tied to the kitchen chair. The camera was running. Nick's mouth was taped shut. Ivy simply said, "Mr. S wants you to see this before you go, Nick…" Nick's face was covered with sweat and the veins in his neck and temples were throbbing. His eyes were widely fixed on the portable player as Ivy pressed the play button. The video started with images and sounds of Stringini's kids playing on the beach, then a shot of eighteen at Shinnecock Hills Golf Club. Finally, Stringini was sitting in a chair in his office. He looked almost human with the real tears flowing. "You broke my heart, Nicky. The kids hate you now," his voice broke. "I hate to do this, but ya' left me no choice. I don't care if I even get the money back, but nobody can steal from me. Nobody. Not even you, Nicky. This guy here is gonna make an example of you, and it's gonna hurt you, but not as much as you hurt me, Nicky. Good bye."

Ivy turned the player off. He stepped over to Nick and pulled a razor blade across his forehead. Blood started rolling down his face. Then Ivy skinned his right shoulder completely. Nick was straining to scream but the tape prevented him. He defecated and pissed his pants. Ivy slit both of Nick's Achilles tendons. Nick screamed and vomited hard enough to blow the duct tape loose where Vinny was standing.

"My god!" Said Vincent, "What the hell did you eat?" Across the front of Vinny and onto the floor, Nick blew chunks of cherries and corned beef. "Damn, Ivy. He stinks like hell."

Ivy precisely lacerated Nick's right jugular vein. At this point, Guy broke through the door. This was the moment Ivy was dreading ever since his first hit. He sliced Nick's throat and Vinny's too. Guy tried to stop him, but sliped on the vomit and fell onto Nick. He could see the resignation in Nick's eyes. It was too late for Nick, but not too late to catch Ivy, who already burst through the front door and ran toward the back. Guy slipped two more times trying to get up and out of the cabin. Ivy ran to his car and sped down M-115 heading for US-131. His only chance, he thought, was to get to a more populated area where he could ditch the car and steal another. He had a couple million squirreled away in the Caymans. He intended to get it and disappear if he could.

AGENT WILLIAMS AND THE SHERIFF

In the motor home, Agent Williams and Sheriff Wheeler saw Nick go in the cabin. Williams made his way to the front door of cabin eleven. When Ivy burst through the door, the door slammed into Agent Williams and he fell backwards, hitting his head on a large rock, a portion of which was exposed above the grass.

Seeing the fall out of the corner of his eye, once Guy got up, he made a quick check on Agent Williams. Sheriff Wheeler rushed over to check on him. Shouting into his radio as he made his way, Sheriff barked orders for EMS to get to the site fast. The EMS crew arrived shortly thereafter and pronounced Agent Williams dead. Sheriff held Williams' head in his arms and although he had just met him, he felt a deep loss.

"Who are you?" Sheriff Wheeler asked Guy.

"I'm Agent Veitengruber from Detroit. Believe it or not, I was up here on vacation when…"

Sheriff interrupted him, "Let's see your badge." Guy showed him his ID.

"Okay. We were expecting you. Go after the bastard now," said Sheriff.

Reaching to the left side of his belt, Sheriff pulled off a radio and threw it to Guy. "It's already set. Keep in touch." Then into his own radio, he said, "Shirley put an APB for a Silver…"

IVY RUNS FOR IT

As Guy flew down Mesick M-115 at over ninety-five miles an hour, he weaved himself around the slow moving traffic. The limit on highway 101 was fifty-five, two lanes and most of it was no passing. He could see Ivy weaving a mile or so ahead. The oncoming traffic made it damn near impossible to pass. The hills didn't help either. Coming up on a van, Guy almost hit it in the rear. As soon as he could, he passed them. The driver and the whole family were screaming and making obscene gestures as he passed. He could not keep up. Ivy had the advantage; Ivy didn't care much if he died. Passing a car into an oncoming semi he jerked back into his lane and watched in his rear view as the semi exploded into the trunk of a massive old white pine, and further penetrated the pine forest on that side of the road. The pines went up like gasoline and the prevailing westerly winds fanned the fire further east and south.

"Sheriff!" Guy radioed. "The son of a bitch drove a semi off the road and the pines are exploding."

Sheriff was stunned. He knew the consequences if this fire got out of control. "Thanks, Guy. I'll keep in touch. You keep following him, okay?"

"Okay," replied Guy.

The flames fed on the under bush like a dog on a hamburger. Pine fires were the worst as they generated high heat that would blow far ahead of the fire. Debris would rise and drift and if the debris riding the upside down, lying on its side "heat tornado" the debris caught fire and the fire would "jump" sometimes as far as a mile ahead starting everything below its path on fire. Sheriff had experienced this years ago when a fire caught the south side of M-72, east of Grayling, a mile in from the road. Sheriff Wheeler had watched as the flames from a mile south of M-72 jumped across the road, exploding the north so quickly that it was impossible to see how the north side fire even started. It was the high heat inversion causing the fire to leap, like an upside down tornado lying on its side. The trees left in the wake looked like expired matchsticks. It looked to Sheriff like a wave curling back where it had come from. The heat was beyond intense, and Sheriff spun around and headed west as fast as he could and did not stop until he got to Acme, forty miles away. The fire leveled over fifty square miles of forest and only stopped because a pounding thunderstorm calmed it enough for the fire fighters to do their job. He had hoped he'd never see anything like it again. Then he was just on vacation fly-fishing the Au Sable River. Now he was responsible for the folks of this county.

Three miles east of the fire, the Trillium Trails neighborhood began to buzz. Trillium was a full service retirement community complete with a well-appointed medical clinic. The native Trillium bordered every home and condo as well as the driveways. All of the other plants and trees were native as well, including a large border of white pine just like those burning three miles away. There were over three hundred residents at the compound and Sheriff acted decisively to move in the first responders and the DNR.

BAD BOY MAKES GOOD

Jack Berridge, the superintendent of the Trillium Center, was moving like a squirrel with his tail on fire. Within an hour and a half, he had set up the make shift gathering hall out on M-115. Jack grew up in Mesick, MI and was the neighborhood bad boy. His parents ran a small animal hospital catering to every kind of creature. They weren't rich by any means, but by Mesick standards they were. Jack had two other brothers, and from all appearances, things seemed normal at the Berridge household. Jack, however, allowed his base nature to control him for many years. When Jack was only fourteen, he and his friend John rode their bikes over to Maggie's house. Maggie and her girlfriend were sun bathing behind a tree house. The tree house was not in the tree but on the ground beside the tree. Everyone called it a tree house anyway. The tree house was a half a mile or so off the road and into the woods inside a clearing under a massive oak tree. The girls were just lying on blankets outside the shaded area of the tree. The boys stayed and talked for a few hours and generally just flirted back and forth. Maggie's friend Julie was a year older than all of them, so naturally Jack saw her as an older woman target. When it was clear that she did not have any intentions of returning his overtures, he became angry and wanted to leave. John, on the other hand, was totally taken with Maggie and didn't want to leave. Given that he was spending the night at Jack's house, he felt it best to leave. Halfway down the pathway back home, Jack turned to Jim and said, "Let's go rape 'em." John stood there in jaw hanging disbelief. "What the *hell* are you talking about?"

"I mean, they're out here all alone. Nobody is around. We could just, rape 'em." At this point, John looked into Jack's eyes and saw that he wasn't kidding.

"Jack, your full a shit. Let's just go home."

Jack protested and turned his bike around heading back to the tree house. He climbed onto the top of the house and watched as the girls turned over on their stomachs and undid the tops of their bathing suits. John couldn't believe it. He peddled back as fast as he could and yelled as loud as he could, "Hey, Jack! Get your ass back here!" Startled by the shout, the girls instinctively looked up, grabbing their tops as they did. Apparently having lost the element of surprise, Jack decided to give up the rape idea and instead just yelled out, "Hey, Julie! I think your left tit is bigger than your right one!" Julie, not to be outdone, yelled back "You perverted, sperm-eating bastard!" Jack jumped off the tree house and peddled back to John.

"What's the matter with you, man!" Screamed Jack.

"What in the HELL is the matter with *you*?" John screamed in his face.

John left and peddled home, and never spent another minute with Jack. John called Maggie to explain, which took him several attempts before she fully believed him. Maggie hated Jack after that for a very long time. Eventually, she came to love John and they were married. A few years later, Jack married another local beauty and a kind of bad girl herself. The problem was that Jack took to beating her on a regular basis, and found himself in jail for breaking her clavicle. When he got out, the court prevented him from seeing their daughter, Sherry, and Jack continued his tailspin through life. He had one redeeming value, though. He was a consummate mechanic and could fix anything, including as time went on, anything computer related. He landed in jail for his fourth time at the age of thirty-eight for accidently killing a man in a bar fight at the Oaken Keg. The fight was over a twenty-one year old woman who had been dating both men. Apparently, the other guy had a weak heart and the blows from Jack's fist sent him over the edge. He was sentenced to five to ten years for manslaughter and was released in five. While in jail, he had a jailhouse conversion and, like most jailhouse converts, no one believed him. He became an excellent mechanic and an all-round handy man. He opened his own business called In HIS Care. After several years of wonderful service to his customers and strong involvement with the local Lutheran church, folks started to believe his conversion. He had an easy way about him now and would share his faith in Christ with anyone. He became a hell of an apologist. He was self-taught to the degree that he could handle any objection to Christ. He was conversant in theology speak and could discuss his faith with anyone from the local grocery checkout guy, to the skeptical Anthropology professor, who spent his summers in town using Jack's service for all his repair needs. John, who ended up marrying Maggie, came to trust Jack again and became good friends before John died. Jack was the real thing and no one could deny it, even if they did not buy into Jack's Christianity. Jack chose to live in a tiny home with a bedroom, bath, kitchen and living room. He built it himself with used lumber and rebuilt utilities. He designed it in a Cape Cod style and the southern exposure allowed in a great deal of light through beautiful reclaimed leaded glass windows. It was somewhat passive solar and Jack had built-in heated floors before they became fashionable. He designed them with glass and plastic tubing imbedded into the concrete. He also had a geothermal system he himself designed and built. The property he lived on was in an isolated section of woods just east of town and he picked it up cheap from one of the residents at the Trillium, who had become quite fond of him. His home was listed in the Tiny Homes Magazine as one of the most beautiful and functional tiny homes in the country. One unique feature was that he had built a small room off the back that housed all the utilities giving him more living space. He was rightfully proud of the home. Because he lived frugally, most of his money went to pay for his daughter Sherry's education and she became a clinical psychiatric research fellow at the University of Michigan Hospital. Sherry had come to truly love her dad and was moved by his obvious desire to see her succeed.

"I made a mess of my life sweetheart, but I'll do everything I can to make sure you don't," Jack said to his daughter Sherry.

"Your life is very wonderful now, Dad, and that's all that matters, right?" Sherry replied.

"Right." He would say, while still harboring ill feelings of himself because of his past behavior.

Seeing the pain in her dad's eyes, "Stop it, Dad. Get off the cross. Christ already paid for your sins and you paid your debt to society. You owe it to Him to forget about 'em." She was a darling and he loved her without measure. His ex-wife was impressed with him as well and after several years, came to trust him again. He was reborn both in the here and now and in the hereafter. Trillium was in good hands, and Jack went to work quickly to take every action to protect the folks there from this latest fire.

MAGGIE TELLS HER DAD GOOD-BYE

Maggie helped the nurse ease her father into the shower. He sat down on a plastic chair with a seat like a toilet. In this manner he could wash himself; 'one of the few dignities he had left. He kept his underwear on until the ladies closed the shower door. Maggie had arranged for the nurse to be there four times a week at which time her dad got his bath and the nurse checked his vitals. He was dying.

"Maggie, when I get out, we need to talk about the will again."

"Okay, dad."

"The will, that damned will," whispered Maggie to the nurse. "It's all he ever wants to talk about. It gets to be a little morbid but I guess it gives him comfort. He wants to get it right. He doesn't have much to leave, but he wants to make sure me and the girls get it not the damned government."

"You're his only child, Maggie, and the girls are his whole world. He's always talking about you girls," the nurse said. "Yesterday he sent me a bunch of emails about Jane's award to study writing at that college in Scotland. He is so proud of her."

"I hope he isn't bombarding you with too much."

"No, Maggie. I like it. His letters are so wonderfully written. So much like people used to write. He uses such descriptive language and proper form. It's a delight, really."

"He's a charmer, that's for sure," smiled Maggie.

"Maggie, he's getting very weak. His blood work is coming back worse each time. He's severely anemic."

"Is he in any pain?"

"No, just very tired and it's likely the cancer will drag him down soon. He'll get so weak all he will do is sleep, and if he is in any pain we will use the opiates like we discussed."

"I wish he would go to the hospital, but he refuses."

"He'll be just fine right here. He really will," the nurse reassured her. "How's it going with the new guy, Maggie?"

"Better than I ever would have expected. I never saw myself falling in love again. When I lost John I just switched off the desire for any man. The girls became my world and they needed that. Helping them grow became my pleasure. I never did mind or care at all. Kirt is a wonderful surprise. I pray it continues to go well."

"Have you gotten, you know, physical?"

"Just necking like teenagers. We don't want to go any further. I'm so grateful that God sent me a solid man, a real adult. Neither one of us want to disappoint our Lord or ourselves. Besides, when I follow His laws it's because He has my best interest at heart. We will wait. But…" she said smiling. "It's damn hard, let me tell you!" The two women laughed.

"Our heads are in the clouds sometimes, but our feet are always on firm ground. So far it's a wonderful balance I never dreamed of having again."

"How's he doing with the grieving/depression?"

"I think it was harder for him because he has had to separate depression from standard grief. He was settling before he ever met me. I cannot imagine the pain of your mind betraying you. Imagine losing your whole family in one day. His parents are wonderful and very much in his corner. I met his pastor, great man, and his shrink, also great. They helped me understand what he has and how successfully he has dealt with it in the midst of the losses. They are amazed that he has come back to himself given his depression."

"Come back to himself?" Asked the nurse.

"Yes, sorry. When a clinically depressed person is not in the midst of a depression they are themselves. In Kirt's case, 'himself' is a very strong, grounded and sweet person. When he is depressed he is not himself. It would be like giving a diabetic an overdose of insulin. It affects their vision, heart rate, everything. When they come back to themselves, things return to normal. In fact, it feels so good to be normal that it can seem like elation for a while. He's a great guy."

"You're pretty great too, Maggie."

"Thank you."

"Ladies, I'm ready!" Said dad.

After the nurse and Maggie were done helping dad, Maggie sat down to review the will again. They finally settled on the last draft.

"Good night, dad," said Maggie.

"Maggie, I love you sweetheart, and I never stop thanking God for the girls you and John gave me. I will be going home soon and you know it. It's time and the Lord seems to be giving me a pretty graceful exit, eh?"

"Yes, He has . When you get there say hi to John."

"I will sweetie, but you know when I get there we'll all be there together. I'll zip out of time and space right to eternity."

"Always the theologian, dad. "

"Yep, you bet. Theology is life. Without my Christocentric trust I would have died long ago from lack of hope based on reasonable evidence."

Maggie smiled. Dad's faith was reasoned, based on a protracted spiritual fight; worked out and solid. He was right—he was going home.

"I'll still miss you, dad," she said while crying.

"I know you will, sweetheart, but not as those who have no hope. I have always left you in Christ's hands and when I'm gone, you'll still be there."

"Good night, dad."

"Good night, Maggie."

They were not their last words, but they were the clearest and Maggie was thankful for the time with her Dad, even as he grew weaker and left this world a few months later.

MAGGIE TRIES TO HELP CY

Maggie was not a complete stranger to the horror of murder. She had witnessed a rather grisly domestic murder as a child when her best friend's father shot his unfaithful wife and himself with a 12 gage pump shotgun loaded with buckshot. He fired four into his wife and one into his mouth. Actually, Maggie did not see anything but because she was spending the night with her friend she saw the results. Her friend was taken down state to live with her grandparents.

She peaked into cabin eleven and the mess that Ivy had left behind. She saw the vomit on the floor, Nick sitting slumped over in the old metal kitchen dinette chair and she stepped, actually she stumbled away, from the door way. She saw Vinny having bled out on the floor. She turned and looked at Cy with her eyebrows forced upward in an upside down V, and her forehead furrowed. Both simply shook their heads as Maggie walked away.

"They told me I could not touch anything until the forensics team was done and that a cleaning crew would come to clean up," Cy said.

"I'm glad they are cleaning it up, Cy. I don't think I would want to."

DON'T DRINK AND DRIVE

Ivy drove into the parking lot of Burger King across from Peninsula drive. Exiting his car, he began to stealth fully look into the windows of the cars in the lot. Bingo, a small Honda Civic with its doors unlocked looked hopeful. In a couple of minutes, Ivy had hotwired and started the car. He pulled out onto M-72 and across to Peninsula drive. Going north, he continued to look into his rear view mirror. Over the years, Ivy had perfected the ability to blend in and fade away whenever he found it necessary.

Driving down M-72, Guy noticed a police car and a man standing in the Burger King parking lot. He pulled into the lot. As he got out he heard, "It was right there and now it's gone. Somebody mustta stole my car."

"Excuse me sir, what color is your car? What year is it?" Asked Guy.

"Hey, wait a minute! Who are you?" The state patrolman asked.

Showing his badge, he said, "Guy Vietengruber. FBI Special Agent."

"Mr. Vietengruber, you're a little out of your normal jurisdiction, aren't you? How can we help?"

"Well, officer…" Guy looked at his shirt to see a nametag. "…Officer."

"Bob Marley. No jokes, please. Just call me Bob," said the Officer.

"Thanks, Bob. I will, and just call me Guy. Look, the car I was tailing is right over there and I bet my ass the *perp* took this man's car. He's a pretty bad character and has killed at least twelve people that I am aware of. We have been trying to find him for years. He's a regular on the list."

"Okay, Guy. How 'bout I check with everyone in the restaurant to see if anyone saw this blue civic pull out of here and in what direction?"

"Thanks, Bob. I'll stay out here and ask the folks in the bank branch over there."

"Sir, 'anything distinctive about your Civic?" Cy asked the man whose car was stolen.

"Name is also Bob," he smiled. "Bob Pingree. Yeah, the civic is a red Si and it goes like hell. I just had the rear and back windows tinted very dark."

"Any membership or political sticker on the car?" Asked Guy.

"Yep. Got a NRA sticker on the rear window and a Brass Roots sticker on the bumper. It's clean too, always keep it clean."

"Thank you, Bob. When Officer Bob gets out of the restaurant he will get the rest of your information. I hope like hell I can find out which direction it was headed in and maybe we can find it soon."

"Thanks Agent Guy," said Bob.

At that moment, Officer Bob came out of the restaurant with a male teenager. "Guy, this young man says he saw the car go up Peninsula."

"Great, 'your name son?"

"I'm Sandy. I saw the car go up Peninsula about ten minutes ago."

"Notice anything special about the car?" Guy asked.

"Yeah, that's one hot little Civic. Had to be one of the new Si's," said Sandy.

"Yeah, it is. Any stickers on the back you noticed?"

"Sure did. I saw an NRA sticker and something else, but I could not make that one out. The other one was definitely a NRA. I noticed it because my dad has one on our car."

"Thanks, Sandy, Officer Bob and Bob," Guy smiled. "Officer Bob, I need to find him right now. 'Catch up with you later."

"Here is my card, Guy. Just give me an update," said the Officer.

"Will do."

~

Heading up peninsula, Ivy noticed the vineyards and cherry orchards and took note of the small roads heading east or west. Halfway up the peninsula he came upon the Chateau Chantal, a vineyard and winery positioned up on a high hill with a road snaking along the side of the hill up to the Inn and tasting room. He turned into the Inn road and drove up the winding trail to the parking lot next to the Inn. While at the top, he looked out at the road to the south to see if he was still being followed. Ivy stood there for over twenty minutes and felt sure he had lost Guy. He decided to get a bottle of wine just to see what all the buzz was regarding the quality of the wine up here. He tried several and settled on the Riesling as it was a great wine and went well in hot weather. The buzz was justified; the wines were excellent. Ivy got back in the civic and started to drive back down the peninsula. He hoped to drive the Civic downstate somewhere, ditch it at some apartment building and steal another car, drive it to Pennsylvania and get a flight out of Pittsburg to New York. Glancing at the bay to his right, following a curve south of the Inn, he saw Guy sitting in a Crown Victoria watching for him to go by. Ivy pretended not to notice him, knowing that the Civic could never out run Guy's standard issue vehicle. Looking to his left he noticed a small road headed east. Quickly, he turned left hard and Guy followed suit. Ivy was approaching eighty miles an hour along the old paved road with Guy right on his rear. Guy knew where this road would lead and was counting on the Civic being unable to negotiate the sharp right turn in order to avoid going into the West arm of Grand Traverse Bay. They traversed several large hills and each time they came down the crest of one, their vehicles scraped across the bottom. The speed limit was forty-five miles an hour and the roads were patched so many times it felt like driving over a pile of giant Hershey kisses. Going up a very tall hill, Ivy noticed that as he came down the other side that at first he saw no ground, just miles of sky and some water. Coming down the other side, he saw a sharp right turn at the water's edge. Not quite the edge, but close enough to frighten the hell out of him. Coming down the hill, Guy backed off the gas as he watched to see the track of the Civic. Just as he had hoped, the Civic attempted the elbow right and slammed into a rock barrier just off the shoreline, tipping into the Bay. Guy sped up and stopped at the curve, while frantically calling Bob back in Traverse.

"Bob Marley? Bob, get up to Gimbals at the curve headed south on the east side of the peninsula."

"On my way!"

~

Ivy was out cold. The water was about six feet deep and azure blue. He was bleeding profusely from the left side of his neck. A bottle of wine had flown off the seat and bounced into the dash with such force that it cut into his neck and imbedded itself. The right side of the vehicle had smashed against the rocks and water was pouring into the cabin. It didn't seem this far out when Guy first saw Ivy plunge in, but in fact it was at least eighty feet and the bottom of the lake here was very rocky. Guy found he had to get a footing and kept slipping as he tried to get Ivy out. Finally, he stopped trying to run, jumped into the water and began to swim. It had been a long time since he had practiced swimming with his clothes and had forgotten how difficult it was. When he got to the car, the water surrounding it was rippled with blood; some of it fairly thick and clotted. Guy dove under the water to check Ivy's status. He was dead, cold and had that bleached look that is magnified under water. Guy came to the top and swam back to the shore just far enough to get his footing. He was exhausted, and this *ghost* of Clio was now dead. He felt extremely unsatisfied. He wanted to know Ivy's history. How had

Karl Schroeder come to this? He was irritated at himself. Why hadn't he given him more room? Maybe he could have cut him off while going south down the straightaway. The truth was, Ivy was not going to be caught. It was going to end badly any way he tried to catch him. But he still didn't know why his life had gone this way and he hated a lacuna.

He made up his mind right there that Karl Schroeder's parents need never know about this. Guy struggled back to shore to meet Bob Marley and explain what had happened. He looked up at the cloudless blue sky. It was seventy-eight degrees and the wind blew lightly from the southwest. It was another beautiful day in the Traverse area.

KIRT AND MAGGIE

Bear sat quietly on the banks of the Manistee River. Kirt walked slowly over to Bear and sat down beside him. Bear put his head in Kirt's lap and Kirt gave him the rub down he knew he wanted. Bear then let out a big sigh and a low contented rumble. "Good to see you again, Bear. I missed you. 'Catch any fish lately?" Bear looked up at him as though he understood everything. Maggie stood by the entrance to Kirt's cabin and watched him huddle with Bear. He looked like a teenager. She noticed Kirt well up again as he seemed to do so easily at things sad or joyful, and he did it without apology or embarrassment. "I'm a weeper," he would say. "Just can't help it nor do I want to." In the few days she had spent with him she already felt comfortable. She liked him. He saw humor all over the place including in himself. He was driven, strong willed and very attentive, very attentive. He listened to her and he had opinions, which she liked, even if she didn't agree with all of them. She liked his friends from Jordan, MI as well. They were like him only much bigger. Both of them were taller, big boned and seemed to have even bigger hearts. When they were there, they spent the night in opposite sides of the house. She had a difficult time trying to sleep knowing he was so nearby. He felt the same. They often met in the living room early in the morning and talked and kissed until the sun came up. Both wanted to explore other parts of each other's bodies, but knew it would only lead to intercourse so they stopped at kissing and talking. They talked just about everything, trying to hear each other's history, family background, Christian journey, career track, hobbies and personal obsessions. Kirt discovered that Maggie was an incredible fly fisher who could read water like no one he had ever seen. She noticed everything; seams, depressions, undercuts, holes, light playing on the water and feeding activity. She was also a gifted gardener. Everything she grew thrived. She was especially good at producing a lot of berries in a small area. She had a small patch of strawberries, blackberries and raspberries in her backyard. She had created a secret garden out there with a winding walkway of crushed granite. It led through a wattle Monet arch that stretched the whole length of the path, about a hundred and twenty feet, and stopped near a small cold Manistee feeder stream around eight feet wide. At this outlet she had crafted two wind barriers four feet high out of red cedar braches covered in clematis. The barriers were angled outward leaving a large opening also covered in crushed granite. On it she had placed an old massive hickory dining table, which she had covered with a heavy plasticized tablecloth, which had been nailed down underneath the table. She said she changed it twice a season throwing the old one out each time. The table itself had been varnished in a marine coating so it shed water very well. The table had been there all the years she raised her girls. It was large enough to hold twenty people, but most of the time she and her daughters sat on one end together. The girls did their homework on it whenever the weather allowed. They used it for crafts and informal gatherings. The table and chairs sat to the left of the opening just far enough from the wind barrier to keep a comfortable distance from any bees on the flowers. It was very feminine and very comforting. The stream held brook trout and the girls would often catch a few for dinner and prepared them in the traditional northern way with butter and sage in a fry pan. He admired the way the girls had rallied around each other to carve out a wonderful family life.

Maggie had kept current with all the technology available. She had a very useful computer system in the house. She wanted her girls to be able to learn how to learn on their own. She saw the Internet as a miracle of information. She had subscribed to a couple of online library databases so they could research anything they wished. She encouraged them all to seek out their own answers to any question. She did not home school the girls, but they spent at least an hour or two each night studying and helping each other to learn. They all read voraciously and were interesting people to be around because of it. Maggie had just embarked upon a theological church history starting with Paul and she was just entering the third century. Kirt had met another woman of substance. He did not fully understand how this could have happened, but it was obvious to those who knew him that he once again had attracted a gem of a woman.

They did not know where this would go, but they loved where they were. As they lay on a big blanket at the opening of the arch beside the stream, they listened to Chet Baker and drank a bottle of Château Chantal's Riesling.

"I started writing again last week," said Kirt.

"Great. What are you working on?" Maggie was genuinely interested.

"I was driving past a small church graveyard in Hadley, downstate, west of Lapeer, small village. Anyway, the church cemetery is small and over two hundred years old. I stopped to look at the headstones. Something I have done for years."

"Why?" Said Maggie

"I guess I see little worlds there. You know, who were these people? How did they live? What did they do? There are people there who lived what *seemed,* to them, to be long productive lives and yet no one cares or even should."

"It seems a little morbid to me," said Maggie.

"All of life is morbid if there is no living God behind it all."

"I guess you're right. You sound like my dad."

"Yes, but like Paul said, 'Christ is real and changes everything or else we are just stupid fools who believe in a lie, a fairy tale'…I stopped to look at the headstones. There was a whole family there—

father, mother and three children. They had all died in the same year. That piqued my interest and I did some research and it turns out many died of malaria back then; it was fairly common. My great Uncle used to say that many in Canada thought of Michigan as nothing but a swamp. Until the floodwaters were controlled, I guess it probably was. Anyway, there were lots of mosquitoes before DDT. They had a very low supply of quinine. The family had come from Philadelphia. Coming to Michigan in the early ninetieth century was very hard. I decided to craft a story based on historical fact; a retelling of a little told story of these Michiganders. What drove them from fairly secure homes in the east? What challenges did they face? What were their relationships like with the Native American groups, the Indian affairs division? How did they live when they got here?"

"It sounds really interesting and requires a lot of good research. I could help you with that."

"Right now I just have a family a little fleshed out. I like to start with characters first, do the research and let the characters tell *me* the story."

"That's a little backwards isn't it?"

"No, the characters are the main point, and if no one finds them interesting the story will stink."

"I guess that kind of makes sense," she said with an, "I don't know about that" look on her face.

"It works. Trust me, it works."

She put her arm around his neck and kissed him long and firmly on the mouth.

"What was I talking about?" He smiled.

"I have to ask you something. 'Not as fun to talk about, but I want to compare notes."

"Shoot," she said.

"I want to see if I can now put it into words. What was it like for you Maggie? I mean, when my girls died it felt like a lie. Like a trick was being played on me. The world got very small. I was alone, completely alone. NO matter who was around or with me, they felt like background noise. I was not able to see beyond the tight world I was in. In the grocery store, the gas station, at work everything was going on like *nothing* had happened. I thought, 'don't they get it? Three precious women are no longer here? How could everyone go on living like nothing had happened? How could three highly animated ladies just lay there like empty husks?' I kept looking at them, expecting them to sit up laugh or start needling each other. There was nothing, not even a wink, a smile, nothing. My girls lived in these bodies and now they were gone, leaving behind a shell that is best thrown away before it starts to stink. Such life cannot possibly just stop. It must have gone elsewhere and even thought I knew that elsewhere was with Christ, it did not bring me much comfort. They still look strange in their macabre mortician's makeup. They seem so much smaller and lighter than before. I now know that the shock of it would not let me acknowledge the facts in too big 'a bites. I remember standing outside my body and watching myself greet friends and family. I was on some kind of social autopilot. I prayed a lot to prayers that only reached the ceilings it seemed to me. I heard someone say they looked *nice*. Nice? Hell they look dead you moron. An unbelieving friend said, 'they are in a better place.' I remember thinking 'what better place are you talking about, you idiot? Especially since you don't believe in Christ. Where do you think they are?' I know they were just trying to be nice but they weren't. They were only showing their desperate need to comfort themselves…The only person to give me any comfort at all was Pastor C, who said little and hugged often. 'I will pray for your recovery, Kirt. It is not easy and we do grieve but not like those with no hope.' He gave it perspective and authenticity. No bullshit, no empty platitudes, just hope in Christ and His resurrection. I stumbled around for months sinking into a deep depression that was made more difficult as I could not separate the depression from the grief. I would drive to our favorite deli off of Twelve Mile Road near Telegraph watching traffic at the intersection. The one thought that haunted me was what they felt at the time of their death. I imagined all kinds of horrible visions of their faces twisted in agony and the look in my wife's eye when she was decapitated. The doctors convinced me that they were dead instantly and even if they lingered for a couple minutes, the shock would have left them in a numb state. I knew they were telling the truth, but the mind plays tricks. It still comes up now and then, but with far less intensity and for very short bursts. It feels strange now knowing if they had met you they would have liked you so much. I have had some thoughts of betrayal because of the deep love and respect I have developed for you so quickly, but those feeling of guilt are false. I now understand the blessings of having loved them and how easily God can heal. Well, easy from His perspective and when I see it in the rear view mirror."

Maggie looked at Kirt, "I guess it was much the same for me. I was closed off for a while but I had to stay present for my girls. If I had not had them and they me, well it would have hard to imagine. I would go through the motions too. I did feel the same way; the world was cruel and heartless toward the loss of John. God seemed a million miles away yet somehow I could detect His Words letting me know He was with me all the way. I attended church and Bible study out of habit; a good habit. The girls were of great comfort to me. I do not know how people who do not have Christ can deal with it. A couple years later I finally began to get my emotional bearings back. I began to feel really good again about things I used to like. Of course, I had to help the girls through their grief too and that in turn helped me. Our devotional life helped too. We all developed a greater compassion and identification for others that are hurting. It's a heck of a thing, but I know I am a better person, more grounded, and more aware of how things really work instead of how I want them to. I'm more patient."

"Well," said Kirt. "I'm glad we can talk about these things. In fact, I can't think of anything we can't discuss and in the process of these conversations I find myself saying to myself, 'How did you ever get so lucky to be with a beautiful woman like this?'"

"I feel the same Kirt. Give me a kiss, you handsome bastard."

Sam, Maggie's daughter, caught a glimpse from the other end of the arch. She had come home for a month from Ann Arbor. She had not yet met this guy but, from what she saw, she knew he must be pretty solid. She knew her mom's mind and heart and trusted her choices. Sam just stood there and watched her mom laughing. She smiled, 'happy for her and she started to cry. She decided to go back into the house and leave them alone. She could meet Kirt later.

GUY DRIVES HOME

Vietengruber could never fold his mind around the reason. What could lead men to such evil? Was it really as easy as it looked to move permanently into that world? Did the conscience disappear or was it simply that the mind invents elaborate rationalizations to justify the behavior? Where was the guilt? Was there ever any guilt? Ivy was one in a long trail of puzzles. The solution was finally confronting Guy, but he did not want to accept it. *Anyone* can allow themselves to become evil because we've already learned to hide our "uncivilized" interior ugliness. Once let out and once you gotten away with, letting it out can become easier and easier. Let the ugly human nature run free and of course it is often easier because it is enjoyable, sometimes euphoric. His colleagues would not buy into this, but Guy felt at some deep level we want to control all around us. We want to be God whether we are aware of it or not. Our best protection against this impulse is civilization; practicing and becoming habitual about doing the right thing, even when we would rather not. No one has to work at being bad—It comes naturally. It was so simple that it made Guy shutter. So it became vital that you never take that first step, that first bad step. Ultimately, that life choice came with a price as Guy had seen so often. Maybe you get caught, maybe someone retaliates, or maybe your mind betrays you and you check out completely. A person, who free flows evil, at some point, becomes numb, mechanical as so much energy is expended to deal with attempts of the civilized mind or residual conscience that is trying to interfere. From what he could tell Ivy had not fully blocked the constant refrain of his originally Christian influenced conscience. Ivy was sort of two people, yet the hit man was winning the battle. Guy made a few pages of notes of his thoughts to discuss with the profiler back in Detroit. He often shared notes with the profiler and this was one of their favorite subjects. She had such a secularized viewpoint that she might not agree with him completely, but Guy was convinced he properly understood it at least as much as it could be understood. Guy carried some empathy for Ivy but no pity. Ivy deserved his end, he earned it, but Guy did not feel any better knowing so. Vietengruber's mind swallowed very hard, he shook his head and got in his car to drive home. He needed a heavy dose of civility that only his partner and his family could provide. He said to himself, "Wash it away."

KIRT'S LETTER OF COMMITMENT

Maggie,

I have traveled this road before.

I know you have too.

I have no doubt that it can't last. Every good thing God gives us in time and space dies because this life is immersed in sin and the fallenness of the cosmos. I have learned a very painful lesson that we do live in the Shadow Lands C.S. Lewis described so well. In fact, Paul described it when he said we see God now as through a dark glass but then we will see him face to face just as he has known us. I intend to live in the Shadow lands and enjoy every minute of it knowing now that all of it is used for our good.

Maggie, you and I have been given a terrific gift and I do not intend to miss any of it. I do not want to be a father again and you don't want to be a mother again. We are both in good health and able to enjoy all that God has for us. My life now is lived in moments and days not weeks, years and decades. I do not have time to see what will happen next. I want to see what is happening now. I was married, fairly successful and deeply in love with my family. These were taken away in less than the seven tenths of a second it takes for a car accident to occur. One of my friends came home one evening only to be told his seven year old child had fallen from the roof of his house to the concrete below, he was dead. A woman of eighty years who had been suffering from a creeping cancer for over twelve years died in agonizing pain, even though the best pain management specialists were there to help. Life, fallen life, is not what God intended for us. He sees the suffering and did something about it. Now the suffering only lasts in this time and space because Christ paid the price for our sinfulness. This single piece of documented fact is all that we need and without it even my love for you means nothing. We are forever creatures and until we leave time and space we are subject to its fallen influence. My prayer has become a prayer for forgiveness, greater trust in Him and greater perspective on the shortness of this life and the glorious eternity of joy to come. I do, however, get a glimpse of His joy and glory every time I read His Gospel or see it in the people I have loved and been loved by.

Maggie, will you marry me?

Just think about it and don't tell me until I get up to see you face to face. I just wanted to put this down on paper so you can fully understand and have time to think about it.

I love you,

Kirt.

Maggie responded in an overnight letter:

Yes, Kirt, I will marry you for as long as He wants it to last!

Sorry, I had to tell you now. Ask me again when you get here and the answer will be the same, only given in a deep kiss!

I love you and I want all of you.

ANOTHER FUN EVENING

He picked up his paper bag and the plastic ones holding the items he had purchased at the store. He unlocked and entered the side door of his business. Inside, he opened the paper bag and pulled out a hooded sweatshirt and a pair of cheap black wrap-around sunglasses. He hung them up in his closet next to a couple other hoodies and two additional pairs of sunglasses. He locked the closet.

What a great night, he thought. *A fourfer and one hell of an audience. Big night for the tow truck too. That Vinny guy even seemed to get a kick out of it and he really put that one guy in his place:* (mock voice), *"ITS NOT FUNNY, ASSHOLE!"* (New York Italian mock voice), *"Yeah, yeah it is!"*

The vigilante sat down in his big chair and laughed until his sides hurt. He was indeed enjoying it a little too much. He poured himself a four finger glass of scotch, lit a cigar big enough to last an hour, turned on the TV to watch a rerun of Northern Exposure and sat back to relax. Just as he was settling in, he heard a knock at the main door of his office and a female voice saying, "Walt, we need to talk…I can hear the TV, Walt."

Walt shouted back, "Yeah, I heard ya', how could I not! Come on in."

Shit, he said to himself. *Almost a perfect night.*